The Painter of Spirits

BY THE SAME AUTHOR

The Wayward Muse (2005)
The Stones of Camelot (2006)
The New Faust the Tragicomique (2007)
The Shadow of Frankenstein (2008)
Sherlock Holmes and the Vampires of Eternity (2009)
Frankenstein and the Vampire Countess (2009)
Frankenstein in London (2011)
Eurydice's Lament (2015)
The Mirror of Dionysus (2017)
The Pool of Mnemosyne (2018)

non-fiction:
The Plurality of Imaginary Worlds (2016)
Tales of Enchantment and Disenchantment (2019)

The Painter of Spirits

by
Brian Stableford

A Black Coat Press Book

ISBN 978-1-61227-900-8. First Printing. October 2019. Published by Black Coat Press, an imprint of Hollywood Comics.com, LLC, P.O. Box 17270, Encino, CA 91416.

CHAPTER I

Paul had been making good progress with the Jeanne d'Arc, although the position of the body was a difficult determination. Although clad in a long chemise, which made the forms of the lower body imprecise, captive in the rising flames, the arms were free and needed to be reaching upwards toward the imagined heaven for which the gaze was also searching.

He had been fortunate enough to find an intelligent model, whose had even read Michelet's account of Jeanne's martyrdom, and had imagination enough to grasp what he was trying to accomplish. She had an appropriate frailty and pallor, but also a kind of innate resolution. Although it was not easy to maintain the requisite pose and the requisite expression for long periods, she showed a rare determination. There were not many pearls of that quality in the Montmartrean mire. He had been fortunate, too, that Juliette was not as much in demand as many of the girls who hung around in the cafés and restaurants frequented by artists touting for such employment, being a little older than most and not as pretty. In consequence, she had agreed to work for a relatively modest fee and also to guarantee him the best of the daylight hours for the four consecutive days that he estimated necessary to complete the central figure of the painting to his satisfaction. The painting would take a good deal longer than that to complete, of course, but he had already sketched and applied preliminary colors to the surrounding composition, and filling in the detail, although slow and painstaking work, would only demand concentration, patience and a steady hand.

Since leaving Jacollet's studio, where he had been a pupil for a year, Paul had not worked extensively with models, painting primarily from the imagination, but he had been criticized for that. Although his Mourgue la Faye had won a medal at the previous year's Salon, he had been strongly advised by friends and critics alike that he could not make a living painting imaginary fays and sirens in numinous settings.

"It's 1901," Victor Marvaud had told him, "the days of the Salon de Rose+Croix are over, and Symbolism is dying. A new era has begun. Your spirit painting might be useful in making contacts and connections, but it's not a route you want to get stuck in. You need to become expert, as well if not instead, in painting mundane portraits of real people. A certain amount of impressionist blurring doesn't hurt, and even an element of caricature, but the real has to be in there if the profession is to provide your daily bread."

Victor was not an artist; he worked in a bank. Nevertheless, he fancied himself as an intellectual all-rounder as well as something of a dandy. He had known Paul since early childhood; they had grown up together in Toulouse, attending the same lycée and maintaining a close companionship while they had continued their studies. Like Gaston Lambrunet, who had completed their trio, Victor had always taken the view that it was up to him, as the son of relatively well-off and settled parents, to "look after" Paul, who was a orphan, and he had somehow appointed himself as a kind of mentor even at an early age, regardless of any lack of qualification he might have to give expert guidance. Victor was never short of advice, or at least of opinions, on everyone and everything.

But sometimes, Victor was right; Paul had to admit that his self-appointed mentor had the gift of adaptation to his social surroundings. Having moved to Paris only a year before Paul—and having played a leading role in persuading Paul that if he really wanted to be a serious painter then he must come to the capital—Victor had become thoroughly Parisian, even losing his southern accent, although refusing to sacrifice entirely his innate braggadocio. Victor seemed thoroughly at home in Paris, just as he had seemed thoroughly at home in Toulouse, whereas Paul....

"Could you lift the right arm a little higher?" he asked the model, his voice a trifle tentative, not yet accustomed to giving such orders. "Rotate it slightly to the right...that's perfect. Hold..."

The door of the studio was flung open, in a quasimelodramatic fashion that only Victor could contrive—and Victor was, in any case, the only person he knew who could have got past Madame Cambourg, the concierge, to whom Paul had mentioned that he would rather not be disturbed. Not that Madame Cambourg was obedient to instruction from anyone, let alone someone as trivial in her estimation as Paul, but there was nothing that she liked better than a license to refuse entry, and she was a dragon that few knights cared to combat—except Victor.

Paul was genuine angry at being disturbed in his work—not only in full flow, but, he estimated, working well—and by someone who really ought to have known better, but the resentful expression that he turned toward the unexpected visitor disappeared immediately when he saw Victor's face, which had a distraught expression that he had not seen for years, since he had seen Victor receive the news of the death of his beloved grandmother. He almost dropped his palette.

He opened him mouth to say: "What's wrong?" but had hardly formulated the first consonant when he was interrupted.

Bounding toward him, the elegantly-clad young man, neat and sharp even in distress, barked: "No time. Got to cut it short. *Palatine* was caught in last night's storm, disabled and driven by the wind toward the Cornish shore. She struck a rock and was badly holed. All four lifeboats were put into the sea, everyone loaded, in as orderly a manner as could be expected. Gaston's safe; he was in the last boat launched, and the first to make landfall—the first, at any rate, within reach of a telegraph office. Amélie and Martine were in the first one launched, with the other women and children—no news of their reaching land yet. Others to inform, must get back to the telegraph—but I can't go with you to Juvisy tonight; I've asked Doctor Cros to pick you up, drive you to the railway station, take you to the Observatory and make sure you get back safely. You mustn't even think of not going—it's too important. I'll get a message to Madame Cambourg as soon as there's any news; if not, I'll come to see you first thing tomorrow morning."

And with that, he turned away—but not without having taken a quick look at the painting, and cast a comparative glance at the model, still holding her pose, perhaps more in shock than professional discipline. There was no approval in his reaction, let alone admiration, but Paul forgave him that; he obviously had more important things on his mind than appreciation of his friend's brushwork.

Paul did not say a word, or even move a muscle, while the door slammed shut again and he heard the sound of Victor's boots clattering down the wooden stairs. Then, and only then, did he feel the need to react—but did not know how.

Automatically, without any conscious decision, his right hand reached out toward the canvas again, as if to apply the brush to the half-depicted arm of Jeanne d'Arc, in mid-martyrdom. But he did not apply the tip of the brush to the canvas. Indeed he drew his hand back as he realized that it had begun to shake, convulsively.

He put the palette down and the brush, and he stared at his hand, as if it had suddenly become an alien object—as perhaps it had, given that it was moving without the slightest volition on his part, not exactly with a will of its own, but perhaps with a panic of its own.

Absurdly, he wondered whether he might have misconceived his painting, whether Jeanne d'Arc, as the flames of the pyre began to rise around her, could possibility have been reaching out in that fashion with deliberate purpose, or at least the illusion of purpose, rather than her flesh reacting of its own accord, without any reference to her terrified consciousness.

The hand was still trembling, not taking the slightest notice of the command that his mind was sending, ordering it to stop, to become steady. *But I'm a painter, he thought, I need my hand to obey my will; if I no longer have that...*

He could not stop his hand from shaking by exerting his will power—but it did stop, eventually. The wrist had been grasped. The model, Juliette, apparently having realized what it was necessary to do, had taken control of the wayward appendage. He looked at her. He could no longer see Jeanne d'Arc in her face, but only anxiety.

"Who was that?" she asked, perhaps feeling that it was the safest of several questions that might have sprung to her mind.

"Victor Marvaud," he told her, and added, automatically: "My friend."

"And Gaston?" she asked. "He's your friend too?" While she was speaking she guided him away from the easel toward the divan on which she had been posing, and sat him down on it gently.

"The three of us grew up together in Toulouse," Paul told her. "Gaston was in Spain, on family business. He was sailing to Le Havre on the *Palatine*, and then taking the train to Paris, so that we could meet up again...it's been a long time...the storm..."

His eyes went automatically to the large bay window of the studio, facing northwards. The city lay in that direction, but the roofs of the houses on the Butte blacked the view of its sprawling extent. From his present position, in any case, all he could see was the sky: the blue, serene, afternoon sky, in which only a few cumulus clouds were drifting, last night's storm in the Channel never having extended its edge as far as Paris, and having doubtless tracked north-eastwards and taken its violence into the North Sea, leaving peace behind...and wreckage...

"And Amélie and Martine?" Juliette asked. "Is it them you're worried about."

Of course it's them..., he began, in the angry turmoil of his sentiments—a turmoil that he had somehow not quite noticed until it was provoked, but his mind caught up with the thought before it could be voiced, as he mustered the awareness that the model could not possibly be aware of the reason for his anguish, and was merely trying to get a grip on what was happening, in a spirit of good will. She was trying to help.

"Amélie is Gaston's mother," he said. "She...well, I had no mother, and she was kind to me...always very kind. I haven't seen her for nearly two years...not since I came to Paris...but...I'm fond of her..."

Her pale blue eyes were studying his face with what seemed to be a remarkable curiosity, although he knew that the impression might only be a result of his own suddenly-heightened sensibility.

"And Martine?" she prompted, again.

"Gaston's sister." He left it at that.

The penetrating gaze was no sham. "And you're fond of her too," the young woman remarked. It wasn't even a question, merely an observation. How much had she observed, Paul wondered—not because he was curious about the precise extent of the model's perspicacity but because he was anxious about the legibility of his thoughts and emotions, the extent to which his inner life might suddenly have been nakedly exposed to an enquiring eye, no more able to hide than his hand had been able to stop shaking. He nodded his head affirmatively.

"But they're safe," the model reminded him. "They were put in the first lifeboat launched, with the other woman and children. All the passengers were taken off, in an orderly fashion—that's what Victor said."

That was, indeed, what Victor had said—except that he hadn't said that Martine and Amélie were safe. How could he? They had been cast adrift in a lifeboat in the pitch dark, in the middle of a violent storm, and hadn't yet reached land, even though the entire morning had passed and the afternoon was beginning to wear away. At least, they hadn't reached land within quick reach of a telegraph office. Paul did not know what the rules were for the evacuation of damaged vessels, but he assumed that there must have been at least two sailors manning the lifeboat, cable of rowing resolutely...but they would surely not have been able to row effectively while the storm was raging, and the boat must have been at the mercy of the wind and waves for hours—desperate hours, in dangerous waters. It could have struck a rock, like the *Palatine*, or capsized...

Deliberately, he pulled himself together. His hand was no longer shaking, and the girl had released it. The idea of picking up the palette and the brush, however...he sat in silence for a few minutes, while Juliette waited, patiently, still observing him.

"I'm sorry," he said, eventually, surprised but gladdened by the seeming calmness of his voice. "I don't think I'll be able to continue, for the moment, but perhaps I've done enough for one sitting." He made an effort to look at her, calmly, like a man in control of himself and the situation. He saw anxiety in her face, which might have been for him, although he did not get that impression.

Absurdly, he said: "Don't worry—I'll pay you for the full session." He realized as he said it that she might conceivably take that as a insult to her concern, but was slightly surprised to see her bite her lip, and her anxiety seemed to increase, as if some plan that she had been nursing, patiently, had suddenly been disrupted.

His eyes strayed toward the door of the studio, to the place where Juliette had put down her bag when she arrived. It had not struck him at the time, his attention being focused on his preparations for the sitting, but it was an unusually large bag by comparison with the handbags that young Parisiennes, of whatever status or profession, usually carried. Thinking back, it now seemed to him that the model had seemed slightly anxious, even before he had asked her to strike the pose and feign the expression of distress appropriate to his subject. He had assumed, without really thinking about it, that she was getting into character. It occurred to him now that perhaps she really had been anxious about something. The bag, though large, was hardly large enough to contain all of a person's worldly goods...unless, of course, the person in question had very few worldly goods...

11

Paul stared at Juliette inquisitively. He had only ever looked or her before as a model, uniquely concerned with her ability to represent Jeanne d'Arc in an admittedly old-fashioned historical painting; it had never occurred to him to think of her as someone with a life, or even an identity, of her own.

He had been acquainted with the girl vaguely before he had asked her to pose for the painting; she was part of the community of the local enclave of the quarter, one of numerous young women who kept company with the artists of Montmartre, in the declining Bohemia that seemed to have lost its impetus when the calendar had imperiously marked the end of the *fin-de-siècle*. He had taken note of her physical appearance with a professional gaze, assessing her as an object...not even that, merely as a potential object. She was not pretty enough to magnetize the eyes in the fashion of some of the other, more flamboyant members of the strange assembly. She was sickly, but that was not unusual—perhaps a little sicklier than most, probably consumptive—but that, he thought, with a sudden twinge of guilt, had merely seemed to him to be a qualification for playing the part of a martyr in his assisted imagination. He had never once wondered whether she might be feeling ill, warranting or deserving of compassion.

"Something's wrong, isn't it?" he asked.

She contrived a wry smile. She took a deep breath, and said: "I was hoping to ask you for a favor when the sitting was over." Then she paused, as if expecting him to guess what the favor was.

He guessed. "You want to stay here until the painting is finished," he said, "because you don't have anywhere else to go, for the moment."

She didn't seem surprised by the guess; she had seen him look at the bag—and his thought-processes were, it appeared, nakedly legible, at least for the moment, in the wake of the shock that he had felt. "I was...thrown out," she said. "I'm sorry..."

"There's no need to apologize," he assured her. "Of course you can stay." He lifted his forefinger to indicate the gallery that ran along the edge of the rectangular room just above head height, like a minstrel's gallery in an aristocratic hall. "You can sleep on the mattress upstairs. I can sleep on the divan down here for a few days; it's no trouble."

He was still looking into her face, and he saw every detail of the change in her expression. As an artist, he felt that he ought to be able to read and interpret that change, but that kind of empathetic deduction had never been his forte. There was a little gratitude there, he felt sure, and surprise, but also disappointment, as if she had taken a punch to the stomach, the reaction to which she was determined to conceal, but could not quite manage.

He realized that when she had formulated the intention to ask him whether she could stay in the studio until the painting was finished, she had taken it for granted that she would pay for the accommodation with the use of her body; she had taken what he had just said as a rejection, a judgment that she was unattractive—a fear that she probably had routinely, doubtless sharpened to a new intensity by the fact that she had been "thrown out?" Thrown out by whom? By a lover, presumably, with whom she had been living, but who no longer wanted her.

Paul had been in Montmartre long enough to understand how some things worked there, even though there were aspects of the quarter's idiosyncratic mores that were not openly discussed. He knew that there were painters who assumed, when they hired a model, that the fee they were paying for sittings included sexual favors as well as posing. There were others who considered that assumption tasteless and unprofessional, and who prided themselves on being above that kind of sordid exploitation. Doubtless the models talked among themselves, and knew what to expect from the painters who asked them to pose, giving them the opportunity to be selective. The general assumption, he knew, was that all of the regular models were prostitutes, more or less, but he was aware that there were infinite gradations within that profession, not merely of price but of appearances, and that there were many who took a pride in some degree or species of virtue. As a relatively recent and still raw recruit to the community, and one who rarely used models—living ones, at any rate—he had never felt any sense of entitlement with regard to the extra favors of the models, and in any case...there had always been Martine, distant but somehow ever-present.

He wondered momentarily how to repair the gaffe he had committed, but swiftly reacted with the thought that he had not really made an error in merely being polite, and that there was, in any case, nothing he could say by way of adjustment that would not make the impression he had given worse.

"I won't be here tonight, in any case," he said. "At least, I won't be back until the early hours. I'll tell Madame Cambourg that I've invited you to stay for a few days and that you can come and go as you please. I'll give you the spare key to the studio door. I'll try not to disturb you when I come in."

The young woman's changing expression was still unreadable, so far as Paul's meager powers of penetration were concerned. Perhaps she was surprised that he was willing to leave her alone in his home while he was away for most of the night, given that her hardly knew her and had every reason to think that she might be a person of low morals, but she probably knew as well as he did that there was nothing in the studio worth stealing apart from paint and paintings, which would not be of any use to her.

When she eventually spoke, however, it was to say: "You're going to Camille Flammarion's Observatory at Juvisy—stargazing, I assume?"

He was not surprised that she knew what Victor had had been talking about, even though his references had been slight and fleeting, but he was mildly surprised that she had taken the wrong inference—unless, of course, she had done so deliberately. Flammarion was one of the most famous men in France, and everyone knew that he lived in his Observatory at

Juvisy—but by the same token, everybody knew that it was not simply "stargazing" that went on there.

"There's a séance tonight," he said, simply. "Professor Flammarion has invited every notable medium in Europe to the Observatory, over the years, to contribute to his scientific research into psychic phenomena. Tonight, he has a new guest, who is rumored to have remarkable powers." *Aren't they all?* he added mentally.

"And he's requested you—or invited you—to draw the spirits his guest evokes?"

Juliette was a reader; she obviously knew something about the nature of Flammarion's research. She could hardly be unaware, in any case, of the stir caused by Théodore Flournoy's recent account of life on Mars, as illustrated and described by "Hélène Smith"—actually a medium named Catherine Müller—given the sensational publicity his book had received in the press, She probably knew as well as he did that, in spite of Flournoy's attempt to explain everything that "Hélène Smith" drew or described in psychological terms, a rich American spiritualist had offered "Mademoiselle Smith" a salary in order to work full time on her visions of other worlds and images of Christ; that had probably caused her to jump to an erroneous conclusion as to why Paul was going to Juvisy. The model had also looked around the studio while posing and while resting between poses, and had doubtless formed an idea, clear if perhaps mistaken, of the kind of work that Paul did when he was not preparing a deliberately retrograde example of pseudo-classical historical art, specifically for possible exhibition at the next Salon.

"Dozens of writers and artists have taken part in Flammarion's experiments in automatic writing and drawing over the last twenty years," Paul said, defensively, "some of them much more famous and talented than me."

"And because the spiritists are a tightly-knit...company," she hazarded, "Flammarion heard what you'd done at Madame Pommerat's séance last week within twenty-four hours, and immediately wrote to you? I presume you haven't been to

Juvisy before, or your friend wouldn't have needed to ask someone to replace him in taking you there and bringing you back?"

Paul stared at her in frank amazement.

"This is Montmartre," she said. "All the gossip in the world circulates here like water around a plug-hole. I'm surprised that I hadn't heard that the *Palatine* had gone down before I came here. There isn't anyone in the local crowd who doesn't know that Henri Lemastur put you into a trance at La Pommerat's last week and that you drew a spirit that poor old Rochemure recognized as his dead daughter. Lautrec and Magre were there, damn it—it might as well have been headline news in the *Petit Parisien*. I guess the hundred jokes that have been circulating since then have all been whispered behind your back, and you've been blithely oblivious to them. That's not good—it's far better to have them laughing with you than at you, and anyway," she took the risk of adding, probably unaware that it made her sound like Victor, "it's not quite the reputation you're trying to cultivate with that." She nodded her head in the direction of the easel, although nothing could be seen from the divan than the back of the canvas.

Paul frowned. "You think I shouldn't go, then?" he asked.

She seemed genuinely startled by that, and suddenly repentant. "I shouldn't have said that," she told him. "I'm the last person entitled to an opinion, and the last one capable of giving you sound advice. Your friend is surely right, though— if you've been invited, you do have to go. There'll be important people there, people who are very useful to know, even people who might give you commissions, if you can put on a good show..."

Paul's pent-up emotion finally found an outlet, and exploded without giving him any warning. "It's not a *show!*" he snapped, furiously. "I'm not some kind of *charlatan!*"

She recoiled slightly, and this time the distress in her expression was far easier to decode. "I'm sorry," she said. "I shouldn't have said that either. I didn't mean to imply...forgive me, please, I'm not quite myself at present, and you're the last person I want to offend, in the present circumstances."

Paul immediately repented of his flash of anger, which he knew to have been quite unjustified. "No, I'm sorry," he said. "I'm...overwrought. The news about the *Palatine*...it really shouldn't have hit me so hard, but it did. Amélie was...not exactly a mother to me, I can't say that, but...well, I don't think Gaston or Victor ever realized how much she did for me, and how much I needed it, at the time. I haven't seen her for so long that it's a trifle absurd, I know, but..."

He had selected Juliette to model his martyr precisely because she seemed intelligent, and sensitive—right for the part and capable of playing it. He realized, therefore, that he ought not to be so very surprised that she actually was intelligent and sensitive, and able to read him like a book in his present condition. "And Martine," she suggested, "wasn't exactly a sister?"

"No," he said, dully. Quickly, he added: "Not that we were lovers." Immediately, he realized how stupid that must sound, and how stupid, in fact, it was to have said it aloud.

"I understand," she said, softly, almost as if she did, although he felt certain, in his admittedly-confused mind that she could not.

There was an awkward pause. Evidently hunting for something to say that was safe, the model eventually said: "Might I have heard of the medium that Flammarion has invited to Juvisy tonight?"

"I don't know," Paul answered, also feeling that it was safer conversational ground and glad to move on to it. "I hadn't, but that's probably not surprising, as I'm even newer to that than I am to this." He waved a hand vaguely in the direction of the canvas. "If by the medium you mean the somniloquist, I believe that her name is Talia Cadelan."

"That's good—somniloquist," the model observed, "Everyone else says somnambulist, even though they don't do any walking. Yes, I have heard mention of her and her partner. Not the conventional double act; her magnetizer is also a woman, something of an amazon, I believe she calls herself Zosima, although I dare say she was baptized a simple Marie or Jeanne, like the rest of us. From Egypt, supposedly—but a hint of the mysterious East is almost obligatory nowadays, so she's more likely from Marseille. Said to be very...talented."

"You're skeptical? You assume that she's a charlatan?"

"Oh, I believe in hypnotism, and the power of suggestion, even animal magnetism...but as for conjuring spirits, that might be a different matter. You're not, then...skeptical, that is?"

"About spirits? Frankly, I don't know what to believe in that regard...but that I see visions, that's a simple matter of fact. Whether they're products of my own mind or whether they come from outside, I'm not sure, but that I have them...and that I can be induced to have them by hypnotism, whether it's really a kind of psychological magnetism or not, isn't in doubt..."

He stopped, thinking that he was letting his tongue run away with him and that he was saying too much, but when she seemed to be waiting for something more, he carried on. "In a way, I'd far rather believe that they were products of my own mind, my own creativity, than that the dead were reaching out to me, intent on communication...but in either case, I'd really like to be able to control the process, to be able to organize it consciously. If Flammarion could help me to do that...or Richet, or Le Bon, or one of the other high-powered scientists who'll probably be present tonight, I'd be very grateful...although I'm sure that their agenda is somewhat different."

Juliette thought about that for a few moments, and flicked a wisp of dark hair away from her pale brow before saying: "You don't believe, then, that you really drew Rochemure's daughter?"

"I believe that Baron de Rochemure is a man afflicted by grief, who was at Madame Pommerat's séance because he was desperate for Lemastur to produce evidence that his daughter still exists somewhere beyond the grave, and that he would dearly have liked to believe that I had seen her spirit, even on the basis of the vaguest of resemblances in a rather poor sketch."

"She didn't identify herself to you while you were sketching her, then?"

"I was hypnotized. I had no consciousness of what I was doing, and I have no memory of doing it." He paused very slightly before adding: "Have you ever been hypnotized?"

"No," she said. "Not knowingly, at any rate. I think I've always known what I was doing, acting within reason...but can any of us be entirely sure, if animal magnetism really exists, of not being affected by it, and not just if we consult a mesmerist physician?"

Paul assumed that it was a rhetorical question. He looked at her curiously, surprised by what she had revealed of herself since the moment when Victor's melodramatic entrance had shattered their previously-comfortable professional relationship. "If I'm not being indiscreet in asking," he said, "how did you come to find yourself suddenly homeless?"

"Indiscreet?" she echoed, wonderingly. "You're talking to a cheap whore who thought you'd be a soft touch for providing a convenient place to sleep while you needed to finish your picture, and you're worried about being indiscreet? Believe me, Monsieur Furneret, that's the last thing you need to worry about—and if you're worried about how you're going to get rid of me when your painting's done, don't. I won't overstay my welcome. I always go meekly."

"That wasn't..." he began.

She raised her hand. "No, of course not—you were just making conversation, and you wanted, entirely understandably, to know exactly what you'd carelessly let yourself in for. I was thrown out, as I said, but you don't need to be worried about the reason. He'd just got tired of me—found someone else. Not as pretty, in my opinion, although God knows that I'm barely fit for posing as Jeanne d'Arc, let alone Venus...but she doesn't cough blood. He's a prudent fellow, and even though I'm not ready for the hospital yet, he knows which way the wind is blowing. So do you, don't you? You only see me during the day, when I'm at my best, but you know what I am—that's why you picked me for your picture, no? Easy to see me as a martyr?"

Paul winced at that, and his inability to deny it. "What will you do, then?" he asked, tentatively. "When the painting is finished, that is?"

"Get a room," she said. "It's easy enough, if you're not choosy. Don't worry about it—but it's nice of you to think that you ought to. Most wouldn't. I won't say that I'll be fine, because we both know that I won't, in the long run—but if I can visit you in your visions afterwards, I will. It would be nice to think that I can continue working, even when I'm dead...if posing counts as work. I won't be able to do the other, of course, but at the risk of being indiscreet, I don't think I'll miss it, if I'm in any state to miss anything."

He wanted to say that he was confident that she would live for years yet, especially if she got away from the polluted air of Paris to the balmy climate of Provence or the heights of the Alps, but he knew how ridiculous those suggestions must have sounded on the numerous occasions that she had presumably heard them before.

"I'm sorry," he said.

"No need," she assured him. "You're being kind. I'm grateful. And you're going to put me in the Salon, as a saint. There are some I know who'll laugh, but that won't stop me being pleased. It might or might not be the only immortality I'll have, but either way, I have every interest in the painting going well."

"You've been in other paintings," Paul said, "even in the Salon. You must have at least half a dozen chances of that sort of immorality."

"As a hackneyed reclining nude or a neo-Naturalist slut? I'll take Jeanne d'Arc, thanks. A better class of Symbolism by far. Be sure to credit me in the press coverage, won't you? Put my name on the record for future generations."

Paul was about to say "Of course," but stopped, embarrassed.

She contrived another wry smile. "You don't know my name, do you" she said.

"Only Juliette," he admitted.

"Scaran," she said. "Two *a*s, not like the writer. Haven't you heard the other girls calling me Scarab?"

"No," Paul admitted. "I don't really talk to them much," and hastened to add: "timidity, not disapproval."

"We'd figured that out."

"Oh?"

This time the smile was almost a laugh. "You think because you don't talk to us that we don't talk about you? That isn't the way it works. We figured you out months ago, while you were still at Jacollet's. Mind you..." She stopped, and frowned slightly before starting again: "You do realize, don't you, that if you tell Mère Cambourg that you've 'invited me to stay for a few days,' the news will be all over the Butte tomorrow? The general opinion for some while has been that you were a fish waiting to be hooked..."

Paul shrugged his shoulders, hoping that the gesture seemed utterly casual. The model was still frowning, so he asked: "What's the matter?"

"Nothing," she said, but then changed her mind. "It's just that, if you're expecting this Martine, and she's important to you...well, I wouldn't want to get in the way. It's one thing for the locals to get the wrong idea, but another for...someone for whom you might have plans. When your friend Victor sends word that she's safe, and tells you when she's due to arrive in Paris...I won't exactly be able to disappear, while you still have to finish the painting, but I'll...in fact, it might be better if you didn't say anything to Mère Cambourg and I'll leave now, as usual. That way..."

"You don't have to do that," Paul told her. "If it's more convenient for you to stay, stay—and you don't have to disappear, no matter who arrives. We don't have anything to hide."

The frown deepened. The young woman seemed to be in a genuine quandary.

A sudden thought occurred to Paul. "Have you had anything to eat today?" he asked.

Juliette blushed. "Have you?" she countered.

"No," he admitted, "and I won't have time to eat at the restaurant at the usual time, because that's when Victor was supposed to be picking me up, and I was planning to have something to eat earlier. If this doctor he's asked to pick me up comes at the same time..."

"Dr. Cros? Don't you know him, then?"

"No. Do you?"

"Only by reputation—assuming that it's Antoine Cros. Old, well-to-do, first-class clientele, but good heart. Does charity work at two or three hospitals. Something of a hero to the poor way back in the Commune, I gather—before you or I was born, obviously—but too well-connected to be shot or sent to New Caledonia. Still something of a legend hereabouts, where legends linger. If you can make a friend of him, he really will be able to introduce you to the right people."

"That's not why I'm going to Juvisy," Paul said, with a hint of snap in his voice again. "I'm going to take part in an experiment, and to make observations of my own. Trust Victor to have a legendary doctor, though, even while he's not really ill—and only he would have the cheek to ask him to give his friend the starving painter a lift to the Gare du Nord and see him safely home from the return train. But we're straying from the subject. The point is that time is wearing on, and I need to get a bite to eat before I get washed and changed to go the séance. Would you like to come with me to a café, or a wine shop—assuming, that is, that the answer to the question you didn't answer is *no*?"

The model frowned again, apparently back in the quandary. "God, I'm stupid," she said. "Why on earth do I suddenly have this strange idea that I ought to protect your reputation. You're a painter's for Heaven's sake. I was perfectly ready to blow it sky high when I asked you if you could stay for a few days, on the assumption that I'd pay for the privilege on my back, so why do I care now that people are going to assume that's the case, when it seems that you don't actually want me. Don't I have my reputation to think of as well?

"Look, how about this: you don't say a word to Mère Cambourg, and we don't go putting on an exhibition in any wine shop. I'll slip out now and buy some fried potatoes, charcuterie, bread and wine, and we can eat it here. Then, when the doctor comes to pick you up, you swan off to Juvisy with him and I stay here. Mère Cambourg will know I'm still here when you go, obviously, and she'll think that I must be still here when you arrive back, whenever that is, but with no explicit declaration, she can't be absolutely sure that I didn't go out while she was in the courtyard, or simply while her back was turned.

"By the time you get back, you'll probably have news of your friends, or, if not, Victor will come to bring you up to date in the morning. Then you can make up your mind what the wisest course of action is. Or, if you prefer, I could just go, and come tomorrow at the same time as today, as if nothing had happened...as, in fact, it won't have."

Paul thought about the options. Then he took out his purse, and shook out a handful of coins on to the divan.

"That's for the food and wine," he said, pushing two coins forward; "and this is the fee for the sitting," he added, pushing two more. "I won't say anything to Madame Cambourg—she can draw her own conclusions, as she pleases—but my offer stands. You can stay here as long as it's convenient for you to do so, and the hell with what anyone might think, including Victor, Gaston, Amélie and Martine...assuming that he latter two aren't at the bottom of the Manche."

She winced at the last phrase, but she took the four coins.

"Thank you," she said and added: "I really didn't want to go. I'm sorry."

"You have nothing for which to apologize," he assured her. "If you hadn't been here, and hadn't been so kind and so sane...I don't think I'd be feeling as sane myself as I am right now. Thank you."

"You're the one who's making me a saint," she told him.

CHAPTER II

Having cleaned himself and dressed himself to the very best of his ability—which was, he admitted, nowhere near Victor Marvaud's standard, Paul made his way downstairs, carrying his hat but no cane. Swagger-sticks, he thought we very nineteenth century, and it was about time that they were laid to rest by practicality, if not by fashion. Victor's, no doubt, would have to be pried out of his rigid fingers on his death-bed.

All he said to Madame Cambourg was that he would be back very late, and apologized in advance for having to wake her up in order for her to lift the cordon. The apology would doubtless have gone down better if it had been accompanied by a tip, but he was all too well aware of the dent that the rail fare to and from Juvisy would make in his limited finances.

He had only been waiting on the sidewalk for ten minutes when a carriage drew up, larger than he had anticipated. It was a four-seater, which was perhaps as well, as he discovered that he was not the only person that Antoine Cros had agreed to escort to and from Juvisy that night. The doctor's other passenger was a small, slender woman in her forties, still serenely beautiful, as Parisian women in their forties often were, especially when delicately built. She was not wearing a veil, perhaps thinking that, like swagger-sticks, they were an affectation that ought to have been laid to rest with the previous century: a neglect that enabled her to wear a small and elegant toque and to show off her luxuriant dark hair. She was elegantly but not ostentatiously dressed.

"Madame Jane de La Vaudère," said Antoine Cros, introducing her. "And you, I presume, are Monsieur Paul Furneret, the artist."

"Indeed," said Paul. "I'm delighted to meet you both, and I'm sorry to have inconvenienced you, Doctor Cros. I've

25

read some of your work, Madame de La Vaudère, and found it very impressive."

The lady only nodded in response to the compliment, while the doctor said: "It's no trouble at all, I assure you. I hope that there is good news of your friends before we return. I called in at the dispatch office on the way; apparently, a second lifeboat has landed safely, with all aboard safe and well, but the other two might have been carried a long way by the tidal current, which began running contrary to the wind not long after the boats were put to sea, making it exceedingly difficult to reach Cornwall. The likeliest contingency seems to be that they would head for Guernsey or Cherbourg, once the weather cleared."

"I hope so," said Paul. "They must have been a long way off course to have struck a rock of the Cornish coat. Do you know how that happened?"

"The engine broke down, and although these mixed vessels carry plenty of sail, there was no way to make use of it. The wind was fierce, and until the tide turned, the current was with it. But the sailors manning the lifeboat carrying the women and children are bound to be old hands who know the waters. Madame Lambrunet and her daughter Martine were dear to you, I understand from Monsieur Marvaud?"

"Indeed. I lost my own mother shortly after I was born, and Gaston's—Madame Lambrunet—was very kind to me when I was a small boy."

"Puerperal fever was still something of a plague twenty years ago," said Cros, with a sigh. "I've been fighting the cause all my life, but hygiene, I fear, has been slow to reach the requisite standards, even in Paris."

"It wasn't puerperal fever," said Paul, automatically making the correction. "She died attempting to give birth to my twin sister, who had perished in the womb." He was within a split second of making a flippant remark, of the kind that he had routinely made in his days as a student, but he glimpsed a brief contraction of the features in Madame de La Vaudère's face, and remembered in time that he was in different company now, where a very different etiquette applied. He blushed, and said: "I'm sorry."

"No, no, my boy," said Cros, quickly. "My fault entirely. I really ought to have mastered the art of setting the professional aside in the social situations."

"No one is at fault," Madame de La Vaudère put in, immediately. "I have had difficulty with the boundaries of the unmentionable myself, as you well know, and I have no need to be shielded from the facts of life. I believe, Monsieur Furneret, that you will be filling the role tonight that I once filled, long ago, in some of Camille's séances—I was an artist before I was a writer, and exhibited at the Salon myself. I produced drawings under the influence of some famous mediums...but nothing like Monsieur Sardou's mages of life on Jupiter, I fear. Automatic writing, on the other hand, has sometimes produced imagery that I have been able to redirect into my works of fiction."

Paul had read "Dans une étoile," but hesitated to mention the fact. Instead, he said: "I'm very new at this, I fear, and I was entirely unprepared for the results of my first endeavor. I don't know whether Victor told you..."

"He had no need, my dear," said Cros. "It's all over Paris, Lemastur is claiming all the credit, naturally, but Madame Pommerot has hardly paused to draw breath. Rochemure is said to have gone to ground, locked away in the company of your sketch—which is rather inconsiderate of him, as there are a dozen people acquainted with his daughter who would dearly like to evaluable the resemblance for themselves. But I understood from Monsieur Marvaud that it wasn't the first time at all—that you've done dozes of paintings based on visions, ever since you were a boy. He says that you've never needed to be magnetized—or hypnotized, as the modern jargon has it—and that you can cast yourself into a trance voluntarily?"

"Victor exaggerates," said Paul, blushing furiously. "I've never claimed to be painting spirits, or to be doing anything other than employing my imagination. I have no reason to think that the people and scenes I see in my mind's eye are anything but evidence of a strong visual imagination, and I'm not convinced that animal magnetism even exists."

Antoine Cros doubtless thought himself qualified to offer an expert opinion on that, but had just been reminded of the sensitive etiquette involved in delving into medical matters in polite conversation. He settled for saying: "Well, you'll find a number of people at Flammarion's who'll agree with you wholeheartedly, as well as a few who'll think you deluded, if you say that in the precincts of the Observatory...but you might find it advisable to hold your counsel for a while, until you see how the land lies there. You'll meet highly intelligent men—and women—tonight, who fill a whole spectrum of opinions, and who like nothing better than debating them; the wisest course might be to play your part in the experiment and let the lions squabble over the spoils, whatever they might amount to, before committing yourself to anything."

"Oh, Antoine, you'll frighten the poor boy," Madame de La Vaudère put in. "It's really not that bad, Monsieur Furneret, and as a debutant, everyone will treat you with the utmost politeness.

"That's true," Cros agreed. "Keep your head down and you'll be absolutely fine. You won't be the center of attention, in any case. Madame Zosima is arriving from the Riviera with a considerable reputation, although some might say that reputations are easily earned in Nice."

"Good hypnotists are ten a penny," Madame de La Vaudère opined. "The medium is the inch-pin of the evocation. Mademoiselle Cadelan is the one that ought to have the reputation—but the art, or the science—is an unreliable mistress, and sensitive mediums tend to burn out all too rapidly. You must be careful, Monsieur Furneret, to husband your resources. Be sparing with yourself, I beg you."

"But I'm not a medium," Paul objected.

"Of course you are, even if we're unsure of exactly what that involves. Automatic writing and drawing are mediumship, just as somniloquism is; they're said only to work well in strong fields of mesmeric force. If that's true, Lemastur isn't wrong to claim his due share of the credit for enabling you to draw what you drew at La Pommerot's last week, but you were the seer as well as the draughtsman. If Zosima has more magnetic force, as rumor alleges, you needn't fear that to-night's experiment will be a failure."

The carriage came to a halt then, outside the Gare du Nord. The three passengers descended, and Cros repeated the instructions that he must already have given the coachman, for the sake of emphasis, before saying: "If you care to escort Madame de La Vaudère to the waiting room, Monsieur Furneret, I'll go and purchase the tickets."

Paul made as if to offer an embarrassed objection, but the doctor silenced him with a gesture. "You're Flammarion's guest," he said. "The old fellow would never forgive me if I let you buy your ticket. I'll be back in a moment, Jane." He strode off, purposefully.

Paul, feeling increasingly out of his depth, looked around for the waiting room. He was familiar with the Gare de Lyon, but had never traveled from the Gare du Nord before. Madame de La Vaudère put her arm in his, gently, and said "It's this way, my dear." As they walked, she added: "I wasn't wrong, was I? About your being afraid that tonight's experiment might fail?"

"Indeed not," he said. "I can't convince myself that what happened at Madame Pommerot's was anything but a pure accident, and that the Baron only recognized his daughter in my rather vague and inept drawing because he was desperate to do so. The thought of repeating the experiment before a man of Monsieur Flammarion's intellect, not to mention the other men of science who might be there...I fear that unreasonable expectations might have been created, in spite of me, and that I might look a perfect fool. Indeed, I fear that I might *be* a perfect fool. In fact, I rather wish that I had seized the opportunity that Victor's bad news gave me in order to send my apologies, but I was too distraught at the time to think of it."

"Well," she said, "I, for one, shall be very interested to see the experiment, and you need not fear any critical reaction from me if nothing comes of it, nor, I think from Monsieur Flammarion. I can't speak for Richet, Le Bon, and the rest, who have always intimidated me too, more than a little, but you will not be alone in a lions' den, as Antoine carelessly implied. He and Camille have known one another for a long time, but have never seen eye to eye—which has never spoiled their friendship. They were both very fond of Antoine's brother, Charles, who was something of a spoiled genius. I knew him when I first came to Paris, but all too briefly, alas. He died of absinthe abuse...spoiled by a woman, alas, as so many men are...although perhaps not as many as the number of women spoiled by a man. I hope that you did not take it amiss that I winced, in the carriage, when you mentioned the circumstances of your mother's death. It was a gesture of sympathy, because I had a suspicion of what you might be about to say. I have such intuitions sometimes, although my friends refuse to take them seriously. Do you have a visiting card?"

Startled by the double swerve in her monologue, Paul was caught at a loss momentarily, but he recovered his poise and pulled out his card-holder. He took out one of the cards and handed it to the lady, who reciprocated the gesture.

"Now that we are formally acquainted," she said, "I will send you an invitation to my next soirée, and I will feel free to call in at your studio in order to examine the paintings that you have drawn from your visions."

Antoine Cros arrived at that moment. "There was a queue at the window," he said, apologetically. "Oh, I should have thought of that, should I not?" He handed Paul a first class return ticket to Juvisy, but retained Madame de La Vaudère's, as etiquette required, and swiftly took out his own card-holder. He held out a visiting card to Paul, who held out one of his own to the doctor, and the ceremonial exchange was completed.

"Excellent," said Madame de La Vaudère. "But beware of summoning Antoine unless you're at death's door, Monsieur Furneret. His consultations are fearfully expensive, and they usually end with a recommendation to go under the knife."

"My fees are a necessary defense," said Cros. "If they were any less expensive, I wouldn't have a minute to myself, and wouldn't be able to escort the two of you to what is bound to be a fascinating evening. And the scalpel, skillfully wielded—including mine, said with all due modesty—has dragged more people back from death's door than all the prayers, animal magnetism and homeopathy in the world, Shall we move on to the platform? The train is ready for boarding, I believe, and the departure is imminent."

They made their way on to the platform, and found an empty first-class compartment without difficulty. As in the carriage, Antoine Cros took a seat next to the lady, while Paul sat opposite them.

"You've known Monsieur Flammarion for a long time, I understand?" Paul said to the doctor.

"Oh yes," Cros confirmed. "Decades. I remember the days when his salon was almost riotous—Villiers de l'Isle Adam used to attend in those days, and Verlaine and Rimbaud dropped in once or twice before the scandal, and Élisée Reclus before he was banished. The gentlemen from the Observatory—the Paris Observatory, that is, before the one at Juvisy was built—were sometimes quite scandalized. We were all young in those days—before you were born, of course, and while Jane was still in the convent. Like you, Monsieur Furneret, she lost her mother at an early age. Victor Hugo was still in exile in those days, but he and Flammarion were in communication. Hugo was a skeptic, but he was persuaded to hold experimental séances in Jersey. Crazy days, but I miss them."

Paul noticed that he had not mentioned his brother, and thought the omission significant, in view of what Madame de La Vaudère had said—just as the mention that she had lost her mother while very young cast a little more light on her enigmatic remark about what Paul might have been going to say—

although surely she could not possibly have guessed that it had been the tip of his tongue to come out almost automatically with the macabre jest that he had often employed defensively in his student days: "I was a double murderer while still in the womb; destroying my sister in the Darwinian struggle for existence, which caused the death of my mother as she tried unsuccessfully to deliver the corpse."

That, he thought now, was an item of black humor that ought to be laid to rest forever.

"What are you preparing for this year's Salon, Monsieur Furneret, to follow your Mourgue la Faye?" Jane de La Vaudère asked. Paul did not take the inference that she remembered the previous painting, even though she would surely have visited the Salon and even though the painting had won a medal; Victor had surely mentioned it to Cros when asking the doctor to substitute for him, and Cros would surely have mentioned it to the lady before they collected him.

"I'm attempting a historical painting," he said. "The execution of Jeanne d'Arc."

She seemed surprised. "A historical painting?" she queried. "Isn't that somewhat counter to the tide of fashion for a young man of your generation?"

"Perhaps," he said, "but I haven't had much success interesting the dealers in the work I've done in the past, and although Mourgue won a medal, most of the critics seemed to think that it belonged to a dying genre—more than one mentioned the Salon de la Rose+Croix, not regretful of its passing."

"So you looked for a historical female figure that you could use as a motif," Antoine Cros put in. "I can see the logic, and I approve. I have my doubts about the modern fashion for wishy-washy landscapes and paintings of ugly prostitutes."

"You're beginning to sound like Rochefort, my dear," said Madame de La Vaudère. Just because you have expectations of election to the non-existent throne of Araucania and Patagonia, it doesn't mean that you have to start carrying on like Var royalty in Nice. I love antique art myself, as you well know, but it doesn't make me disapprove of Monsieur Cézanne, or of Naturalism. Art is a broad church, and should be. And whatever anyone might think of Sâr Péladan as a would-be Magus, his Salon provided a forum for some wonderful works of art. Doubtless the critics to whom you're referring thought it an insult to suggest that your Mourgue la Faye would have been at home there, but in my opinion, you should take it as a compliment, and I thought it an excellent piece of work, thematically and technically. You did not use a model, I assume?"

Paul, peculiarly embarrassed by the implication that the lady had, indeed, remembered his painting, said: "No, it was pure imagination, an entirely hypothetical *femme fatale*. Some critics mentioned that, too..."

"And is your Jeanne d'Arc entirely imaginary too?" asked Antoine Cros, a trifle maliciously, evidently having followed the implication of Paul's remark.

"No," Paul admitted. "Imagination seemed the appropriate source for a imaginary character, and a real model for a real one. I was fortunate enough to find one who matched and helped to focus my idea of the character."

"I shall be very interested to see it," said Madame de La Vaudère. "and your other paintings too."

"Whenever you wish," Paul said, in a rather faint voice, hoping that its weakness would not be taken amiss—but the lady's intuition came into play again, and she did seemed to understand perfectly why he was so nervous.

"There's no need to be apprehensive of the consequences of tonight's experiment, whatever they might be," she said. "I fear that Antoine and I have alarmed you slightly—you didn't know did you, that there had been so much talk about what happened last week at Madame Pommerot's? But it really doesn't matter. As the late Monsieur Wilde said, the only thing worse than being talked about is not being talked about. People like us—you and I, that is, artists, meaning no disrespect to you, Antoine—can't afford to worry too much about what expectations have of us and what they expect of us. We have to follow our own path, and have confidence in our own vision, wherever it comes from."

"In spite of being excluded from your generalization," the doctor put in, "I agree with you wholeheartedly—and you can take her judgment seriously, Monsieur Furneret, coming as it does from the most scandalous woman in Paris."

Jane de La Vaudère pulled a face at that, but did not seem entirely displeased by the judgment, even though it was exaggerated. Paul knew exactly what Cros meant—he had read her "magical Hindu novel" *Le Mystère de Kama*—but he knew that no *succès de scandale* achieved by a book could possibly compete with the dizzy heights of scandal attained by actresses and courtesans.

"At least I shall be able to present Monsieur Furneret with a reassuring example," said the author. "Although people in other sectors of Parisian society are beginning to treat me as a pariah, there will be nothing of the sort in Juvisy. Those gentlemen will treat me with the utmost politeness, just as they will Madame Zosima, even though there will be no one there who does not know that she is a notorious lesbian. Like Antoine, they might regard both of us—and you too, Monsieur Furneret—as specimens for observation and psychological analysis, but they will be exceedingly polite while doing so, because they believe it to be a necessary corollary of their scientific objectivity."

"You're doing us an injustice, Jane, and mischievously," Cros objected, smiling. "My politeness has never lacked sympathy, as you know very well. Flammarion, Le Bon and their friends are genuinely good men, even though some of them are a trifle lacking in healthy skepticism, and that's why you have nothing to worry about, Monsieur Furneret, whatever your experiment in automatic drawing produces, or doesn't produce. They'll be understanding, and they'll be generous. Yes, they'll be observing you as a phenomenon, as I will myself, just as those who have read *Le Mystère de Kama* will have combed it for psychological insights into Jane's supposed neuroses, but those who know her, as I do, love her as well, and those who do not will, as soon as they get to know her. They will like you too, Monsieur Furneret, just as we do, even on the basis of such a short acquaintance."

As morale-boosting speeches went, Paul had to admit, that seemed to be the work of an expert psychologist. He was beginning to understand why Antoine Cros had to charge high consultation fees in order to avoid being swamped by demand—and why he still made time to visit the hospitals. He hoped that Juliette, when the time came, might find such a doctor there to care for her in her final hours—but then he felt a sharp twinge of guilt, at having made the careless assumption that the poor girl might have to rely upon a charitable doctor, because there might be no one else to lend her moral support. He had not known her for much longer than Doctor Cros and Jane de La Vaudère had known him, but he and she had broken bread together now, and he was making her a saint, albeit in his imagination, which surely implied some kind of moral responsibility. Why, otherwise, would he have insisted that she stay when she had offered him the opportunity to let her go away in immediate search of some dismal mansard in a furnished hovel?

When he could find no reply to the doctor's kindness, Madame de La Vaudère came to his rescue again.

"Forgive my curiosity, Monsieur Furneret." she said, "but might I ask you what attracted you to the motif of Jeanne d'Arc, who seems to me to be the opposite of Mourgue la Faye, a supreme victim rather than an arch-manipulator?"

Paul blushed. "I honestly don't know," he said, "there wasn't a process of conscious reasoning by which I made the decision. I was just...drawn to the one as I had been drawn to the other."

"Which is perfectly understandable and right," said Cros, perhaps still deploying his bedside manner. "Analysis of the unconscious creative processes involved in the production of works of art is probably best left to psychologists. Artists are wise who simply follow their instincts. Once they start thinking hard about what it is they're doing and how their work often becomes formularistic, detached from its source."

Ouch, Paul thought, all too well aware that he had begun thinking very hard about the possible sources of his work since his experience at Madame Pommerot's soirée, and had so far discovered nothing but confusion. He hoped that the doctor's prognosis was not a prophecy of doom.

"I'll try not to take that observation too personally, Antoine," the author responded, "but once again, you're exaggerating, and perhaps being too idealistic. We—again, I mean artists like Monsieur Furneret and myself—can't rely entirely on the promptings of the unconscious, surrendering entirely to the unreliable whims of inspiration. That way lies sterility as well as starvation. The optimum strategy is to work consciously in collaboration with the unconscious, to learn how to stimulate it, to maintain its flow and to direct it productively, in a fashion analogous to the way in which the most successful mediums interact with mesmerists—although few such alliances seem to be made in Heaven, and the same is true, in many instances, of the relationship between artists' conscious and unconscious minds. You're correct, obviously, in suggesting that some artists build dams that enable them to accumulate a reservoir than can be tapped routinely and repetitively, but there are infinite gradations between the extremes, and the fortunate imagination can and ought to interact fruitfully with method, without being destroyed or spoiled by it. Don't you agree, Monsieur Furneret?"

"Entirely," said Furneret. "The difficulty, alas, is in striking the balance, in discovering the kind and extent of the analysis that will help the endeavor rather than confusing it and bleeding life from it. That's what I'd dearly like to find, and fear that I might never achieve."

"Amen," said Cros. "And you're fortunate that Jane is one of the few followers of her profession honest enough to tell you that everyone has the same fear, and that few, if any, every attain the holy grail."

"You see, Monsieur Furneret," Madame de La Vaudère retorted. "Always exaggerating. Believe me, there are more honest writers and painters than he's implying. He knows that, but it's the way he operates—it comes of being a surgeon you see. A trenchant personality."

Cros laughed. "Jane has difficulty accepting compliments, at least in the spirit in which they're offered," he said. "But her objection doesn't touch my point: the grail is difficult, perhaps impossible, to attain. Be kind to yourself, Monsieur Furneret, and don't expect too much too soon: that's a certain prescription for failure. Be content to make slow progress. And don't be intimidated by the people you'll meet tonight. Not all scientists are saints, by any means—far from it—but Flammarion's crowd is exceptional."

"As the present company demonstrates," Madame de La Vaudère added. "Although I must admit to being a great anomaly, at Juvisy as in the Faubourg Saint-Germain—Antoine is much less so, in spite of his virulent skepticism, his checkered past and aspirations of royalty."

Cros sighed. "If you'll agree to leave Araucania and Patagonia out of the discussion tonight, Jane," he said, "I'll leave *Les Demi-Sexes* out, although I'm sure that Monsieur Furneret has heard scathing mention of both."

In fact, Paul had not, but was not sure that he would make himself look better or worse—or merely foolish—if he protested that, in spite of having been in Paris for nearly two years, he was still almost entirely detached from Montmartrean gossip, let alone the conversational topics of the salons of the *haut ton*. Fortunately, he was not required to say anything, because Antoine Cros continued after the slightest of pauses: "You really have no need to be embarrassed, Monsieur Furneret, about what we might have heard said about you in the last week. By comparison with what you might have heard said about the two of us, it's trivial. But as you can see, Madame de La Vaudère and I have survived it all, and remained sane, cheerful, and productive. I have every confidence that you can do the same."

"Thank you, Doctor Cros," said Paul, wishing that he was capable of thinking the same. "You're very kind—both of you."

"But not very persuasive, it seems," judged Jane de La Vaudère, gazing at him with an uncomfortable penetration—although he tried to persuasive himself that it was a mere semblance, caused by his own oversensitivity, and that it was, in any case, not at all fitting for him to be mentally comparing the eyes of the serene and supremely stylish author with a Montmartrean model who had casually offered to sleep with him in return for a few nights' emergency accommodation.

"At the risk of making things worse," the lady said, pensively, "it isn't just the reception that you might receive at Juvisy that's worrying you, is it There's a deeper anxiety than that. You're afraid that what you're doing might be dangerous, aren't you? No—don't answer that. As Antoine advised you earlier, hold your counsel. But for what it might be worth, there was a time when I was very anxious about the possible dangers of what Antoine would probably call dabbling with the occult. Don't ask him about it—he probably has half a dozen case studies to cite that would make your hair stand on end—and I probably shouldn't try to offer myself as a shining example either, but I do know that such dangers can be met and overcome...which is as well, because, as I'm sure you've already discovered, they can't really be avoided. If the visions come, they'll come; you can't block them out, or at least, if you can, that can be just as bad for you as falling victim to them.

"Look round tonight, as I'm sure you did at La Pommerot's last week, not just at the scholarly observers but the believers. There are people among them who've been exposed to the dangers, who know them, and have come through them, triumphant if not entirely unscathed. Take heart from that. I do. And don't be afraid of Madame Zosima. If she's a charlatan, she's harmless; if not, she's not your enemy and might be a valuable resource. If she really can enable you to see something, whether it comes from within you or without, it's a treasure of sorts. Don't fight it, use it. And don't give a damn whatever anyone else might think—but if that's too difficult, remember that there are people there who are entirely on your side, and not just scandalous Jane, the tender butcher Antoine Cros and dear old Uncle Flammarion. You're by no means the only one who's been there, believe me."

Paul knew that what he had obtained on his journey, as the train drew to a halt at Juvisy, was an infinitely better quality of reassurance than he could possibly have obtained from Victor, even though Victor was his best friend and wished him nothing but good.

"Shall we hunt for a cab, my dear?" asked Antoine Cros, mildly, as he helped Madame de La Vaudère down from the train.

"Don't be ridiculous, Antoine," she replied. "I'm not an invalid; I can walk, and it's no distance at all. And you know what they say about three in a fiacre."

Paul didn't know that either, and rarely traveled by cab, but it wasn't difficult to imagine that it would be rather cramped, even though Madame de La Vaudère was so slender. He didn't think to offer her his arm, and blushed when she took possession of it blithely, having refused the arm offered by the doctor.

"No offense, Antoine," she said, "But I have my image of consider. What would people think if they saw my clinging to an old fogey like you, while there was handsome young man walking on the other side? Please try to look like an idolater, Monsieur Furneret, rather than someone out for a sedate walk with his mother."

She must have realized as soon as she had said it that it might be undiplomatic, in view of what she had heard when they had first met, but she followed her own advice and simply ignored any possible reaction.

"It's an honor, Madame de La Vaudère," he assured her, "and there's no effort involved in such idolatry."

She laughed. "Oh, you really must come to my next soirée," she said. "No animal magnetism, I promise you. No young women either, I fear—I can't abide competition that I can't win—but you might find it an interesting study regardless. Lead the way, Antoine."

The doctor, who had not forsaken his cane, and probably never would, swung the implement in an expressive fashion, and set forth into the darkness, heading for the Observatory— from which, Paul thought, if the sky had been somewhat clearer, it might have been possible to take a close look at the face of the moon, or even the tiny bloody disk of the planet Mars.

CHAPTER III

To begin with, so far as Paul was concerned, Camille Flammarion's soirée was simply dizzying, consisting of one introduction after another: a blizzard of names, some of which he recognized, but the number of which posed such a severe test to his memory that he knew full well that he would only be able to retain a few of them, even those that were of highly significant weight: Gustave Le Bon, Charles Richet, Gilbert-Augustin Thierry, Jules Bois, Oliver Lodge. He was whisked away from the protective custody of Jane de La Vaudère—which he could not help thinking of a maternal, in spite of her injunction to pretend to be her cavalier—and felt its absence more than he would have expected. He would have been grateful to keep Cros by his side, but the doctor knew almost everyone present, and launched himself into enthusiastic circulation. It was something of a relief when Camille Flammarion exercised his authority as the host to draw Paul magisterially to one side in order to monopolize him for a few moments. As soon as they were in confidence, the astronomer became avuncular, as Cros and Madame de La Vaudère had prophesied

"Thank you for accepting my invitation," he said. "Monsieur Marvaud speaks very highly of you, and was very insistent that I ought to invite you to participate in one of our sessions. In a minute, I'll take you to meet Madame Zosima and Mademoiselle Cadelan, but I wanted a private word with you first. You've done this before, I understand, so you know what to expect."

"Only once, I fear," Paul hastened to say. "At Madame Pommerot's last soirée."

"Oh?" Flammarion queried. "When I spoke briefly to Monsieur Marvaud, he implied that you had more experience than that, but no matter. Are the chair, the drawing-pad and the charcoal adequate to your needs and your comfort?

"Perfectly," Paul assured him, and then became tongue-tied.

"You're nervous," Flammarion observed "That's understandable—but I've done this hundreds of times before, as have many of my guests, and I sure you that we don't have unreasonable expectations; our sympathy is guaranteed in advance. It's difficult, I know, not to be intimidated by the intellectual stature of some of the people here, knowing that they have come to observe you, and knowing that some of them have preconceived ideas about what might or might not happen and how it might be interpreted. For myself, I try my utmost to keep an open mind. Many people think me utterly credulous because of the phenomena I choose to investigate, and because I occasionally dabble in hypothetical fictions, which adopt an imaginative stance of *what if?* without any implication of committed belief, but in fact I'm curious without being yet convinced. I wanted to tell you that, because I can't be sure what impression you might have gained from what you've heard people say about me in the drawing rooms of Paris."

"I had no preconceived opinion," Paul assured him, thinking that assertion safer than the admission that he had seen exceedingly few Parisian drawing rooms, "and if I had had any, Doctor Cros and Madame de La Vaudère would have dispelled them in the train on the journey. They were kind enough to prepare me in advance for what I would encounter here."

"I dare say they did," said Flammarion, sounding less than confident that the groundwork those two individuals had laid would meet with his entire approval—although Paul thought his anxieties unjustified. "Having said that, might I enquire as to what you consider to be happening when you make art-work of the sort you made last week under the influence of Henri Lemastur's hypnosis?"

42

"Like you, Monsieur Flammarion," Paul told him, "I have yet to make up my mind. I simply cannot tell, as yet, whether my visions come from within or without, nor can I judge with any degree of certainty what contribution hypnotism might make, or how. Monsieur Lemastur seems certain that he generates a kind of field of force analogous to the one that surrounds a magnet, which acts upon the human mind in a fashion analogous to the manner in which a magnet acts upon electric wires, inducing some kind of psychic current...but I am not sure how far his analogy can be trusted."

"Excellent," said Flammarion. "You will be as interested, then, to observe the experiment as I shall, or Professor Lodge."

Paul permitted himself a small ironic laugh. "I would," he said, "if I were capable of observation, but I fear that my watchful consciousness goes to sleep, or otherwise absents itself, while I'm under the influence of inspiration—if you'll forgive my use of the ancient term rather than the modern analogy."

"Of course," said Flammarion. "From your viewpoint, as an artist, it is the more accurate terminology. And it is by no means unusual—indeed, the reportage of participants in the experiments to which I play host suggests that it is almost invariable. Perhaps there is a paradox in the very idea of being able to take the backward step necessary for the intellect to observe the mind's creative process. Nevertheless, whatever the results of the experiment might be, I would like the opportunity to discuss your personal experiences further. Would you be prepared to visit Juvisy again, when it is convenient for you? In the evening, perhaps, when the light is not conducive to your ordinary labor?"

Paul thought it undiplomatic to confess that he often worked by lamplight, because it would have seemed to be a protest rather than a mere point of information.

"I'd like that, Monsieur Flammarion," he said. "It would be very interesting for me to discuss the various theories that have been formulated and published, and to obtain your expert opinion."

"You're not afraid that such discussions might disrupt your creative processes? I've known painters—including some you've certainly heard of and some you may know—who have refused point blank to involve themselves with my research, thinking it dangerous. It's not unlikely that once the word gets around that you've been here, some of your colleagues might elect to give you their advice."

"I can't say that I'm completely unafraid of that," Paul admitted, although he had already decided to give his preference to Jane de La Vaudère's advice on that subject, "but on the whole, after what happened last week, I think I'm more afraid of going on without at least the beginnings of an understanding. To be honest, when your invitation came, I was delighted by the thought that I might have an opportunity to consult you. As you say, there are painters in Paris who would probably think me foolish even to listen to your advice, let alone to prefer it to theirs, but I think I'd like to make up my own mind. I can't do that without knowing the facts, and I strongly suspect that you have more facts at your disposal than any painter in Montmartre or Montparnasse, precisely because you're an astronomer and a naturalist rather than an intuitive impressionist or a focused portrait painter."

Flammarion seemed pleased by the compliment. "I hope I can justify that trust, Monsieur Furneret. We'll make an appointment for a private conversation before you leave, but I must introduce you to Madame Zosima without further delay. She and Mademoiselle Cadelan are in my study; they didn't want to face the crowd beforehand, but Madame asked to see you, given the role you'll be playing."

"You mean that she wants to hypnotize me in advance?"

"I don't think so, but if she asks, the decision is entirely up to you. Lemastur didn't, I understand—at least, not explicitly, with the standard rituals?"

"That's correct. As a firm believer in magnetism, he said that it was only necessary for me to be within the field of his effluvia while he concentrated his mental force."

"He belongs to the old guard—one of the last of the dedicated Mesmerists. Zosima is...well, let's go, and you can make up your own mind."

Flammarion ushered Paul into another room, smaller than the large drawing room but still quite capacious, where the scientist obviously did much of his writing, although it had presumably been tidied for the occasion. Zosima was sitting at the desk, while Talia Cadelan was sitting in an armchair set against the side wall, opposite its twin positioned against the far wall. Flammarion did not make any gesture to move the armchair or to invite Paul to do so; both women stood up, and the four met in the middle of the room; introductions were swiftly made.

Madame Zosima was not tall—a few inches shorter than Paul—but she seemed robust and solid, giving an impression of masculinity that was further enhanced by the fact that she was clad in a man's suit and had her black hair cut short in a kind of bob. Her face, however, surprised Paul by its beauty, more Classical in its style than Jane de La Vaudère's; while she probably would not have been chosen as a model for Aphrodite, she might well have made a Hera or an Athene. In spite of her apparent claim to an Egyptian origin, there was little sign of it in the cast of her features, although her complexion was dark. Her age was difficult to estimate, but Paul found it difficult to believe that she was very much older than forty, and probably much the same age as Madame de La Vaudère. She was considerably more striking than the medium, who was small, thin and rather sickly.

Unlike Zosima, whose eyes were dark, Talia Cadelan had pale blue eyes, but they were not as bright as Juliette's, and her wispy ash-blonde hair contrasted strongly with Juliette's dark hair. Their complexions were similar, though, with the slight chlorotic tint symptomatic of the early phases of tuberculosis. The medium could not have been much more than twenty, in Paul's estimation.

Both women were studying him intently, but Paul was much more conscious of Zosima's eyes searching his face, with an appraising gaze that put him in mind of a Norman horse-dealer assessing a colt.

"You've worked with Lemastur, I believe," she said. Her voice was soft, and although the question as a trifle blunt, it did not seem rude.

"I wouldn't call it working," Paul said, "but I did volunteer to execute a drawing under his influence, perhaps unwisely."

"You're a medium, then?" she queried, still scrutinizing him closely.

"Not to my knowledge, but I often slip into a dream-like state of semi-consciousness when I'm painting—dream-like not only because it brings on brief visions but because I usually can't remember the experience afterwards in any but the vaguest terms. I've been assured more than once that it's a hypnotic state—a trance akin to somnambulism—but I'm not sure about that."

"Can you induce it?"

"Not by an actual effort of consciousness, but I can create circumstances which it's more likely to happened."

"A low level of light, but not darkness? A susurrus of sound or soft music, but not silence?"

"That's right. You're familiar with the phenomenon, then?"

"Of course. Any touch sensation? The brush of invisible insectile winds, a prickling sensation in or under the skin."

"The latter, sometimes—not necessarily."

"Good. Don't expect too much tonight—I generally work better with women than men. I'm surprised that Lemastur found you a good subject. Perhaps you went to the soirée with a mistress—or a potential mistress?"

Paul blinked in surprise. The voice was still soft and casual, but he felt that the boundary of decency had definitely been crossed. "No," he said.

"No matter. Tonight you'll have Talia close at hand. Do you think you can bond with Monsieur Furneret, Talia?"

Automatically, Paul looked at the younger woman, who had been studying him closely a moment before, but dropped her gaze immediately. "I'll try," she murmured, in a tone far more redolent with negation than a simple *no* would have been.

"It's not essential," Zosima said, with a resignation in her tone that suggested a dire lack of confidence. Paul couldn't help wondering whether it was all an act for Flammarion's benefit, preparing excuses in advance for her probable failure to incorporate Paul into her standard performance. He summed that the astronomer, with his decades of experience, must be well accustomed to that kind of maneuver.

Zosima's tone hardened slightly as she became more businesslike in addressing her unwanted extra assistant. "You probably noticed that your table in the drawing room is positioned directly facing the chair in which Talia will be sitting. When I command her to relax, she'll slip into a trance state and close her eyes. When that happens, I want you to keep your eyes on her face. Don't look at me. You'll hear me murmuring, but don't look, and don't try to make any sense of what I'm murmuring. Just consider it as empty noise. Focus your attention on Talia. Imagine that you can see through her closed eyelids, as if you were looking into her mind. Don't put too much effort into it; focus, don't strain. Don't rush it. Just let your mind drift. I can see that you're nervous, but there's no need. If we're all relaxed, the process will go smoothly, once it has gathered momentum. With luck, you won't even hear me when I begin to address Talia, or her replies. Don't try. Just let your mind and your hand drift. The spirits will come. It will take time, but the conditions are right. Don't worry if the spirits are crowded or confused; it's quite usual for several to jostle for attention, but it's rare for the contest to go on for long; order should follow. Take your time—and if some kind of conflict does develop, don't panic. You're in safe hands. And when I snap my fingers, loudly, that will be the signal for you both to resurface and resume consciousness. It's all quite simple. Any questions?"

Paul had dozens

"The spirits will come?" he quoted. "Where from?"

If she was startled by the question, or its bluntness, she didn't show it. "I don't know," she replied, frankly. "Nor, apparently, do they. They can become articulate, with an eloquent medium, but when they do, they recall feelings much better than locations."

"And where do they come *to*?"

"Hereabouts. They'll be most evidently manifest within your skull—visible to your mind's eye, given that you're a seer, whether you remember having seen them consciously or not, but they're not restricted to the volume of your brain. Sometimes, they can form apparitions, or move objects, or touch people, and even speak without using the medium's vocal cords, although it's not easy—not easy for them, at any rate, to make sense."

"And will the same...spirits...come into my mind as into Talia's?"

At last Zosima's expression gave a slight hint of surprise. "That's an interesting question," she admitted. "Sometimes, yes, even though that gives the implication that they're manifesting in two places at once. More usually no, I suspect—but I rarely work with two mediums simultaneously, and I wouldn't be doing it now if it weren't for the fact that Monsieur Flammarion is intent on putting both of us to the test, laying down a challenge, wanting us to do more than is...comfortable."

Paul glanced at Flammarion, but the astronomer made no protest, content to observe the dialogue with a scientific eye.

"Comfortable?" he said to Zosima. "Do you mean safe?"

"No, I mean what I say. You're evidently uncomfortable and so am I. Even Talia is uncomfortable. The situation is new, awkward. There's no danger, I can assure you of that, but sometimes, I've observed that if two mediums respond simultaneously to the same stimulus, especially if there's a conflict of manifestations, things can become confused. You might find that disturbing, but no more so than a mildly disturbing dream."

"A nightmare?"

"If you like, but I've never witnessed anything akin to a violent nightmare. It's just...strange."

"But by your own admission, you don't do it frequently, and you prefer not to work with male subjects. You might not have seen the full range of phenomena."

While the hypnotist drew breath, Paul glanced sideways at Flammarion again. The astronomer was still impassive, but Paul got the distinct impression that he was pleased, perhaps being drawn into an area of observation that was new even to an investigator of his abundant experience.

"That's possible," Zosima admitted. "If the prospect frightens you, you're free to refuse to take part. I'm sure Monsieur Flammarion would understand."

That, Paul knew, was blatant hypocrisy—and a challenge. The alleged Egyptian was perfectly sure that Flammarion would be very disappointed if Paul decided to back out at the last minute, and she was confident that he wouldn't want to display that kind of cowardice. On the other hand, she hadn't contradicted him when he pointed out that she couldn't have seen the whole range of the possible phenomena that her ability might provoke, if she did have any kind of uncanny ability.

"If you'll forgive me saying so, Mademoiselle Cadelan," Paul ventured, addressing the younger woman, "You don't look entirely well. Are you sure that you're up to...experimenting tonight?"

The young woman formed a wry smile. "Thank you for your concern, Monsieur Furneret," she said, "but I'm quite well, and I'm curious to see what you draw, and to compare it with what I'm reported to have said while entranced, and any fragments of memory I can retain. I have complete faith in Zosima; she won't allow any harm to come to me."

Paul looked at Flammarion.

"I don't want to say too much," the astronomer said, "lest I plant suggestions prejudicial to the experiment, but I have supervised hundreds of experiments of this general sort. I can't guarantee, obviously, that I've seen the whole range of possible phenomena, but I have seen a great many. I have seen mediums and artists become disturbed, in the manner that Madame Zosima has described, and mediums often faint—but none has suffered any serious harm here at the Observatory."

Paul took note of the fact that his host had felt it necessary to qualify the word "harm" with the adjective "serious," and assumes that Flammarion must suspect that many of the fainting fits to which he referred were tactical losses of consciousness rather than reactions to real or imagined spirit phenomena, but he was prepared to accept that anecdotes about mediums being scared to death by the spirits they evoked were simply improvised horror stories, and he had never heard an anecdote about an automatic artist or writer dying of effects of their endeavor. If any ever had, he suspected, the tale would surely have been added to the rich urban legendry of the City of Light.

"All right," he said, "I've got the instructions clear in my mind; I'll do my best to follow them. Let's go.

Flammarion nodded. Zosima smiled. Talia remained impassive.

All four of them made their way into the drawing room, where there was a sudden bustle as conversations began to fall silent, and the members of the audience who had been standing in groups searched for seats in an array whose order was deliberately not geometrically regimented.

Paul had heard accounts of séances in which the participants formed a circle and held hands, but that had not been the format at Madame Pommerot's soirée and it was not the format here. Knowing that he would have his back to the audience when the séance began in earnest, Paul took a long look round before sitting down, noting the positions Antoine Cros and Jane de La Vaudère had taken up, some way behind the ragged front rank of armchairs, which was occupied by Oliver Lodge and the other leading scientists, in something approximating their order of prestige. They did not seem unduly intimidating, certainly not hostile, or even severe.

The atmosphere in the room, where the lights were subdued, but still allowed faces to be visible and discernible, seemed relatively relaxed, although no wine had been served during the interim while Paul was being interrogated and asking questions in his turn. All but a few of the audience members, Paul judged, were regulars who knew one another well and had seen similar occasions several or many times before. They were all comfortable with it—which reassured him a good deal more than the elliptical comments made by Zosima and Flammarion regarding things they had never seen.

Paul took his seat, took a piece of charcoal between the thumb and forefinger of his right hand, and gazed at the large square of blank paper in front of him

Zosima came to lean over him. "You're in safe hands," she assured him, again. "Just relax, let yourself go. Keeping looking at Talia, imagine that you're gazing at the mind behind her eyes. It's easy."

The she went to Talia, who was sitting in an armchair facing him, already apparently relaxed and thinking of nothing in particular—surely not about him, in spite of her false promise to attempt a connection. Zosima stroked her hair, closed her eyelids gently, kissed her softly on the forehead, and whispered something in her ear, inaudible to anyone but her. Then she disappeared—not literally, but simply moving away in order to take up a position a fraction outside Paul's peripheral vision.

Silence had fallen in the audience. As Zosima had announced, she began murmuring, but without producing intelligible words—not, at least, in French or any other language that Paul could recognize. He thought that it was probably a kind of vocal music, a sonic background rather than an incantation or an evocation.

He looked at Talia's closed eyes, and, obedient to the suggestion he had been given, he imagined that he was looking through her closed eyelids into the private area of her mind: her peaceful, dim, almost quiet mind.

But why make that assumption? he asked himself. Outwardly, yes, the young woman was placid, colorless, and meek—but what reason was there to assume that such an exterior mirrored her inner being? Might her mind not be turbulent, seething with emotion? What emotion? Pal tried hard to keep ideas of lesbian lust at bay, but could not. Zosima, who had organized her appearance as a walking cliché, made that impracticable.

Paul had never been introduced to the painter Louise Abbéma, who moved in social circles distant from the Butte of Montmartre, but he had seen her at the Salon, dressed as Zosima was, with an entourage that included frail adolescent girls as well as other amazons and stylish aristocrats who were above criticism, if not above suspicion. He knew nothing at all about that private world, that not-so-secret society, except what he had read in Catulle Mendès' *Méphistophela*, which clearly went far beyond belief; he had not read the book that Madame de La Vaudère and Antoine Cros had mentioned in the train as a topic best avoided for this evening, *Les Demi-Sexes*, but his reclusiveness had not insulated him entirely from gossip, and he had heard of it, as her first *succès de scandale*, now outshone by *Le Mystère de Kama...*

But such imaginations were surely the very last thing he ought to be thinking about now, in spite of the fact that Zosima had actually gone out of her way to plant them there. Why? Did she really believe that there was a sexual component to the way in which the magic of spiritism worked, that Lemastur's "magnetism" ought to be construed metaphorically, or even euphemistically? But who was he trying to fool? The painter of Mourgue la Faye, Jeanne d'Arc and countless ethereal female "spirits" that originated, or at least passed through, the murky depths of his own mind? What on earth was the point of pretending that that his work was not essentially erotic in nature, even if he had refused Juliette Scaran's naked offer of sexual intercourse...because of Martine, because the model was a part-time prostitute who might well be carrying some kind of infection, and because of any other excuses he could invent for his reluctance, but not because he did not feel...and all through the journey here he had been sitting in close proximity with Jane de La Vaudère, who was very beautiful, and scandalous, even if she was old enough to be...

He cursed himself volubly. Was this where his mind went when he let it drift? What on earth as wrong with him? He was taking part in a scientific experiment, concerned with matters of life and death and hypothetical forces and energies, on which important theoretical matters might depend, not to mention his own ability to obtain a greater measure of conscious control over the practicalities of his career, his vocation, his obsession...could he not, should he not, must he not keep his mind on higher things than...

And in any case, he told himself, sternly, look at her, look at Talia, at that pale, sad face, that victim of the early stages of tuberculosis and the machinations of that fake Egyptian...

But again, he knew, without really thinking about it, he was letting his imagination run away with him. Was Talia really sad? Was she really a victim? Was she not, first and foremost, placid, relaxed, entranced. Was she not letting herself drift, as she was supposed to do, opening her mind, her self, not to any kind of vulgar groping, but to the advent of delicate, phantom entities hardy capable of appearing of touching, as harmless anything imaginable, open, as he ought to be open, to inspiration, to connection...

And even if he could not find her physically desirable, even by comparison with Juliette, let alone Jane de La Vaudère or the memory of Martine, surely, as an artist, he ought to be able to empathize with her, to form with her a mystical triangle with the magnetic Zosima? Should he not be able to appreciate, esthetically, the delicacy, sensitivity and serenity of her beautiful mind, her almost quiet mind...?

Almost quiet?

He felt, although he did not know how he felt it, or how it was possible to feel it, that there was a mind, which was perhaps not Talia's, nor Zosima's, nor even his, but was nevertheless a mind, and nevertheless *there*, or at least thereabouts, and that it was almost quiet.

Almost, but not quite. There seemed to be sound there, which was not Zosima's soothing murmur, and also, as Paul stared, into what ought to have been a void behind Talia's eyes, a glimmer of light. That impression of light fascinated him. It began as a dot, but slowly expanded to become a curve, whose end arched back toward one another but did not meet. Then the lines of the curve became jagged, zigzagging as the curve continued to expand, or inflate.

That was not odd, because Paul had seen that phenomenon before, in his own eyes, persistent no matter whether they were open or closed, but always seemingly on the surface of his own vision, not imaginatively projected as it was now, so that it seemed to be beyond Talia Cadelan's eyes, in the depths of her drifting—or entranced—mind.

He wanted to think about that, to consider its implications, but simultaneously, he didn't want to think about it at all, now or ever; he just wanted to experience it. He didn't want to think about the significance of the curve, or its jaggedness, or its gradual inflation; he didn't want to find meaning where there was none; he just wanted to drift, like the curve, and expand, like the curve, and try as he did so to iron out the zigzags in his soul, to smooth himself, to open himself, to allow himself to be empty in order that he might not be empty any longer...

And he went to sleep.

CHAPTER IV

At least, Paul assumed, subsequently, that he must have fallen asleep, probably not at that moment, when the jagged curve of light had expended beyond the periphery of his vision, although that moment was the last of which he had even a vague memory of a describable perception, but some time thereafter, perhaps a long time thereafter, while he had been dreaming without being able to retain anything that could later qualify as a memory *per se*...but he did have the vague feeling that it had not been unpleasant, to begin with, that he had indeed been in safe...no, not hands, not hands at all, but safe nevertheless...not a *place* of safety, because he didn't seem to have a particular location, but a safety, a kind of limbo, where there was peace...sound, yes, but soft sound, and light, too, but soft light, no longer curved or jagged, and where a soul could drift, and where such drifting was, as Zosima had promised, easy...

Until it wasn't.

Then, things seemed to happen rapidly, although it also seemed, when he tried to remember them, that the rapidity had be a temporal illusion, that things had actually happened quite slowly, but that his mind had compressed them and compacted them, and squeezed them into a single moment...

Things?

No, it hadn't been *things* that had happened. What else could it have been? He had no idea...he just had a feeling that *things* was the wrong expression, that whatever had happened, slowly or quickly, had not been events, as such. Visions, perhaps, seen and perhaps even touched, but nevertheless invisible and intangible...but no, that didn't even make sense.

But wasn't that the truth of the matter? Wasn't the whole point of the experience that it hadn't made sense, and couldn't make sense, because that was not the kind of experience it was.

Wherever or whenever he had been, he concluded, much later, it had not been hostile to paradox or any other kind of impossibility: quite the reverse. Wherever it was, if there could be any graspable meaning in the word "where" in that context, it was neither earth nor Mars, and whenever it was, if there could be any tangible meaning in the word "when," it was neither now or then.

He heard a scream. *Then* there was a where, and a when.

Then, distinctly, in spite of the scream, he heard fingers snap. Then, obediently, he woke up.

Dazed and confused, he found that he was staring, with his eyes wide open, not at Talia Cadelan, but at the square sheet of paper in front of him: the large square sheet that was no longer blank, because a swift hand...surely it had been swift?...had made four drawings. Four! There were four separate figures, three of which were very recognizably faces, and the fourth of which surely wasn't, only bearing the vaguest resemblance to a bloated, distorted head. Two of the faces were female, and one male. They were sketchy, dashed off in charcoal who relatively few strokes and only a little shading, but they were perfectly recognizable—recognizable, at least, as individual people, but not necessarily recognizable in the sense that Paul recognized them by virtue of knowing who they were.

He barely glanced at the male face and one of the women, looking at them just long enough to be certain that he didn't recognize them, that he didn't have the faintest idea who they were.

But the third face—the fourth entity—he did recognize. And that was when he did what he vaguely remembered having been told not to do, at some stage, by someone...he panicked.

He didn't scream. Unlike Talia, he didn't scream; but an irrational terror suddenly overwhelmed him: not the terror of what he saw, or even the terror of what it might imply, if he really had been drawing spirits, if he really had be drawing the souls of the dead. It wasn't the terror of dire suspicion, although he would surely have been entitled to that, but something deeper, an existential terror in the very core of the soul.

He was suddenly ashamed of having thought, earlier, that if mediums often fainted in Monsieur Flammarion's séances, they alas did so strategically, as a tactic of evasion. If even one of them had experienced something akin to what he had just experienced...

But the mere fact that he had been able to think that was evidence that he was not lost, not doomed...

He also knew—in that moment, in spite of all his careful intellectual uncertainty, he felt that he *knew*—that the inference that the recognition of the face had forced him to draw was impossible. He could not be drawing the souls of the dead, he had to be drawing figures from his own imagination, from his own ignorant imagination. He had to be, because otherwise...

He was aware of people clustering around him, leaning over him—not leaning over him because they were concerned for him and wanted to help him in his distress, but leaning over him because they wanted to see the pictures, *the goddam pictures!* They wanted to see what, or who, he had drawn. They wanted to see whether there was anyone there that *they* could recognize. And while they were pushing and shoving one another and craning their necks, Paul thought that he could easily have died. He thought that he might literally have died, that he might have been about to plunge into some spaceless, timeless, horrible well of souls, from which he would struggle for all eternity to emerge...except that there was absolutely no way that he was going to let that happen, even if he had to fight his way through that stupid, inconsiderate crowd of great intellectuals with his young fists.

In the event, he did not have to do that. Just when he was clenching his firsts, ready to smash Oliver Lodge or Jules Bois in the face, salvation arrived—or rather salvation had already been there, craning its neck with all the others, but had realized all of a sudden that assistance was necessary, that Paul was in difficulties, and fighting to remain conscious in the grip of vertigo—and he heard a voice, the voice of Antoine Cros—telling everyone else to get back, to get out of the way, to give him room. Then he felt Antoine Cros grab one of his arms, while someone else grabbed the other, and they pulled him away from the table, away from the fatal sheet of paper, toward the door to Camille Flammarion's study.

There was a problem at that point, because Zosima and someone else were half-carrying Talia in the same way that Antoine Cros and someone else were manhandling him, and Cros had to stand aside for a moment to allow Talia to be transported through the doorway first; but Paul then he was bundled through, and deposited in one of the two armchairs positioned on opposite sides of the room, while Talia was placed in the other. Then Antoine Cros seemed to become all arms and legs, hustling people back through the door and shouting; "Out! Out! And don't let anyone else in until I say so!" before slamming the door behind them—everyone, that is, except Zosima, who was bent over Talia.

The doctor returned to his patient with all possible rapidity and knelt before him, putting his face very close to Paul's dazed and confused face.

Paul tried to formulate the phrase *Thank you*, but couldn't

But to his utter astonishment and alarm, what Doctor Antoine Cros said, or whispered, or hissed, was: "If this is some trick cooked up by you and that fop Marvaud, believe me, you'll regret it!" He looked, for a moment, like a man capable of doing murder.

Paul had enough presence of mind to be glad that the doctor didn't have a scalpel in his hand, and enough to find his voice and croak: "What trick? I swear to God I don't know what you're talking about! Help me!"

Then, abruptly, Cros became all doctor again, all concern for his patient, at least momentarily. He put his hand on Paul's forehead, loosened his collar, and took his pulse. Then, finally, he said, still whispering: "All right. I believe you, but tell me: why the fit? What did you see that scared you half to death?"

Paul, still started and distressed by the catastrophic failure of the physician's bedside manner, croaked: "Martine."

There was a moment of utter puzzlement, and then enlightenment dawned

"The girl in the lifeboat!"

Paul nodded.

"One of those faces was the girl in the lifeboat! And when you recognized her, you thought, if you really had been drawing spirits, that she must be dead!" The doctor had a quick mind. He had summed up the situation with striking exactitude. Paul nodded again.

Cros softened his attitude considerably, and said: "Paul, this is very important. Did you recognize either of the other two faces?"

"No," Paul said, managing to sit up straight. "I've never seen either of them before. I'm certain of it."

"Wait here," said Cros, although Paul had certainly not been thinking of going anywhere. The doctor reached the door in two strides, flung it open, and shouted: "Jane! Where's Jane?"

A moment later, he pulled Jane de La Vaudère into the room, and slammed the door again behind her. He was still whispering, but Paul could hear what he was saying, although he did not think that Zosima could, from the other side of the room, where she was absorbed with Talia. Paul could see that Talia, too, was trying to sit up. If she had fainted in the drawing room, she had come round. She seemed disorientated, but not frightened

"Did you recognize anyone?" Cros asked Jane de La Vaudère, bluntly.

"Yes," she said, positively. "It's been a long time, but I remember—and when I saw Flammarion recognize him too, I was certain."

"Flammarion will keep quiet for now, in the interests of the experiment. Is there anyone else in the audience who might have recognized him?"

"I don't think so—not immediately. Nobody said anything in my hearing. As I say, it's been a long time. but the face isn't unfamiliar; it's been reproduced frequently. But surely Paul couldn't..."

Cros silenced her with a curt gesture. "He recognized one of the women as the girl in the lifeboat, Martine Lambrunet. The idea that she might be dead hit him like a sledgehammer—he's obviously in love—but nobody else knows her. What about the other? Did anyone show any sign of recognizing her?"

"Not that I saw. As for the blob..."

"It wasn't a blob," said Cros. "We can leave that until later. Flammarion will take possession of the paper, as always. He won't rush into an announcement until he's made a thorough investigation. He'll make sure that everyone gets a good look at the paper, and he's doubtless soliciting and collecting opinions as we speak. If someone recognizes the second woman, that will cause a stir, but if not...we're probably the only ones who know exactly what happened, the only one who can evaluate it sanely. Paul and I have a personal stake in it. We need time to think about it, time to weigh it up..."

He had not noticed, while intent on his tête-à-tête, that Zosima had come up behind him, and must have overheard at least a part of his final speech, in spite of his scrupulously low tone.

"Either I'm much mistaken," the dark-haired woman said, sarcastically, "or this young man has just provided spectacular proof of my power as a generator of mesmeric energy, and you're discussing ways and means of suppressing the information." She did not seems particularly angry, but nor did she seem amused.

"That's not what's happening," Cros told her. "At this moment in time, the evidence that we and Flammarion have is decidedly ambiguous. In order to determine whether this fellow really can commune with the spirits of the dead, with the right assistance, we need to investigate much more carefully. We don't want to rush to publicity until we're sure, and Paul and I both have a personal stake in being sure. If possible, we need to identify the third face that he drew, and we need to wait, at least until the morning, and perhaps longer, for one more crucial item of evidence."

"And may I join your little cabal," the Egyptian said, sarcastically, "given that I too have a personal stake in this, at least as great as Paul's, and greater than yours?"

"Of course," said Cros. "How is Talia?" As he spoke, he moved to cross the room, in order to check the younger woman's condition for himself.

"Better, now," Zosima called after him. "It was just a shock." She glanced at Paul, meaningfully "As I said, there was no real danger."

And as I thought, Paul thought, *there was no way that you could be sure of that.*

Meanwhile, Jane de La Vaudère put her right hand on his forehead, in a maternal fashion, showing an evident concern that did not seem to be feigned. He opened his mouth, but she immediately moved the hand to put her finger over his lips. "Hold your counsel, for now," she advised. "One step at a time." He noticed that she had positioned herself between him and Zosima, protectively.

Having checked Talia swiftly, and evidently satisfied himself as to her condition, the doctor patted her on the shoulder, paternally, and crossed the room again. "Why did she scream?" he asked Zosima, bluntly.

"She says that doesn't remember. She thinks she saw something horrible, but she says that doesn't know what it was." Zosima turned to Paul, and took advantage of the fact that once Cros had returned, Jane de La Vaudère had abandoned her protective position. "Who did you recognize, Monsieur Furneret?" the magnetizer asked, with careful politeness, although her soft voice seemed to Paul to have taken on a feline quality.

Paul could not think of any good reason not to tell her. "Martine Lambrunet," he said. "She was aboard the *Palatine*, which struck a rock and foundered off the coast of England last night. We know that she was put in a lifeboat, but so far, we don't know whether the lifeboat made it safely to shore."

"Ah!" said Zosima. "I see why you need to know before jumping to any conclusion. And you?" she asked," turning to Cros. "Who did you recognize?"

"My brother Charles," Cros answered. "Jane knew him, and Flammarion too. They both recognized him."

"But he's definitely dead? And Monsieur Furneret never met him?"

"Yes, but that's not conclusive. He was a famous man, in his time. He published books, which still have some reputation, and he invented the phonograph before Edison. His photograph appeared in numerous places where Paul might conceivably have seen it. My first thought, when I saw the drawing, was that it must be a practical joke, hatched by Paul and the friend who arrange for me to bring him tonight, but that was unworthy of me, and I owe Paul an apology for my reaction. I'm convinced that he's honest. He doesn't remember consciously having seen a photograph of Charles, but if that memory is stored away in his unconscious mind...he met me for the first time today; that could have caused it to surface, in the context of a vision, without my brother's soul having anything to do with it. That's why Monsieur Flammarion needs to identify the third face, if he can, in order that we can evaluate that evidence, if it is evidence...while we wait to find out whether Martine Lambrunet is alive or dead."

Prudently, Zosima did not venture an opinion on that. Instead, she said: "You believe that he's honest, but you still have doubts about me. Well, that's understandable; a superabundance of charlatans has made it virtually impossible for most magnetizers and mediums to convince anyone other than prejudiced believers, no matter what evidence they produce. If Talia levitated and circled the room, half those old men in there would cry miracle and the other half would proclaim it an obvious case of collective hallucination. But I need to know what happened in there even more than you do. Your young friend was right: I hadn't seen the full range of possible phenomena. I'm reluctant to put Thalia through that again immediately, even if it was just a nightmare."

Jane de La Vaudère, who was still half-crouching beside Paul's chair, whispered: "And you ought to think very hard about putting yourself through it again, no matter what happened..."

Cros had heard her, and he turned round.

"Exactly what did happen, Paul?" he asked. Whether the use of his first name was a gesture of alliance or the fashion of a doctor addressing his patient, Paul could not tell.

"Exactly what you said," Paul told him. "I saw Martine's face, recognized her, thought it might be evidence that she was dead, and reacted badly. I reacted almost as badly when Victor told me that the *Palatine* had hit a rock. I'm sorry. Far too sensitive."

"Not if I was right about your being in love with the girl," Cros opined, and waited for confirmation.

Paul remained silent, leaving the three of them to interpret his silence any way they saw fit.

The door opened and Camille Flammarion came in, scanning the room anxiously. "How are they?" he asked.

"Fine," said Cros. "Shaken, but not hurt. Nothing that we haven't seen before."

"It seemed more violent," Flammarion observed, uneasily.

"Perhaps a touch of *folie à deux*," opined the doctor. "Whether it was a contact with the *au-delà* or mere psychology, the fact that they were under the spell together exaggerated the response—but like you, I've seen deliberate fakes and I've seen the sincerely deluded enough times to convince me that I know the difference. These two—these three—aren't fakers. Exactly what that remarkable sheet of paper is evidence of, I don't know, but even if it's only evidence of the richness of Monsieur Furneret's imagination, there's genuine wealth in there. It's a pity that Charcot's not here—but Richet is, and if it's grist to his mill, we can be sure that it'll be finely ground. Have you left the paper on the table?"

"Yes. They're calm now, there's no possibility of it being damaged while they're all trying to snatch it at once. They're already forming groups, and the arguments are starting. If your patients have recovered fully, shall we submit them to the Inquisition?"

"No," said the doctor, decisively. "Not now. We need to wait—it's vital, not just to the investigation, but for Paul's peace of mind."

"Why so?" the astronomer asked, in a level tone that implied that he would not ream of contradicting the doctor's opinion.

"Because the latest news we have of one of the women he drew is that she was put into a lifeboat in the early hours of this morning and set adrift in a storm. We need to know whether the boat made it to shore before we can decide what the drawing might signify."

"Ah!" sad Flammarion. "In that case, it's a pity that Myers isn't here—but Lodge will undoubtedly report he case to him when he returns to England, no matter how it turns out. Do you think that the fourth face might be that of an extraterrestrial?"

"No," said Cros bluntly. "I can assure you that it isn't."

"Really? How?"

"I'd rather not say, for the moment," the surgeon replied. "When I've investigated the matter further, I'll let you know."

The astronomer was not the only person present who felt that reply inadequate, and who looked at the doctor a trifle resentfully, but precisely because Cros was a doctor, and had assumed responsibility for both Paul and Talia as patients, he evidently felt that he had the authority to dictate the terms of the situation—or, at least, he was prepared to adopt that pretext.

"Professional reticence, Antoine?" Flammarion asked, gently.

"If you like. Or experimental conscience. You and I know only too well the dangers of suggestion. I don't want to disclose my hypothesis until I've checked it, any more than I want to alarm my patients unnecessarily. The matter needs further investigation, delicately—not in that lion's den out there. It's worse than usual, and there are strange faces in the crowd—unknown to me, at any rate, although they obviously have your permission to be there."

He glanced at Jane de La Vaudère then, very briefly, and Paul, who was still very close to her, saw a flash of enlightenment dawn in her expression—but she controlled it immediately, and Paul got the impression that, having guessed the reason for Cros's discretion, she had immediately consented to maintain the same discretion.

"Antoine's right, Camille," she said to the astronomer. She turned to Zosima. "Am I right in thinking, Madame, that you have no interest in facing the inquisition that's waiting for you outside immediately, given the circumstances?"

Zosima nodded. "I can talk to them, if you wish," she said, "but they'd know that I was being evasive and might take the wrong inference. The doctor is right, as you say. We need to know all the facts—or as many as we can obtain—before we draw any conclusion, and until we reach a conclusion on our own account, any hypothetical discussion in a crowd would probably be futile."

Camille Flammarion frowned, but his reflection was immediately interrupted by a knock on the door. He went to answer it, and then turned to Cros. "A colleague would like to speak with you," he said.

Cros nodded, and left the room.

"I don't want to make any difficulties," said Paul. "If you need someone to take questions from your guests, Monsieur Flammarion, I'm willing to do it. I'm the one who made the drawing, after all—it's me they'll want to interrogate."

"No," said Jane de La Vaudère, immediately. "You can't ask him to do that, Camille, not now. Antoine and I both assured him on the way here that he had nothing to fear, and I

65

don't want to be proved wrong. The boy has had a bad shock, on what was already a terrible day; it's not fair to make him—or even to let him—expose himself to that kind of probing, however polite it might be, and I've seen the intensity of the argument break the boundaries of politeness too often. He has too much at stake. If you want to tell them about him recognizing the girl in the lifeboat, go ahead—that will explain to them why he's in no condition to do or say anything further tonight—but I won't let him go out there. For his own good, Antoine and I need to take him home, as Antoine promised his friend to do."

"I'm not a child," Paul protested, although he knew how impolite and unreasonable it was for him to protest against what was in fact, an act of kindness.

"Of course not," said the lady, "But humor me, will you, Paul? I have far too few opportunities to exercise my maternal instincts, and I'd like the opportunity to strike a different pose, for once. Being the author of *Le Mystère de Kama* can become a little wearing. Allow me to play guardian angel for a little while, if you can bring yourself to do it."

Paul could not imagine that there was any possible reply to that. He and Madame de La Vaudère both turned toward the door as Antoine Cros came back in, frowning. In response to four inquisitive gazes, he said: "You're going to hate me, I know, but there's been a further development, about which I can't tell you, for reasons of...well, patient confidentiality might not be putting it too strongly. Anyhow, I don't want to make it public yet, and I can only apologize, Camille. I'll explain everything to you as soon as I feel able to do so, but this labyrinth is even more complicated than I thought. If it's convenient, I'd like to take Monsieur Furneret away in order to consult with him in private, wherever he feels most comfortable."

"I was just saying that we need to take him home," Jane de La Vaudère said, swiftly. "Even if you don't feel able to talk about confidential matters while I'm with you, you can't leave me here. You can speak to Paul alone when you get him back, if he's not too tired—or you can make an appointment to see him tomorrow. He wants to go out and talk to them, but you took responsibility for him when he fainted, so you can order him, as his physician, to let us take him home."

"I didn't faint," Paul said, weakly, as a point of information rather than a protest, but Antoine Cros waved the objection away. "Jane's right, Camille," he said, addressing Flammarion. "I've taken responsibility for the boy as his physician. I can't see him exposed to further risk. In view of what's happened, my professional opinion is that it would be best if he went home, and not alone. I'm sure that he doesn't think that he requires mothering, but he was relying on us to take him home in any case."

"Very well," said Flammarion, a trifle reluctantly. "But Monsieur Furneret and I had already agreed that we would meet again, in private, to discuss...matters of common interest. Subsequent developments—including the ones you seem intent on keeping quiet, Antoine—have only made me, and, I suspect, Monsieur Furneret, more anxious to have that discussion. May I, then arrange such an appointment for tomorrow, by which time we will probably know about the fate of the lifeboat?"

"Just a moment," Zosima put in. "Haven't we agreed that I have as much interest this matter as anyone? I need an urgent private consultation with Monsieur Furneret too."

"So do I," another voice put in from behind the Egyptian.

Everyone turned to look at Talia Cadelan; Zosima was by no means the least surprised by the unexpected interjection.

"Why?" the Egyptian demanded, with her customary bluntness.

Talia blushed. "I can't tell you that, Zosima" she said. "Not yet—but I do need to talk to him."

Paul felt that the situation was becoming positively surreal. He stood up, and took out his card-holder. He handed cards to Zosima and Talia. Flammarion already had his address, and Cros and Madame de La Vaudère had his cards.

"I think, on reflection that Doctor Cros is right," he said. "It might, indeed, be more...comfortable if I allowed myself to be taken home. Monsieur Flammarion, I'd be grateful if you could make my apologies to your other guests, and explain to them why I'm...indisposed. Anyone who wishes to speak to me privately, for whatever purpose, is welcome to visit my studio tomorrow, although I'd prefer that they did so in the early morning or the evening, because I have a painting in progress and a model booked for a sitting from late morning until mid-afternoon. For personal reasons that you'll understand, however, I'd dearly like to know that Martine and Amélie Lambrunet are safe...or not...before I enter into any further discussion of the drawing that I made a little while ago. Hopefully, news will have reached Madame Cambourg—the concierge of my building—by the time I get back to Paris. If not...well, as soon as there is news, I'll telephone you, Monsieur Flammarion, and I'll notify anyone else who cares to give me a number where I can reach them, or an address to which I can send a pneumatique. Is that agreeable to everyone?"

"Of course," said Flammarion, instantly. "I do apologize, Monsieur Furneret—I've been rather inconsiderate...as have we all, I think, except for Madame de La Vaudère. Consideration for you should have been uppermost in all our minds...and for Mademoiselle Cadelan. My other guests will understand perfectly, and I shall promise them to keep them apprised of further developments in the situation so far as I am able to do so. I'm sorry that the evening has been so stressful for you both."

"My fault entirely," Paul murmured. "I'm the one who made the drawing."

"That was certainly no fault," the astronomer assured him. "Whatever kind of marvel it might ultimately return out to be, it is most certainly a marvel, of considerable relevance to science, quite apart from any personal relevance it might have."

"Enough," said Jane de La Vaudère. "Enough, for now. Antoine and I will take the matter from here. Antoine, there must be at least a dozen carriages waiting in Monsieur Flammarion's courtyard. Find someone sympathetic prepared to lend us the use of one for the few minutes necessary to take us to the station, while Monsieur Furneret and I take our leave of present company, and make our way down by the service staircase."

Cros nodded, and left the room, while Madame de La Vaudère did as she had said, ceremoniously, imperiously speaking for Paul as well as for herself; then she took possession of his arm, in the same fashion as she had when they had emerged from Juvisy station.

"Please forgive me, Paul," she said, as they made their way down the service stair. "I'm behaving like a tyrant, I know—which I've become increasingly inclined to do as I've grown older, I fear. It comes, I think from having been obliged to be so meek and obedient as a child, an orphan abandoned in a convent. It was an experience from which I have never entirely recovered, and against which I still have fits of reaction."

"There's nothing to forgive," Paul assured her. "I'm very grateful to you. I dread to think what would have happened if I'd followed the original plan and come with Victor. Then, you and Doctor Cros would only have been members of the audience, and even if Doctor Cros had come to help me...anyway, I'm very glad to have made your acquaintance beforehand, and that you felt an obligation to intervene on my behalf. You've been a godsend."

She laughed. "Hardly that," she said. "Scandalous Jane, remember? That fake Egyptian witch and half the audience will think I'm a predator swooping on a handsome innocent. We'll be fortunate if it doesn't make the gossip columns. But have no fear—my motives are pure, and when your lover arrives, having run aground at Land's End or on the Scilly Isles, too far from the nearest telegraph to save you from worry earlier, I'll make sure that there's no possibility of a misunder-standing."

Paul hesitated, but then said, shamefacedly: "I fear that there has already been a partial misunderstanding. Yes, it's true that I have been in love with Martine for years—all my life—but I doubt that she's aware of the fact, and I'm certain that the feeling isn't reciprocated. She isn't in any real sense, my lover."

"Ah!" she said, perhaps more surprised by the fact that he had made the revelation than its content. "Yes, it's a situation I've described in more than one of my novels—something of a cliché, I fear...but no less painful to endure, as I know only too well. Shh! Here's Antoine. Neither he nor anyone else will hear the secret from me."

CHAPTER V

"I've borrowed a carriage," Cros said, as he guided them across the courtyard to the vehicle in question. "There'll be a short wait for the train, but not too long." He assisted the author into the four-seater carriage, and sat beside her as he had previously, He seemed preoccupied, and did not say a word on the brief journey to the station. Nor did he seem any more inclined to speak in the waiting room, although that seemed more reasonable, as there were several other people waiting for the Paris train.

When the train arrived, however, they had no difficulty in finding a empty first-class carriage, and when the train pulled away, Jane de La Vaudère said: "Are you really going to take refuge in the fiction that Paul is your patient not to say a word all the way back to Paris, Antoine? He's far too polite to say anything, I'm sure, but he must be burning with curiosity to hear what you've deduced or discovered, and so am I. Is it really the case that you can't say anything to him in front of me?"

"It's not that simple," Cros replied, and was plainly hesitant as to whether he ought to say any more.

"I'm truly sorry to have involved you in this, Doctor Cros," Paul said. "I think I've pieced together what must have led Victor to ask you to pick me up in Montmartre on your way to the Gare du Nord. Victor is a thoroughly good fellow, and a good friend, but he's something of an *arriviste*. He wants me to be successful, not just for my own sake but for his, because he's like to be the friend of a famous artist. In the same way, when he needed to consult a doctor—he never told me for what, but I can guess—it would never have occurred to him to consult one that wasn't famous, in order that he could then salute the doctor in question in the street and qualify as an acquaintance...which doesn't license, I know, him asking the favor of you, but I hope you can forgive him, even if it has turned out badly for you."

"Badly?" the doctor queried, a trifle sharply. "For me? Are you assuming, then, that if I hadn't accompanied you to Juvisy, you wouldn't have drawn my brother in your trance?"

Paul had not been looking at the matter from that point of view. "I don't know," he said, finally.

"Neither do I," said Cros. "But if anyone owes anyone an apology, it's me, for the way I spoke to you when I bundled you into Camille's study. I was taken by surprise, and leapt to the wrong conclusion. I know well enough what your friend Victor is, and why he took advantage of a very slight acquaintance—and the fact that he knew that I was coming to Juvisy tonight, obviously—in order to engineer a meeting between us, and I know that it wasn't part of a nefarious scheme that you had cooked up with him to set me up and win you some cheap publicity. If that had been the case, you wouldn't have done the other three sketches, and I can't figure out, as yet, how you could have drawn one of them without some kind of supernatural involvement—in which I'm extremely reluctant to believe. And even if there's no mention of Charles when this affair reaches the papers, you and I might both get more publicity than either of us wants...or, at least, publicity of a distinctly troublesome sort. My colleague swore to keep silent, but one way or another, the information he gave me will probably leak out. There were a lot of people there, and they're talking behind our backs right now."

"It won't do any harm," opined Jane de La Vaudère. "Publicity blows over—believe me, I know."

"I fear not, Jane," said Cros, "in this instance, it might blow up rather than blowing over. Look, I'll talk if you want me to, but there might be things in what I have to say that neither of you will like, and you *are* both my patients, even if I haven't taken a fee from Paul and have no intention of asking him for one. Are we all friends?—because no matter how this matter works out in the long run, we might have to be, if we're to work out what on earth has happened...assuming, as I do, that it really has happened entirely on earth?"

"Of course we're friends," said Madame de La Vaudère, positively. "We've only known one another for a few hours, but we're already calling one another by our first names. If your skepticism is so indomitable that you think you can explain what happened without recourse to the other world, spit it out, Antoine."

"Do I have your permission to be dreadfully indiscreet, then?"

Jane de La Vaudère rolled her eyes. "Yes, of course."

When the doctor looked at Paul, Paul nodded his head although he was utterly mystified as to what sort of indiscretion Cros might have in mind.

He did not have to wait long to find out.

"You were a student of Jacollet's until recently, were you not?" Cros said.

"Yes."

"And were you the student featured in the anecdote that Jacollet was putting round in the salons a while back: the one who joked that he'd murdered his twin sister in the womb in the struggle for existence, and thus caused the death of his mother when she failed to deliver the corpse?"

Paul felt as if all the blood were draining from his heart, as he realized that Jane de La Vaudère really had known exactly what it was on the tip of his tongue to say when he had unwisely mentioned his mother's death.

"It was a stupid joke between students," he murmured. "I never thought..."

"Damn it, Antoine, why did you have to bring that up?" Jane de La Vaudère demanded. "Don't you think the poor boy's been through enough?"

"Because it's important, damn it," said Cros. "Because when people say things like that, in conspicuous jest—not realizing, obviously, that even a student quip can run all over Paris in a matter of days if those who hear it think it amusing enough to help fill the eternally challenging void of salon conversation—are sometimes using humor to conceal the fact that they have real anxieties, and before I tell you why it's important I need to say two things to Paul, which he might think he knows, but which might also concern things that he isn't admitting to himself."

"I know that I didn't really murder my twin in the womb," Paul was quick to put in.

"My point exactly," said Cros, "You know that rationally—but do you really believe it, unconsciously?"

""That's a silly question, Antoine," the author put in, evidently still annoyed, perhaps because she was the one who had told Cros the anecdote and was now regretting having done so. "How can he possibly know what he only believes—or doesn't believe—unconsciously?"

"It was a rhetorical question," Cros said, mildly, not sounding contrite, obviously having taken seriously the permission he had been granted to be dreadfully indiscreet. "The first point I want to make, Paul, is that if you ever took the proposition seriously, even for a moment, as a possible consequence of Darwin's theory of evolution—the survival of the fittest in struggle for existence, as it's vulgarly called, although that's a mistaken interpretation—then you're entirely wrong to do so. If, perchance, someone once told you that non-identical twins might be naturally bound to compete for resources in the womb, with the result that the stronger might sometimes starve the weaker fatally, that's a gross misreading of the logical consequences of Darwin's theory. If you care to read *The Descent of Man*—as few God-fearing Frenchmen bother to do, alas—you'll see that in Darwin's view, the evolution of humankind from animal ancestors, under the impetus of natural selection, has far more to do with the improvement of parental care and family bonds than with slaughtering one another. So you're absolutely right to think, rationally, that you didn't murder your sister in the womb, and you were not, in consequence, the indirect cause of your mother's death, and you need to convince yourself of that completely, if you can, in the hope that you can liberate yourself from any suspicions

and feelings of guilt that might still be lurking in your unconscious mind, suppressed there, as such feelings sometimes
are."

"I don't see what this has to do with what happened at
the Observatory," Paul said.

"I know—but if we're to search for an explanation that
doesn't require spirits, it's in the depths of your mind that we
have to search for the origins of the images and the reasons
why they surfaced when and as they did. I warned you that it
might be uncomfortable, especially with Jane present—but
she's in involved in this now, and she needs to hear what I
have to say as well if we're to examine the hypothesis fully.
Shall I continue?"

"I still don't see what my student joke has to do with
what I drew in my trance."

"Because, if my hypothetical interpretation is correct—
and it's only a hypothesis—as an account the source of the
second image that you drew on the sheet of paper, as well as
the image of Martine Lambrunet...it will encourage us to
search for similar explanations of the remaining two."

"The second image?" Jane de la Vaudère queried, before
Paul could get a word in. "You're suggesting that the other
woman might be his mother?"

"No," said Cros, "I'm suggesting that the blurred image
of the human fetus might have been his sister."

"The human fetus?" Paul said, dismayed as well as taken
aback.

"That's right," said Cros. "I'm not surprised that many
people in the audience didn't recognize what it was right
away, on the basis of a somewhat impressionistic sketch, because it not the sort of image they would come across if they
never had reason to consult anatomical textbooks, but I knew
what it was, and so did at least a dozen other people at the
Observatory. As far as I know, though, I was the only one who
had heard you mention your mother dying in childbirth, with
such an odd combination of embarrassment and indiscretion. I
was thus able to connect it immediately with the anecdote that

Jacollet had spread around the salon, and the fact that I'd accidentally reminded you of it at a moment when your nervousness was at its peak, when you had just climbed into a carriage with two people you only knew by intimidating reputation, in order to travel to an unfamiliar destination for a very challenging encounter. So I was the only one, so far as I know, who could construct an instant hypothesis as to why that image might have surfaced in your mind when the hypnotic trance left your right hand at the mercy of your unconscious."

Paul was dumbstruck. Jane de La Vaudère had become very pensive, and was presumably still following her own train of thought, and she was the one who broke the silence. "Do you know for sure that the other woman wasn't your mother?" she asked Paul. "After all, you never saw her, did you?"

"I have a portrait," Paul said. "I don't think it was her, but I suppose, if the unconscious plays tricks..."

"I doubt that it played that one," Cros put in, "If you had drawn your mother, I think it unlikely that you wouldn't have recognized her—given, as you say, that you've long been familiar with a portrait, at which you've presumably looked often and intently over the years, and given that another suggestion has been made to me regarding the identity of that person. Before tackling that enigma, though, I'd like to address the simpler one. You knew that Charles Cros was my brother, of course? Even if you don't consciously remember having seen a portrait of him, you knew his name. How much did Victor tell you, when he first boasted to you about having consulted me, because of my slight celebrity?"

Paul had no difficulty deducing the chain of argument that the doctor was trying to fit together.

"You might think me very stupid," he said, "but consciously, at least, I didn't even know you that you had a brother until Madame de La Vaudère mentioned the fact at the Gare du Nord. It would, I agree, have been entirely in character for Victor to boast about your being his doctor when he consulted you, but if he did, the name he cited made absolutely no im-

76

pression on me, and it still didn't when he called at my studio this afternoon to tell me that he couldn't pick me up in a cab to take me to the Gare du Nord and that he had asked you stop for me on your way there. Your name meant nothing to me, and it wasn't until the model sitting for my Jeanne d'Arc, who overheard what Victor said, commented on your name, that I had any idea that you were famous. So I have no reason at all to think that your brother's image might have been lurking in my unconscious mind, ready to be produced in your presence."

"That doesn't necessarily mean that it isn't what happened," Cros said, stubbornly. "Let's accept that you had no idea who I was until you stepped into my carriage—but you knew my name then, and merely on the basis of the name, your unconscious mind might have connected one Cros with another, especially after Jane, as you've just said, told you at the Gare du Nord that I had a brother, and doubtless mentioned that he was a poet and the true inventor of the phonograph."

"You know me so well," the lady murmured

"And if I had previously read about a French inventor of the phonograph," Paul supplied, dubiously, "with a portrait attached, you think it's the sort of thing that might have stuck in my conscious mind, even thought my conscious mind had lost the memory?"

"Exactly," said Antoine Cros, almost as if he had just proven that Paul had not been communing with spirits at all, but that what had happened had been a case if what Théodore Flournoy had recently called cryptomnesia. Whether it was a likelier hypothesis than the alternative—that the spirit of the dead poet and inventor really had been making an effort to contact him in his trance—Paul was unsure, given that any assessment of likelihood depended upon the beliefs that one brought to the interpretation, Cros, as a skeptic, was coming from a mental direction directly opposite to the one adopted by the Baron de Rochemure at Madame Pommerot's séance.

But where do I stand? Paul thought. *Where should I pitch my tent?*

That, he realized, was the whole point of what Cros was doing, not only as an interested party but as his physician...perhaps even as his friend

Jane de La Vaudère was still listening intently, perhaps searching for further opportunities to test a skepticism with which she did not agree, but whose strength and ingenuity she presumably knew of old. "But that isn't all, is it, Antoine?" she said insistently. "Whatever was said to you in the drawing room while I was helping to comfort Paul, it had something to do with the fourth image didn't it? Who recognized her, and why did they feel the need to communicate it in confidence?"

"The person who whispered the suggestion to me was a venerable colleague, Doctor Roimantel," Cros said, with the ghost of a sigh. "And he whispered it confidentially partly because he was far from certain in his judgment, at an interval of more than forty years, and partly because he was afraid of upsetting you, Jane, knowing that the subject was touchy. He said that he recognized the second woman, not as Paul's mother, but as yours."

"That's impossible," said the lady, flatly.

"That is exactly what I said to myself, at first," Cross agreed. "Quite impossible—because I'm a skeptic, who took it for granted that the drawing could not possibly be that of a spirit attempting to employ a medium in order to make contact of a kind with someone in the audience. Knowing your beliefs, however, it's not obvious to me why you're so quick to judge it to be impossible, even if none of the numerous mediums you've witnessed in performance during the last twenty years has ever announced to you before that your mother's spirit was trying to contact you. Firstly, though, may we attempt follow my chain of reasoning and work through the possible consequences of the premise that the means by which that image came to be on the piece of paper might have been natural rather than supernatural?"

Jane de La Vaudère looked at Paul. "This is nonsense," she said. "You need to know that Antoine has spent a great deal of effort in recent years doing what the Americans call debunking—explaining away the phenomena produced by mediums at Flammarion's séances and elsewhere. He's not just a skeptic, but a spokesman for skepticism, and a very ingenious one—but the explanations he suggests are sometimes far more bizarre and implausible than those he is trying to dispute and he has been quite carried away by his admiration for Doctor Flournoy since his book became a best-seller. Beware of his intellectual conjuring."

"Jane is right, of course," said Cros, mildly. "Objectivity, like credulity, is a pose—and I might be wrong. But you have the most important stake in this matter, and she is far too generous a person to refuse to let you hear an argument that might be crucially relevant to your understanding of what happened to you tonight, and what abilities you might have, just because it might cause her some slight embarrassment. On the other hand, if you would rather I discussed the matter with you in private..."

"Damn you, Antoine!" the lady said. "You can be so infuriating at times! Get on with it—I'm sure it will be a bravura performance."

The doctor inclined his head; his expression was one of practiced professional gravity. "Firstly," he said, "let's examine the suggested recognition. Roimantel is no fool, even if he is more than seventy years old, and he claims to have known Madame Scrive well, in the early 1850s, while your father, Jane, was serving in the Crimea."

All the color had drained from Jane de La Vaudère's face. "What are you implying, Antoine?" she demanded.

"Absolutely nothing," he replied. "I'm merely reporting what Roimantel said to me. He did not suggest that there was anything untoward in their relationship, merely that he knew your mother well. Like your father, he was a physician; there is no cause for astonishment in the fact that the families were acquainted, moving in much the same stratum of society as you and I now move."

"But I hardly know the man!" she protested.

"That's not surprising, given that you belong to different generations, nor is it surprising that he is a good deal more aware of your presence in society than you are of his. The point is, though, that his tentative identification of the portrait is not inherently implausible. Now, am I right in assuming, Paul, that you had no idea, when you came down to meet my carriage this evening, that Madame de La Vaudère might be in it?"

"None whatsoever," Paul confirmed.

"Had Victor had not mentioned her to you as someone who might be at the séance?"

Paul hesitated. "Actually, he did mention her name when I confirmed that his maneuvering had been successful and that Flammarion had invited me to the Observatory," he said, "but that was because he had previously mentioned her to me in a completely different content. He had told me that I absolutely must read *Le Mystère de Kama*—that all of Paris was talking about it."

"And did you?"

"Yes, I did." Paul glanced at Jane de La Vaudère, who was still very pale. "It's a fine book," he said. "I loved it."

"You might be well-advised not to say that too loudly," the author murmured. "The prevailing opinion in the circles in which I move seems to be that it's pornographic trash, fit for burning."

Paul was about to argue against that, but Cros cut him off. "What else did Victor tell you about Jane?"

"Not much. He said that I really ought to read 'Dans une étoile' as well—that it was a brilliantly graphic dramatization of Flammarion's ideas about interstellar reincarnation, with a remarkable twist of her own."

The author formed a modest moue.

"And did you?" asked Cros, again.

"Yes," said Paul, and added boldly: "He was right—it's magnificent."

"So, when you got into my carriage and were introduced to Madame de la Vaudère, you not only knew who she was, but had been impressed by her work?"

"Yes."

"The name struck a resonant chord. Magnificent, you say—and that's not just simple flattery? You're speaking as an artist, and the story in question has some very striking visual imagery...dream imagery, explicitly drawn from the unconscious, by a process akin to automatic writing. You felt a strong sympathy with it?"

"Yes, I did," Paul said, forthrightly. "The symbolism of the chimera..."

"Let's not get into literary criticism, for the moment. So, when Jane asked you to take her arm, when we descended from the train at Juvisy, and asked you to try to feign idolatry, and you said that no effort was required, even though you were both being conventionally flippant and slightly flirtatious, you meant what you said, didn't you?"

Paul said "Yes" without hesitation.

The interrogation continued: "Did you, perchance, know that her maiden name was Scrive, and that she was the daughter of a one-time Surgeon-General of the French army?"

"No," said Paul, flatly, "And if you're going to say that I might somehow have known it unconsciously, that would become a license to say anything at all, wouldn't it? Consciously, I know perfectly well that the moon isn't made of green cheese, but how can I know whether my unconscious mind might not be convinced that it is? The simple fact is that even I had some way of knowing what your brother looked like before Madame Zosima started muttering in my trance, there is absolutely no way that I could have known what Madame de La Vaudère's mother looked like."

"There isn't even any way that I can know what she looked like," Jane de La Vaudère put in, adding her own challenge to Paul's. "You've been in my home, Antoine. Have you ever seen a portrait of her there?"

"No, I haven't," Cros agreed. "Which is pity, is it not? If there were one there, with which we were both familiar, perhaps we could have recognized Paul's sketch."

"Unless, obviously, it wasn't and isn't my mother," she insisted.

"Which is an interesting insistence of your part, given that your spiritist beliefs certainly don't rule out the possibility that it was, and that you might be expected to be prejudiced in the other direction. So, let's examine that question further: how might we confirm or disprove Roimantel's identification? Does your sister have a portrait? Or, being slightly older than you, might she actually remember what your mother looked like?"

"No," retorted Jane de La Vaudère flatly. "And in anticipation of what you're going to say next, leave my husband out of this. He doesn't know either. He never met my mother. You'd have to find someone else of Roimantel's antiquity—preferably a woman."

"Why preferably a woman?" queried Cros.

"Because women have better memories, and they don't make sly insinuations."

"Not necessarily," the doctor countered. "When it comes to gossip...but that's not the point, is it? Undoubtedly, there are women still in society, albeit rather aged now, who knew your mother during the Crimean War. It was a long time ago, but, as you say, some of them have good memories, perhaps remembering the Second Empire better than the Third Republic, nostalgically, as a kind of Golden Age."

"I wouldn't know. I couldn't give you the name of a single person who might have known my mother before I was born. I couldn't even have named this Roimantel fellow."

"Which is another interesting point, my dear," said Cros, "in terms of what it implies about your attitude, conscious and unconscious, to the mother who died, tacitly abandoning you, as a small child, and thus consigning you to a convent, of which you have such mixed memories."

"You're overstepping the line, Antoine. My mother didn't abandon me deliberately, and I don't resent her for it, consciously or unconsciously. In any case, the point is that there's absolutely no way that Paul could know what my mother looked like? Absolutely none."

"Yes," said the doctor, "that is the point. But it isn't *absolutely* impossible, is it? Just because you don't have a portrait of your mother, it doesn't mean that none exists—it just means that you've never taken the trouble to look for one. But that's by the by. I've been dangling a hook, but Paul hasn't bitten, so he obviously isn't going to. Flammarion didn't say anything either, so perhaps it's my imagination that's playing tricks, but Paul, at the risk of putting ideas into your head, when you first looked at those four drawings you'd made, did it not strike you that there was a certain resemblance between Jane and the picture of the second woman—the one who wasn't Martine, that is? It clearly wasn't a portrait of Jane, but didn't it strike you that there was a...family resemblance?"

"Not that I noticed," Paul said, defensively.

"No, of course not—you were intent on the one that you recognized. But I once had a patient, a skilled artist, who had an odd talent for aging images. He could look at a girl of eighteen, or even sixteen, and he could sketch her as he said she would look at fifty. People inevitably called him a fraud, as you would expect, so he would routinely invite his listeners to bring him a portrait of a woman at twenty who was now in her fifties—someone he didn't know—and undertook to construct the present face from the past image. He was uncannily good at it. He could do it the other way around as well: he could look at a fifty-year-old face and reconstruct it as it must have been at twenty. How old would you say the person in Paul's fourth sketch was, Jane?"

"It wasn't me," she said. "I know perfectly well what I looked like twenty years ago, when I was twenty-four. Believe me or not, I don't look so very different now. It definitely wasn't me."

"No, it wasn't," Cros agreed. "But as I say, my first impression, when I looked at it, was that there was a family resemblance."

"So you're suggesting," Paul put in, "that I might actually have imagined what Jane's mother might have looked like, merely by virtue of seeing her...and that I might have imagined it accurately enough to facilitate a tentative recognition?"

"Not *merely* by virtue of seeing her," the doctor said. "Seeing her in a particular way, from a particular viewpoint, knowing that, like you, she had lost her mother at a very early age...and having read, and loved *Le Mystère de Kama*."

"You're being silly, Antoine," said Jan de La Vaudère. "This is utterly ludicrous, and far beyond the bounds of plausibility?"

"Well, perhaps it is," the doctor acquiesced, without putting up any further resistance, "but if, by chance, we were able to find someone else who could confirm or deny Roimantel's identification, we would be obliged, would we not, to find some explanation? I wanted to put the possibility on the table, as it were, so that we might be a little clearer in our own minds as to what the parameters of the problem are. What do you think, Paul? You have no idea what was going on in your unconscious mind while you were making the sketches, obviously, but you had just walked from the station to the Observatory with a beautiful woman on your arm, whom you had said in so many words that you could idolize without effort, although she is, in purely literal terms, old enough to be your mother. And you had just been given the opportunity to compare and contrast her with a calculatedly exotic lesbian who had, if I'm not mistaken, commanded you to stare at her slip of a sweetheart and let your mind drift while she talked you into a trance. Where it drifted, obviously, I have no idea...and I wouldn't want you to say a word about something so private and personal, but at least ask yourself: is it really impossible that you might have drawn an image of Jane's mother—an image as recognizable to a prejudiced party as the image you drew at La Pommerot's was of old Rochemure's daughter—without any necessity for her spirit actually to appear to your mind's eye from whatever world beyond the world that the dead go?"

Paul, having been given permission to say nothing, remained silent. So did Jane de La Vaudère. When the pause became embarrassing, Cros murmured: "I warned you that you wouldn't like it, but if we're really to get to the bottom of this conundrum, we do need to consider all the possibilities, in context." Then he stood up, because the train was pulling into the Gare du Nord. "Let's hope that my coachman can follow instructions," he said. "You know what they say about three in a fiacre."

Paul still had no idea what they said about three in a fiacre. Fortunately, the doctor's coachman was perfectly capable of following instructions, and the carriage was waiting for them directly outside the station entrance. It was past midnight, and there had been little competition for the best parking spots. The three of them climbed aboard. Jane de La Vaudère sat down next to Paul, opposite the doctor.

"You don't mind, I hope?" she said

"Not at all," Paul assured her, sincerely.

As the carriage accelerated down the hill in the direction of the Seine, Paul looked the doctor in the eyes, and said: "One thing that puzzled me is that Talia said that she needs to speak to me urgently—obviously somewhat to the astonishment of Zosima, who clearly took the implication that her...sweetheart wanted to speak to me without her being present. Given your exercise in psychology, what do you think that signified?"

"I haven't the faintest idea," said Cros, "but if the kid manages to get away from the tigress, you'll presumably find out."

"Tigress?" queried the symbolist novelist. "I thought she was trying hard to play the sphinx."

"Of course," said Cros, but a sphinx with stripes—and a false face."

"Wordplay," said the author, dismissively. "Would you like my opinion as to what Talia wants of you, Paul?"

"Yes," said Paul, already having an inkling of what the author of *Le Mystère de Kama* might suggest—but he was mistaken.

"She looked at you and saw herself, with a slight difference in the pubic region. She wants to speak to you as one medium to another, to compare experiences, and most of all, to ask you why she screamed."

"To ask *me* why she screamed? It was nothing I did."

"Of course not. She knows that, and she's obviously not afraid of you. But she also knows that you were looking into her face, and perhaps into her soul, when she was entranced. Perhaps she thinks you might have seen what she can't remember. You can tell her whatever you like—she'll probably believe it. But if you want my advice, whatever else you do, don't let her persuade you to make love to her. It wouldn't be fair. She's too vulnerable—and the sphinx might tear you limb from limb."

"I had no intention of doing any such thing," Paul said.

"I believe you," she said, "but little girls like that can sometimes slither past intentions. I have a responsibility to you now, remember. I haven't sworn the Hippocratic oath, like Antoine, but I've sworn the oath of amity. Whatever happened to you tonight, and wherever the images that you drew came from, I wouldn't want any harm to come to you as a result, from any direction." She looked at Cros, with a suggestion of accusation,

"Nor would I," said the doctor, mildly, "having not only sworn the oath of amity but the Hippocratic oath as well. You're my patient now, and no one is going to stick any kind of knife in to you except me, if can help it. And on that note, given that the Butte is already dead ahead, I hope with all my heart that the lifeboat carrying Madame Lambrunet and Martine has made landfall safely, and that there will be a message waiting in your concierge's lodge to tell you so. Either way, I'll come back tomorrow morning, at least briefly, in order to obtain news and for a further consultation, if you're still prepared to talk to me."

"You can add the whole of my heart to that," said Jane de La Vaudère, "and I'll come too, as Antoine says, at least to obtain news." She did not mention the possibility that he might not want to talk to her, evidently finding that impossible to imagine.

Paul just had time to thank them both effusively, and bid them a suitably fond and ceremonious area before leaping out of the carriage and ringing the bell to ask Madame Cambourg to lift the cordon, which she did with reasonable promptness.

The carriage waited until Paul put his head out of the door again and shook his head. The two figures silhouetted vaguely in opposite sides of the portière knew exactly what the negation signified, and the doctor ordered the carriage to pull away without further ado, while Paul made his way up the dark stairway.

CHAPTER VI

Somewhat to his surprise, there was a lamp lit in the studio. When he opened the door he saw that was set on a table beside the divan, on which Juliette Scarran was lying, reading a book. She stood up when Paul came in, holding the book in her right hand with her thumb between the pages, marking the place that she had reached.

"Is there any news?" she asked, immediately. "About the lifeboat that is?"

"None," he said, a trifle curtly.

Obviously embarrassed she searched for a safe remark, and held the book aloft. "Have you read this?" she asked.

He peered at the cover of the book, and was not in the least surprised to see that she was holding *Le Mystère de Kama*. All Paris was reading it, after all. What else would she have picked off his shelves, even though there was a tolerably wide and varied choice?

"Yes," he said.

"It's absolutely filthy."

"That, I'm told, is the general opinion. I disagree. It seems to me to be a genuine attempt to examine the mystery of the title—the mystery of erotic attraction—which can only be done effectively by transgressing the boundaries of the conventionally unmentionable. It's lurid, to be sure, but in a worthwhile cause."

"Well, you're a man...and an artist. You're entitled to your opinion, and to spout pretentious nonsense defending it." She paused, and then said: "Did you have a productive evening at Flammarion's Observatory?"

"Interesting, but rather troubling, in more ways than one. You're up very late."

"Not for someone in my profession. My other profession, that is, when I'm not pretending to be a saint." She returned immediately to her own topic: "Did you draw any spirits?"

"That's currently a subject of hot debate. There are probably people there who are convinced that I did, or would like to be convinced, but Doctor Cros has just spent a long time trying his utmost to convince me that I didn't. He claims that it was entirely in my interest, because he seems to have adopted me as a charity patient, but I don't believe him. At any rate, he hasn't convinced me yet, and he certainly didn't convince Madame de La Vaudère."

"Madame de La Vaudère?" the model glanced down at the cover of the book.

"That's right. She's a friend of the doctor. He escorted her to Juvisy as well as me. It more than doubled the interest of the journey. You can meet her tomorrow, if you like, and give her your opinion of her book."

Juliette was astonished. "She's coming here?" she queried.

"It seems so. Doctor Cros is coming too, but separately. There might well be others dropping in; whatever else I did, I certainly stirred up a lot of curiosity. Unfortunately, I don't think it's the kind of curiosity that sells paintings—but who can tell? The séance might be reported in the morning newspapers, but what they'll say about it I have no idea. And what they'll say if the worst comes to the worse and the *Palatine*'s first lifeboat had foundered...well, I might have helped unwittingly to turn a tragedy into a sensation."

"How?"

"I drew a picture of Martine while I was in a hypnotic trance. Flammarion has probably told the entire gathering that she was aboard the missing lifeboat, and that nobody in Paris knows, as yet, whether she's alive or dead. If it turns out that she's dead, every true believer in the land will take it as proof of my ability to see dead people. By the way, have you ever heard of Doctor Cros's brother, Charles?"

"Of course. Everybody has. He invented the phonograph before Edison."

"Have you ever seen a portrait of him?"

"Not that I recall, but quite possibly. Why, did you draw him too?

"Yes."

"Without ever having seen a portrait?"

"Without ever having consciously seen a portrait."

"Ah. What else? There is more, I take it, from the mysterious way you're talking?"

"That's where it becomes even more controversial, and ominous. According to Doctor Cros, I drew my twin sister."

"You have a twin sister?"

"Had. She didn't make it out of the womb, and my mother died trying to expel her. I didn't know what the thing was that I'd drawn; I thought it was just a blur—apparently not to the medically-trained eye, although I'm not completely convinced that it really was a human fetus."

"Even if it was, who would Doctor Cros think that it was your twin sister?"

"That's where psychology comes in. He's not just a surgeon, obviously. Everyone's a psychologist nowadays. It's all the rage. For psychologists trying to explain neuroses, a twin sister that died in the womb is pure gold, in terms of burdens of secret guilt. Suppressed guilt is very much in vogue. Mercifully, he only voiced that one in the train on the way back, so that it would remain strictly between the three of us."

"Except that you've just told me."

"I'm relying on your discretion."

"Well, I was about to say: 'But you don't have any neuroses.' Now...you actually trust me with a secret? There are some who'd say that you're completely mad."

"Not me. I do trust you. For me, you're Jeanne d'Arc, and you know that I see you that way, so I know that you won't let me down. And even if you did, what would it matter? Apparently, everybody in Paris knows that I had a twin sister and that I think I murdered her. It's a popular salon anecdote."

"I never heard it."

"Well, not quite everybody in Paris, then. Do you happen to know what they say about three in a fiacre?"

"Yes of course. They're a crowd." Paul assumed that he must have looked puzzled, because she continued: "You know the saying: Two's company, three's a crowd. It's a lame joke, because the saying's usually meant metaphorically, but in a fiacre, three people really are crowded—its either an awkward squeeze, or somebody has to sit on someone else's knees."

"I see. A pity we didn't try it, then—but at least I got to offer Madame de La Vaudère my arm, and pretend to be her gigolo for five minutes or so."

The model's eyes narrowed, in a fashion that the angle of the lamplight exaggerated. "Is she pretty?" she asked lightly.

"Truly beautiful," Paul said. "Old enough to be my mother, though, and she seems only to have maternal sentiments for me."

The model looked down again at the book that she was holding. "Yes, I can believe that," she said, in a tone suggestive of the exact opposite.

"Authors are no more like their books than artists are like their paintings," Paul said. "Even if the book were pornographic, which I don't believe it is, it wouldn't imply anything about the author's morals or conduct."

"Pull the other one," she said. "And what makes you think artists aren't like their paintings? Do you really think that Jeanne d'Arc is more me than you?" she paused briefly, and then said: "Sorry, I shouldn't have said that. It's late, and I've switched without thinking from meek model timidity to whorish banter. Give me a break. It was bad enough for my ailing self-esteem when you didn't want to screw me because of the girl in the lifeboat. Now that you don't want to screw me because I can't compete with the truly beautiful author of *Le Mystère de Kama* either, my self-esteem is totally ruined." She hastened on, in order not to give him an opportunity to respond. "You must be tired. I ought to get out of your way. Let me take the divan and you take the mattress. It's no better, but it's presumably familiar."

"I am tired," he admitted, "and tomorrow threatens to be an extremely busy day. When I agreed to see one or two of the interested parties again I specified that I'd be busy on the painting during the best hours of daylight, but I don't suppose that anyone will have taken any notice. We might be interrupted...continually."

"Do you want me to make myself scarce, so that we won't be seen together?"

"Absolutely not. I want to get on with the painting, if I possibly can. And there's no reason why you shouldn't be seen with me given that you're my model. Quite the contrary."

"But if you're interrupted, and the painting takes longer than you anticipated...and you're still expecting your friend, from the boat that did reach land..."

"Gaston won't leave Le Havre, even if he gets that far, until the other boat is found and he's reunited with his mother and sister. Please don't worry—you can stay here as long as you need to, and it really doesn't matter what conclusions anyone might draw. I might not have known what people say about three in a fiacre, or that half of Paris had heard that I was a double murderer before being born, but I do know what people say about artists and models, with an invariable snigger, and I know that those of my colleagues who don't automatically bed their models simply shrug it off rather than issuing denials that inevitably ring hollow. So will I. On the other hand, if you're desperate to leave because you feel insulted and demeaned by my treating you with undue politeness, you're certainly not under any obligation to stay."

She seemed stunned by that, and there was a pause before she said: "You're right—everyone's a psychologist nowadays. It's all the rage. I'm trying to read your mind and you're trying to read mine. And you're right, too, that I'm an ungrateful bitch, who ought to be delighted that you not only agreed to let me stay here for a couple of nights when I asked, without an instant's hesitation, but didn't expect payment in kind. But if you knew what a mess I am, and how hard it hit me when the bastard who'd used me up threw me out, and took back all his presents when he did it, barely leaving me the clothes I was standing up in, knowing that I already look too sick to attract much quality custom, in spite of the rumored fashionability of screwing consumptives on the threshold of death...but throwing myself on your mercy is exactly what I didn't want to do, precisely because I knew that you were too much of a plaster saint not to let me wind you round my little finger. Call it perverse—that's what it is, I guess. So, I'll stay, if you don't mind, and I'll try not to feel too guilty if you end up regretting it, as you probably will, even more so if you end up weakening and screwing me than if you don't."

She sat down then, put the book aside without marking her place any longer, and burst into tears. Obviously, it was so late that she had passed beyond the phase of whorish banter. Not for a moment did he consider the possibility that what she had just said was a mere ploy.

"You're tired," he said, "and you should have gone to bed instead of waiting up for me. We've both had an exceptionally disturbing day, it seems, yours worse than mine. So let's get some sleep—and however absurd it might be for me to tell you not to worry, take what comfort you can from the fact that at least you have somewhere to be for the next few days, with nothing to do but pretend that you're being burned to death while an inept painter tries to capture the essence of your saintly suffering."

She wiped away the tears. "I'm being stupid," she said. "Also selfish. You're the one whose lover is lost in a lifeboat after a catastrophe at sea. Nothing has happened to me that isn't routine for the life of...someone like me."

The psychologist in him took note of the fact that she had refrained, or once, of castigating herself with a nasty word descriptive of a situation to which she surely had not been reduced by choice. He reached out and took her wrist, in order to ease her to her feet. Then he took her to the metal spiral staircase leading up to the gallery that passed for a meager living space, leaving the floor of the high-ceilinged room entirely free for the apparatus of his art—save for the sink in the corner, which had to do double service.

"Sleep," he commanded, as he pushed her on to the staircase. "And if you happen to wake up early, try not to wake me. Tomorrow might be a very busy day."

Obedient to his assumed authority, Juliette went up the stairway and disappeared into the gloom of the gallery.

Paul took off his outer garments, but didn't change into a night-shirt. There were cushions piled up at the foot of the divan, and a blanket for possible use by models required to pose in scanty attire, so he had no difficulty arranging himself a comfortable accommodation for sleeping before extinguishing the lamp.

Actually going to sleep, however, was a different matter. His mind was far too full of anxieties and obsessions, all of them amplified and made more acute when he could no longer avoid turning his psychological analysis on himself.

He knew that the most sensible matter on which to focus, and perhaps the most important as well as the safest, was the theoretical question of what the drawings he had made actually signified. There had been no point in becoming unduly obsessed with the drawing he had made in Madame Pommerot's séance, given the dubiousness of Baron de Rochemure's identification, but there was no doubt whatsoever about the identity of two of the people he had drawn earlier in the evening, and the question of how and why he had drawn those images was urgent, even though the exact nature of the urgency would not become clear until he knew whether Martine was alive or dead. But that was not what preoccupied him most.

Perhaps absurdly, and perhaps an interesting psychological observation in itself, what sprung to the forefront of his mind, for the moment, was the awkward confession he had made on another spiral staircase, to Jane de La Vaudère: an entirely unnecessary confession, which had probably been far better left unvoiced.

Was he really, in any meaningful sense, in love with Martine Lambrunet? Could he possibly be "in love" with her, given that he had not seen her for nearly two years, and that he had never confessed the feelings to her that he had in the days when he saw her routinely, in Gaston's house, albeit almost always in company with Gaston or Amélie. But how secret could his feelings really have been? Might it not have been the case that she was fully aware of them? But if so, why had she never given him any indication of it? Was she merely waiting for him to speak, as a well brought-up demoiselle as supposed to do? Or had she wanted to refrain from lending any encourage to a sentiment that was unreciprocated? And whether or not Martine had been aware of his feelings, had Amélie guessed, or Gaston, or—even worse—Victor? Perhaps they had all been aware of it, and had even joked, behind his back, about "poor Paul's crush." And perhaps, if Martine had held her own counsel, as Cros and Jane de La Vaudère put it, it was because she had secret feelings of her own, not for him, but for her brother's other friend, Victor, more handsome than he was, with far better prospects for the future? And if so, how did Victor, the fop, the rake, the arriviste, feel about her? Was he not already seeking explicitly, to make himself an advantageous marriage in Parisian society, preferably in the Faubourg Saint-Germain? Surely, if he had any feelings for Martine, he would never let them take priority over his ambition? Was that a good thing or a bad thing, from Paul's pint of view? Good, if it meant that it eliminated the possibility of competition, but bad if Victor took it into his head, as he might be capable of doing, to seduce Martine and discard her, thus breaking her heart, and Amélie's, and Gaston's too. But that judgment took it for granted that Paul's love for Martine was real, and not a mere illusion, a mere excuse for his dire timidity in seeking other relationships, even causing him to refuse explicit offers from young women to whom he could not help but feel physically attracted, in spite of all the rational reasons he could produce for letting her well alone. And however absurd it might be for him even to be able to ask the question, what did he really feel for Martine? Was it possible that he actually did not know, that he had not the slightest idea whether what he felt for her was or was not what other people, and books, called love? How could be so uncertain? On the other hand, philosophically speaking, how could other people—anyone—be certain that what they felt for someone else was the same thing that other people felt when they termed it love? Was he even capable of "true" love? Was anyone? Was it not possible that the very idea of "true" love was merely a myth, an unattainable ideal, like the holy grail, imagined and propagandized by writers like Jane de La Vaudère...and which they sometimes questioned themselves in cynical texts and enquiring texts, which deliberately called into question the entire mythology of love and erotic attraction, brazenly and painfully attempting to address the mystery of Kama, without any possibility of finding a key to the enigma, and at the risk of their hypothetical endeavors being thought mere pornography and exposing their defenders to the accusation of spouting pretentious nonsense...which was drifting away from the point, which was, how did he really feel about Martine, and what was he going to do about it if and when that accursed lifeboat beached on Guernsey or Herm some other remote spot, and she contrived to make her way to Paris, and a confrontation in the flesh with her idolater...and why was he only thinking about it now, when there as a possibility that she might not return to Parris, when he had not been thinking about it with any similar intensity when he had simply taken it for granted that the *Palatine* would dock at Le Havre and she would take the train? Had he been deliberately excluding from his mind, even though it had obviously been lurking in his unconscious, ready to spring forth as soon as he was hypnotized...

Except, it suddenly occurred to him, it had not. Was it not a significant fact, now, that when Henri Lemastur had hypnotized him—allegedly—he had *not* drawn Martine, but another young woman entirely, perhaps Baron de Rochemure's dead daughter and perhaps some entirely imaginary person who simply happened to resemble Rochemure's daughter, just as the other woman he had drawn tonight happened to resemble Jane de La Vaudère enough to be mistaken for her mother? If his unconscious mind that was producing these images in response to its secret stresses and torments, why had he not drawn Martine at Madame Pommerot's séance? Why had he not drawn a fetus then? Why, if he were responding to what he knew of people in that audience, had he not drawn someone recognizable to Gabriel de Lautrec, whom he knew, rather than Baron de Rochemure, whom he did not? And to whom could he look for help in trying to sort out these multiple enigmas? To Antoine Cros, a surgeon who fancied himself a psychologist, a debunker of charlatans and, it appeared, the potential heir to an imaginary kingdom, about which he must remember to obtain more information from Jane de La Vaudère? Or to Jane de La Vaudère, to whom he had already made a reckless partial confession, whose own explorations of the mystery of Kama, although graphic, had not actually produced anything resembling a conclusion, but who might, at least be sympathetic? At least she would probably be more sympathetic than a lesbian striped sphinx who seemed every inch a charlatan but who nevertheless really was a clever hypnotist, and who really had liberated something from the recesses of his mind, and was now as interested as the other involved parties to know what and how. Or an aged astronomer who had been trying for decades to assemble conclusive evidence of the existence or non-existence of spirits without ever achieving certainty, or a tormented model grasping at straws in order to preserve some semblance of a meaningful life in the knowledge that it might not last very long...although even they, however weak or strong their qualifications might be to offer him useful advice or sympathy, were less intimidating as possible confidants than the one person to whom he really ought to confide, at last, the elements of his predicament: Martine herself? Even if she were alive—especially if she were alive—how could he possibly tell her even the smallest fraction of what he had just been thinking, when doing so would surely destroy any chance he had of giving her the impression of someone that she might love in her turn. If, that is...

But at that point, consciousness gave up. He lost the thread of his thought, such as it was, and fell asleep.

CHAPTER VII

He woke up to find someone shaking him, and opened his eyes reluctantly. It was broad daylight, and he had to squint against the glare in order to identify the person leaning over him.

"Victor?" he said, finally. "What time is it? Has the lifeboat made landfall?"

"Half past eight. Sorry to wake you so early, when I know you had a late night, but I couldn't wait—no, there's no news yet of the lifeboat. The other three have all been found with all personnel aboard and no serious injuries, but there's no news of Amélie and Martine. Sorry."

"Why couldn't you wait, then?" Paul demanded, peevishly.

"Because I wanted to hear your news. It's all over Paris already that there was a sensation at Flammarion's séance last night, but nobody seems to know the full details. You certainly put Madame Zosima and her medium in the shade, though. The girl only babbled and screamed, it appears, but you drew a whole host of spirits. Everybody expects me to have the inside information, and you surely owe me that, given that I made sure that you got there. I came as soon as I thought I could decently wake you. I'm sorry—you must have been tired if you couldn't even make it up the staircase to your little nook up in the gallery—but..."

Paul raised a hand defensively, as he looked around for his trousers. He would have preferred to put on his working trousers, but they were up in the gallery, and he did not want to go up there while Juliette might still be asleep—and even less if she were awake. He settled for pulling on the formal trousers that he had worn the previous evening—but his smock was hanging on a hook, so he put that on rather than donning the formal jacket he had worn to the séance. Once he felt suitably armored he turned back to face his friend.

"What have you heard?" he demanded, brusquely. "And how can it possibly be 'all over Paris' at half past eight, when the séance can't have ended before midnight?"

"Well, perhaps not all over, yet," said Victor, "but rumor gets up early hereabouts—and it will be all over soon, trust me on that. Oliver Lodge was there, and Jules Bois, as well as Thierry and the usual crowd. A lot of interest had been attracted in advance—by you as well as the Egyptian amazon and her juvenile partner. The dailies that have already hit the streets only have a single line in the latest news and I doubt that any will be able to get a formal 'account rendered,' but the later editions will flesh it out as and when they can. I'll use the pretext to drop in on Cros myself, obviously, but where better to get the real story than straight from the horse's mouth, so give?"

Paul stared at him. "You can actually think about that while Gaston's mother and sister are lost at sea. Why aren't you at the telegraph office with his cousins, waiting for the clicker to start chattering?"

Victor looked sheepish for a moment, but then moved to counter-attack. "I could ask you the same question," he said. "Where do you think I've come from—do I usually look this disheveled? And you're the one who's supposed to be in love with the girl."

Paul's blood ran cold. He hesitated over what reply to make, before hazarding: "Is that going to be 'all over Paris' too?"

"Quite possibly," Victor answered. 'Why on earth did you tell Flammarion that you'd drawn Martine, and explain why you couldn't know whether or not she was a spirit, if you didn't want that to be the headline in the reportage? You must have known that even if Flammarion only passed on the bare fact, the further reporters were bound to make a romance out of it. Do you think Martine's going to thank you for it, when she eventually gets back to France and sees the papers?"

Paul hesitated again before saying: "No, I suppose not. But surely that can't qualify as news?"

"In 1901? It adds exactly the kind of fuel to the mystery of the missing lifeboat for which the papers are avid. They can't keep reporting old mariners' speculations indefinitely as to why the boat hasn't come ashore."

"What speculations?" Paul asked, sharply.

"Unpredictable and changing currents in the Manche. The boat might have broken a rudder, or lost its oars in the storm. Not knowing their exact position, the sailors might have tried to make for Guernsey and missed it—but that one's wearing thin, as the boat ought to have reached the French coast by now if it was heading in that direction. If it's adrift and helpless, though, every ship within a radius of two hundred kilometers has been warned to keep a lookout. This is 1901, as I say. If it's out there, it'll be spotted before nightfall. The boat had some water and food stowed—not much, but enough to make sure it won't turn into the raft of the *Medusa* any time soon. There's no reason for despair for at least another twelve hours. Now..."

"And you think that Flammarion's note will refuel the story?"

"Bound to—and there's the mystery woman angle too. You drew more than one, apparently, and Flammarion's asking around trying to find someone who recognizes her—or who's prepared to guess. I wouldn't be surprised if your drawing is in all the evening papers with a caption asking anyone who recognizes her to contact the paper."

"They can't do that. They can't copy my drawing without my permission."

"Maybe not, but when it's a matter of hot news, editors tend to print first and worry about permission later. It's all come together, you see, at the right time—or the wrong one, if you take that point of view. So, what's the real story?"

"You seem to know as much as I do," said Paul, bitterly. "More, in fact—God, this is a mess."

"No it's not, it's publicity. It's a chance to get your flagging career off the ground. And stop trying to dodge the issue. I got you there, and you owe me the details."

"So you can feed them to the papers?"

"Nothing that you put a veto on. I'm your best friend, remember. And I've known that you were dotty about Martine for years. So has Gaston, so if you're worried about that secret causing any surprise, don't. Now..."

He got no further before there was an imperious rap on the door. Paul went to open it, and Antoine Cros swept in, fully dressed and looking a good deal more elegant and spruce than Victor, even though the latter hardly warranted his own description of "disheveled."

"Bonjour, Paul," he said "Bonjour, Monsieur Marvaud"—Paul was certain that Victor would have noticed the difference in the mode of address—"I'm afraid I haven't much time; no end to consultations, except when I have to ply the lancet. I'm terribly sorry, Monsieur Marvaud, but do you mind if I ask you to allow me to speak to my patient alone? The obligation of confidentiality, you understand."

"Patient?" Victor queried.

"Indeed."

Doctor Cros didn't add another word, but Paul, unbound even by imaginary obligations of confidentiality, said: "Dr. Cros was kind enough to help me yesterday evening, when the séance left me a little...drained. I'm sure that it won't take him long to check me over...but you'll probably want to get back to Gaston's cousins at the telegraph office in any case." He turned to Cros in order to add: "We're still waiting for news, alas. We're very anxious."

"Of course," the doctor said, and looked at Victor with an expression that spoke volumes.

"I'll come back later, then," Victor said, meekly. "I'll bring news, if any arrives." He picked up his hat, gloves and cane, and left. His boots could be heard clattering down the stairs in their usual careless fashion.

"You didn't want him to stay, did you?" Cros asked.

"No, I didn't," Paul conformed. "Come over to the window, Doctor, where we can sit down. I haven't anything to offer you, I'm afraid. I haven't had a chance to make coffee, or go to the bakery. Victor woke me up." He looked down at his ill-matched smock and trousers, as if to provide an explanation.

Cros took the chair that was offered to him, and Paul moved another into an appropriately confidential position.

"First of all," said the doctor, "I need to apologize for last night, and for springing my theories on you in front of Jane—but in the circumstances, it seemed necessary to make it a three-way investigation rather than a duet, at least to begin with. What I said about her mother won't have ruined my relationship with her, even though it's always been a touchy subject—as her doctor, I have a certain license, and she'll understand that I had to ask you about it. She seems to have a soft spot for you, but that's not surprising. Anyway, there are more important things to discuss. You seem to be a remarkably level-headed young fellow, by the standards of accidental seers, so I'm assuming that my attempt to explain how you might have made those drawings without any input from the spirit world didn't cause you any profound offense?"

"Certainly not," said Paul. "In fact, I'm profoundly grateful to you—I could never have worked that out on my own, and although I can't say that it has cleared up my confusion, at least it has made the parameters of the problem much clearer. Obviously, you have an interest n the matter yourself, but even so, it's kind of you to make such efforts on my behalf."

"On your behalf?" Cros echoed. "Don't exaggerate my altruism. I can assure you that I was thinking first and foremost about myself. My brother's fate is a sore point, even after all these years, and unlike Jane's hypothetical feelings about her mother and yours about your sister, there's nothing suppressed about my guilt feelings, of which I'm acutely conscious. I was supposed to look after him, but it was, to a degree, my fault that he became addicted to absinthe. I introduced him to Nina de Villard, you see, and her mental breakdown factory, as Goncourt called it. I didn't know that she'd become besotted with him, or he with her, and by the time I tried to break it up, it was too late. I introduced him to Flammarion too, and I did my utmost to find him financial support for his inventions, but I failed, over and over again. He was a hero, you know. During the Commune, he was my aide, although he was little more than a boy, in some truly horrible situations—he saved lives; and even that came uncomfortably close to getting him arrested and tried as a collaborator, or unceremoniously shot like poor Tony Moilin. So, you can understand that the idea that I might be confronted by his spirit isn't a consoling one. In a way, he already haunts me, and I don't want the haunting to become any more explicit. Nor do I want the fact that you drew him to become a focus of attention in the papers—which is why I'm selfishly glad to let you take that particular fire, although I promise you that I won't throw any oil on it."

"There doesn't seem to be any need or that, alas," said Paul. "And I'm still very grateful for everything you've said and done. I'm fortunate, it seems to me, that your interest in the mater seems to have coincided with mine. I can't guarantee, I'm afraid, that your explanation of how I came to draw your brother's image is the correct one, but I certainly can't contradict it, and if it turns out that Martine is, in fact, dead..."

"Don't think that yet," Cros said, swiftly. "Catastrophes like that are best not anticipated; it only makes them worse, when it isn't wasted anguish. I wish that I could wait with you, but I told your friend the truth, alas. I really don't have much time, for the present—but I'm delighted to find you taking such a reasoned attitude to your situation, and I really would like us to discuss it together at length some time, in private. In the meantime, will you come to my house for dinner tonight? I've already invited Flammarion, and Jane, obviously, and I had to invite Zosima and Talia as well, not only because of their declared interest but because they really might be able to offer us some useful insight. I realize that your situation is more delicate, but..."

"It depends...," Paul said, uncertainly.

"Of course. In a sense, everything depends on whether the lifeboat turns up—but if it does, your friends won't reach Paris for at least another two days, and if it doesn't...well, it might be a good thing of you were among friends tonight, and with all due respect to Monsieur Marvaud, I'm not sure that he'd be the ideal person, in the circumstances. Obviously, you haven't known us long enough for us to qualify as real friends yet, but Flammarion is one of the best men in the world, and Jane...well, Jane is Jane, and that's far from being a bad thing, especially if she likes you. And it might be a good idea for you not to be at home, if the press takes as much interest in the affair as now seems possible. You might find yourself under siege from reporters. God only knows what scurrilous nonsense they might pick up from your concierge and the local cafés, where everyone will suddenly pretend to know your most intimate secrets."

Paul's heart sank. "Damn," he said, softly, and almost left it at that, but pulled himself together enough to say: "Yes, thank you very much—you're absolutely right. I'll come—but I can't promise to be very good company, if..."

"As I've already prescribed, don't think that yet. I'll send my carriage to pick you up at six o'clock. No, don't protest. I'm not being excessively polite, just selfish. And until then, get as much painting done as you can." As he spoke, he stood up and strode over to the easel on which the Jeanne d'Arc was standing.

Cros removed the dust cover unceremoniously, and studied the unfinished painting for some time before nodding. "Good," without further elaboration. "I'm truly sorry, but I must dash now. I'll see you this evening—without fail." He was already heading for the door. Paul was still standing by the painting while the doctor's footsteps faded away on the stairs, more discreetly than Victor's, although Antoine Cros must have been considerable heavier than the slender dandy.

Juliette Scarran came down the spiral stairway, wide awake and fully dressed.

"I thought I'd better hide until they both left," she said "Do you want me to put the shift on and pose now?"

"Not yet," said Paul. "I need some sustenance first. I'll go down to the bakery and get some croissants and bread, and buy some coffee."

"Let me go," she said. "I can get a newspaper as well, and some other necessities...if you can let me have a little more money. I still have yesterday's posing fee, but..."

"It's all right," he said. "I didn't have to pay for my train fare last night, and it looks as if I won't have to take a cab to the doctor's house tonight. Get what we need...and be sure to keep enough back for your dinner at the restaurant this evening. There's a basket in the corner."

She disappeared, making hardly any noise at all on the stairway, although she was certainly not wearing satin slippers. Paul busied himself with his toilette, and unified his clothing, putting on his working trousers and folding his evening attire carefully, ready for further deployment later. Then he went downstairs himself, in order to pick up his correspondence from the lodge and warn Madame Cambourg, in a suitably apologetic fashion, that other people might be calling for him, and that she might be approached by newspaper reporters in quest of information.

As he went through the door of the Madame Cambourg's lair, however, he stopped dead in frank astonishment. The old women had a guest of her own, with whom she appeared to be engaged in polite conversation.

When she saw him, Jane de La Vaudère—who, as on the previous evening, was not wearing a veil—stood up from her armchair. "I do apologize, Madame Cambourg," she said, "but I need to look at Monsieur Furneret's art work. It really has been interesting talking to you. Bonjour, Monsieur Furneret; may I see the paintings now?"

Dazedly, Paul could only contrive to say: "Are there any letters, Madame Cambourg?"

The old woman, who had come to her feet simultaneously with her interlocutor, handed him a package that was noticeably thicker than usual, but he barely had time to glance at the address on the topmost item, and had no opportunity to made any further remarks to the concierge. Although she did not seem to move with any undue hurry, or to put any undue pressure on him, Jane de La Vaudère somehow managed to maneuver him out of the room and back on to the staircase. She put her finger over her lips surreptitiously, to bid him to remain silent, until they had climbed four flights of dimly-lit stairs all the way back to the door of the studio, which he had left open. When they were inside, she closed it carefully behind them.

"I'm sorry about that," she said. "I had intended to come up as soon as Antoine left, but I was sidetracked, as you saw."

"You came with Doctor Cros?" Paul queried, puzzled.

"No, but when I arrived I found his carriage waiting outside. Joseph—his coachman—told me that he would only be a moment, because he had to drive him to his first appointment He offered to open the carriage for me, so that I could wait in it, but I said there was to need. He bowed, but as I was about to step into the building he told me to beware of the concierge, who was a living legend among her own kind—he's been with Antoine for years, so there's a certain familiarity between us, permitting such remarks. That one, however, was heard by the concierge in question, who emerged from the door like a dev-il-in-a-box, and told him that there was no need for him to issue warnings, that although I probably wouldn't remember her, she had known me for many years—and she invited me, very ceremoniously, to wait in her 'parlor' until the doctor came down."

Paul was amazed. "You mean that she recognized you?"

"She must have heard Joseph address me as 'Madame de La Vaudère,' and recognized the name—and knew enough about me to be able to tell me that when she had last seen me I had been Mademoiselle Scrive, and only a little child. I'm trying to avoid recognizing the hand of fate in this, but she claims...and I have no reason to disbelieve her...that she knew my mother. What a remarkable room this is, Monsieur Furneret. Surely that can't be a minstrel's gallery?"

While she was speaking she had taken off her hat and mantle and handed them to Paul, who had placed them on the stand bedside the door. Slightly flustered by the swift change of subject, and unable to feel a slight twinge of regret that she was continuing to use a formal manner of address, he felt obliged to skip over the most interesting remark that she had made and answer the final question.

"No, it isn't," he said. "Long ago-back in the days of the Second Empire, I presume, although I don't know any precise dates, this space comprised two rather low-ceilinged rooms—servants' attics, I presume. It was adapted by an artist specifically to make a studio, with the large north-facing window. The floor of the upper room was removed, except for one section, with was then equipped with the waist-high side-partition, in order to improvise a space for sleeping, with room for a wardrobe and a chest of drawers, while the floor and its furniture could be reserved for painting and the accumulation of the artist's equipment. Since then, it's always been rented to painters as a live-in studio. I don't know how many others have preceded me here—at least four, perhaps half a dozen."

"Well, the big window certainly provides a good light—gloriously bright after that gloomy stairway and the Stygian landing." She had already moved to inspect the canvas on the easel, which he had not covered up again.

Like Cros she studied the embryonic painting for some time with an appraising eye, and then nodded. "I'll come back when it's finished, if I may," She looked around the room at the various paintings resting on shelves and stacked against the wall, all or most with their faces invisible.

"You should put them on display," she said to him. "Discreetly, of course, so as to give the appearance that they have been carelessly placed, but in order that their best features can be noticed, and attract attention. Then people will not have to ask you, as I am obliged to do, to pick them up and show them to me one by one." She was already moving away toward the nearest stack.

He began to do as she had demanded, while she said: "You haven't had a chance, obviously, to have a meaningful consultation with Antoine—he had to rush off. He barely nodded to me as he left, and seemed slightly envious of the fact that I might be able to speak to you at my leisure, although I fear that I might be almost as rushed. He had already sent me a note inviting me to dinner tonight, but I really think he might have spared me the time to apologize for last night. He's been my doctor for years, but even so, there's a line that shouldn't be crossed. I've decided to forgive him, though, in view of the fact that the matters discussed, precisely because they were so awkward, required the triple input. Have you forgiven him?"

"There's nothing to forgive," Paul said. "I was immensely grateful to him."

"Have you forgiven me?"

"Again, there's nothing to forgive, and I was honored by your company as well as grateful for your kindness."

"In that case, you have my permission to continue with your outrageous flattery. I wish, though, that I hadn't repeated that anecdote to Antoine on the way to pick you up. I can't claim ignorance, you see—as soon as he mentioned that you were an ex-student of Jacollet's—which was practically the only thing he knew about you apart from the business at La Pommerot's, I just came out with it, almost automatically, not caring whether it might or might not be you—and then, when Antoine prompted that confession about our mother...I had to wince. That was your model I saw going out with the basket, I assume? Will she be gone long, do you think?"

Paul hoped that he was not blushing as profusely as he suspected that he might bed, given the warmth in his cheeks and neck.

"We're not..." he stammered.

She seemed surprised by his confusion. "I only ask because I wouldn't be comfortable talking about what we discussed last night in her company, and that's why I feel some sense of urgency."

"We're not...involved," Paul contrived to finish, although he had already realized that it might have been better simply to keep quiet. "The only reason she stayed here last night is that she lost her previous accommodation, and couldn't go in search of a new room during the day because she was posing for me."

"I seem to have embarrassed you," she said. "That wasn't my intention. Perhaps I'd better explain that that when I saw the young woman go past I had no reason to assume that she had come from your apartment rather than one of the others, and Madame Cambourg didn't say a word about her—but when I saw the painting on the easel, I recognized the face. I like this one. Is it sold?"

Paul had not even glanced at the painting that he was holding up for inspection, and looked down. It was, in fact, one of his favorites: a painting of a wistful siren.

"No," he said, and risked adding: "You said that Madame Cambourg knew you went you were a little child?"

"So she says. Apparently, she was obliged to move to the Butte because her previous house fell victim to Baron Haussmann. You've probably heard her long speech about how it was one thing to knock down filthy hovels to make new boulevards, but quite another to demolish decent houses and force honest concierges to move from respectable situations to the scandalous slopes of Montmartre, but if you haven't, you surely will. I can understand why Joseph asserted that Mère Cambourg is a legend among concierges, although it wasn't a legend that had ever been reported to me. You wouldn't think there would be a society of concierges, would you? with their being confined to their lodges all day every day, but there is. She didn't say a word to me about you, even when your model went past the lodge, because I'm from what she thinks of as the upper echelons, but believe me, if you think you have any secrets, you don't."

Paul took note of the fact that the author had made no further mention of Madame Cambourg having known her mother, and deduced that it was not something she wanted to discuss, for the moment; he did not feel entitled to interrogate her, so he remained silent and kept turning paintings over for her inspection.

"That's it, keep going," she said. "I like the textures of the atmosphere—a nice impression of dynamism. The water symbolism is good, too, although you might be overdoing the mythological inclusions. Trees, not so good—you need more practice with foliage, especially if you're going to concentrate of the peaceful aspects of scenery, quiet beauty but not much sublimity. But a lot of the repetition is presumably due to the fact that your student work is still piled up here, with a strong underpinning of Jacollet's penchants and techniques.

"Counting the trees as earth, that only leaves one element, but fire doesn't seem to have been your thing—Jeanne's pyre seems to be a new departure. Don't worry, I'm not wasting your time, or mine. I'll buy something, but I want to see them all before I make up my mind. Ah! A chimera! I like chimeras—as you know." She looked up, and met his eyes before he could look down, but his peripheral vision informed him that she was looking at one of his earlier student paintings—one of the most fanciful, and most numinous. It did, indeed, feature a winged chimera, but not one that bore a close resemblance to the heart-collecting monster in Jane's story.

"It's early work, not very good, I'm afraid," he murmured.

"I didn't say it was very good," she told him, mildly. "I said it was something I like. You do understand why, don't you?"

He looked down then, and studied the painting more carefully. "Not exactly," he admitted, hesitantly.

"Keep going, then," she said, moving on. Her tone became more pensive "You really have read my double star story, and *Kama*? And it wasn't just flattery, when you praised them?"

"It was an honest judgment," he told her.

"I believe you. You understand, then, that I really was drawing upon...inner resources. They're not automatic writing, because automatic writing, even at its best only produces sense in short bursts, and it's difficult for the pen to keep up with the imagery. I was extremely impressed by the speed with which you were able to work last night. I've seen caricaturists like Sem dash off likenesses in a matter of seconds, which were recognizable as well as being satirically distorted, so I know that an artist's hand is a lot quicker than a writer's hand, but even so,...anyway I envy you that speed. I have to work much more slowly, so the extent to which I can rely on the automatic component is very limited, and the material routinely gets confused, especially when you have to integrate the material with some semblance of a plot. The unconscious mind doesn't conceive plots, because that isn't the way it works. Again, the freedom of collage is something I envy visual artists...but I simply wasn't adept enough as a painter, to capture the impression of what I wanted. I needed the supplementary effort of input of the conscious mind, the method...but the essence of the work...the most personal work, that is...look here's another, naïve again, not expert, but raw, visionary...because the real essence of true endeavor comes from the visionary element."

She looked at him again, in search of some kind of prompt, looking for some endorsement of her desire to see him as a kindred spirit—exactly as she had suggested that Talia Cadelan would.

"Yes," he said. "I do know what you mean. I do understand. Yes, that one did come straight from the unconscious; I was in a virtual trance when I painted it. It's a trifle banal, though, the numinous female figures, like English fairies...but not really spiritual beings, certainly not the spirits of the dead. I wouldn't care to subject it to Doctor Cros's psychoanalysis now I've seen him in action, though. That could be a trifle uncomfortable"

She permitted herself a slight sigh. "Good," she said. "Now I've seen this, and the chimera paining...and the siren, too, although that's more accomplished work, presumably more recent, I have more confidence in what you saw in *Kama*, and what you liked in it. I'd like to think that you genuinely understand why it's the way it is, and that you appreciate that it isn't just a sordid attempt to make money from fervent eroticism, as some people think. This painting, and the chimera—which are, as you say, not very good, and which I wouldn't actually hang on my wall—are what I came here looking for, because I can recognize their source more easily. This one is naïve, and inept, but it comes from...I'm tempted to say the double star, but it's not a star, is it? Flammarion spread his visions all over the universe of astronomy, and invented souls that could travel faster than light in order to give him an imaginative viewpoint, but he wasn't really seeing life on Mars, any more than Mademoiselle Müller was. The visions come from stranger places than that, don't they?"

She paused again, and waited for an answer.

"Yes," he said, "I believe that they do, but exactly where, and how..."

"Indeed. A conundrum—and without wanting to depress you, I've been trying to solve it for a great deal longer than you, without much success. But it seems to me that what you're doing, in some of your paintings, and what I try to do in some of my writing, is genuine exploratory work, attempting to go deep...and perhaps and to try to make sense of it."

"Yes," he said, "I believe it is...except that I can only reproduce the visual imagery, and hunt for explanations separately. As a writer, you have the potential to combine expression and explanation..."

"Potential, perhaps. Actually doing that...it's very difficult. Do you find that it hurts?"

He only hesitated for moment before saying: "Sometimes."

"If you keep trying, it will hurt more, and more frequently. Trust me on that. You won't stop, I know, and you won't even be careful, because I look into your eyes and like that child last night, I see myself, and just as you already feel sorry for her, even though she's probably only a couple of years younger than you, certainly not twenty years and more, I can't help feeling sorry for you, because I have some suspicion of what you're going to put yourself through, and I know that it's even more dangerous for you than it has been and will be for me, simply because the artist's hand is much quicker than the writer's hand. May I give you some advice that you probably won't be able to take?"

"Please do,"

"Beware of the sphinx. Not just the Egyptian—she probably won't do you any harm, because she doesn't like men, and if she tried to seduce you, you'd probably jump like a scalded cat—but a time might come when you meet a similarly powerful magnetizer who will have everything required to seduce you...and I mean everything. You probably won't be able to help yourself, but if you can avoid falling, cling on to whatever comes to hand. If your Martine turns out not to be dead, and if, when you get round to telling her how you feel, she's able to reciprocate, make the most of her, because she might be your only hope, and will surely be your best one. It hasn't worked for me, but that's probably as much my fault as the other people that I blame. And I'm sorry this all came out in a ludicrous rush, but even if your model doesn't come back soon to put on her shift and play the martyr, it won't be long before other people are hammering on your door. Has Antoine invited you to dinner tonight?"

"Yes"

"Did you accept?"

"Yes."

"Good. I was hoping that he would, and that you would. It might be difficult, I know, but remember, then and always, that there's at least one person relatively close at hand that has some understanding of what you are and what you see. It might help. Would you like to paint my portrait? I can't promise that it would do much for your future career, but I'm at a

114

point in life when I'd like to have my portrait painted by someone who might be able to catch a glimpse of my soul as well as my face-paint. Will you?"

"Of course," he said. "It would be a privilege."

"Good. We can make arrangements for sittings tonight, or in a few days' time, when the situation is clearer and calmer."

The door opened at that moment, and Juliette came in carrying the laden basket in both hands. Without pausing, Jane de La Vaudère raised her voice and said: "I'll buy the first one that I said I liked, Monsieur Furneret. That one I can hang." Effortlessly, she strode forward to meet Juliette, who had stopped dead. The author inclined her head and said: "Bonjour Mademoiselle. I'm Jane de La Vaudère. I won't get in your way—I presume that Monsieur Furneret will want to start painting, now that you've arrived. I recognize you from the canvas, of course as Jeanne d'Arc, but I fear that I don't know your name."

"Juliette," murmured the intimidated model. "Juliette Scarran."

"Like the famous author?"

"No, two *a*s."

"You're very pretty my dear, and very fortunate to be able to pose for Monsieur Furneret. He'll be a great painter one day—but before then, he'll put you on display in this year's Salon as a saint and martyr. Immortality awaits you." Then she turned to Paul, who had put down the painting he had been holding and had hastened to join her. She offered him her gloved hand, which he shook, uncertain as to whether he ought to have kissed it instead.

"Thank you so much for showing me your paintings, Monsieur Furneret," she said, "and all my hopes and prayers go with you, in your present troubles. *Au revoir*." She glided around Juliette, made her exit through the door, which was still open, and disappeared.

After a few seconds of silence, Juliette said, incredulously "*That*'s the author of *Le Mystère de Kama?*"

"In person," said Paul, with a wry smile. "I told you that authors don't resemble their books"

"Still not convinced. I see what you mean by truly beautiful, though, even if she is old enough to be your mother. Which one did she buy?"

Paul stepped back, found the painting of the wistful siren and displayed it to the model.

"Really? No lascivious dancing girls capering round lingams? No sinister snake charmers who can induce orgasms by telepathy?"

"Not really my stock-in-trade—and she wanted something she could hang. She moves in polite circles, and hosts upmarket soirées."

"I'll bet she does. Well, at least she didn't arrive before I went out."

"She was in the concierge's lodge when you went past. Mère Cambourg didn't say anything, apparently, but as soon as she came up she recognized you in the painting."

"Ah! That's why she gave me such a dirty look, then. I thought it was just habit."

"I thought she was very polite to you."

"Exactly—but there's nice polite and there's look-what-the-cat-dragged-in polite. Now that she thinks you're screwing me, you probably just went down ten points in her estimation, but I'll bet she hasn't scratched you off her dance card. And you'll be seeing her again tonight, I gather, with the fellow who's all in a twist about his dead brother?"

"You weren't supposed to overhear that conversation, and the decent thing to do would be to forget that you did. And I think you're being unfair to Jane. You really shouldn't let your false impression of her book prejudice you. I think she's wonderful."

"You would," she said, with a sigh. "Have you boiled the water for the coffee?"

"I haven't had time."

"I'll do it, as soon as I've unpacked the basket. In the meantime, have a croissant."

Paul obeyed, and bit into the warm croissant gratefully while he went to tidy away the paintings that he had disturbed while exhibiting them. He only just had time to replace the siren, however, before Juliette exclaimed, in a tone of mingled anxiety and anger; "Who the hell are you, and what the hell are you doing here?"

He looked up at the gallery, and saw someone stand up, who had evidently been hiding there while he was talking to Jane de La Vaudère, exactly as Juliette had hidden while he was talking to Antoine Cros.

It was Talia Cadelan—and she looked down at Paul with an expression on her face that seemed close to panic terror.

"I'm *so* sorry," she said. "I didn't mean to..."

CHAPTER VIII

"But how did you get in?" Paul asked, when he had finally calmed both Juliette and Talia down and sat the medium down in one of the armchairs by the window while the model made coffee up in the gallery.

"It was stupid, I know," she said. "When I arrived and came in—very nervously, I fear—the concierge and somebody else were in the lodge together, talking, with their backs to the door. I couldn't see who it was, and...well, I just slipped past and started coming up the stairs, because I wanted to talk to you in private, Monsieur Furneret, and I was already on edge because I'd had to give Zosima the slip. I had your card, so I knew the number of your apartment, but the corridors are so dark, and the chalk has worn off some of the doors. Anyway, I finally got up to the top floor, still not knowing which door to knock on, and I was on the dark landing when you suddenly came out and started down the stairs—you didn't see me. And I know I should have called out, or said something, but you'd left the door open, and...well, I thought that I could just wait inside for you to come back. But when you came back up, you weren't alone, and...I just panicked, and I ran up the stairs, and I hid. That's what I do, you see...all my life. I hide. I wasn't really eavesdropping, just hiding. I didn't do it so that I could listen. I heard Madame de La Vaudère say that she hadn't got much time, and I thought she might leave you alone, so that I could...but then...well, I just kept hiding, until the young woman saw me. It was stupid, I know. I'm *so* sorry. But I had to see you, and I wanted to see you on your own."

"Why?" Paul asked, speaking as gently as he could. He had sat down in the other armchair, in order not to seem intimidating by looming over her.

"Because...well, because I wanted to tell you what I saw...or felt...last night, because I thought you needed to know, and I didn't want to do it in front of all those people, especially Zosima, because...it's too personal...but you looked into my head...all the way, and I know you saw and felt...what I saw and felt. Nobody's ever done that before. I didn't even know it was possible. If Zosima knows, she should have told me...but she wouldn't. To her, I'm just an instrument, not a person. Everybody thinks that I'm her lover, but I'm not. I'm just...part of the act. Not that I'm complaining, you understand. She doesn't mistreat me. She just...doesn't love me."

"Part of the act?" Paul queried. "You mean that you and she are charlatans."

"No, of course not—you know that. But Zosima says that it isn't enough to be real, because the reality of what we're doing is too uncertain, too often incomprehensible; it has to be managed, and packaged, or it's impossible to make a profession out of it. She says that we can't make progress with the science without working on it, and we can't do that by locking ourselves away. We need audiences—and we need quality audiences; not just the converted, who are ready to believe anything, but genuinely inquisitive people, even skeptics—not because she wants to convert them, but because they're a test, a challenge, and without tests and challenges we can't make true progress. But in order for them to help us, we need to know about them. So we try to find out about them, not because we want to cheat by pretending to discover things by supernatural means that we've actually found out by other means, but in order that we might be able to understand and evaluate the things we see and discover magically, by putting them in context."

Juliette rejoined them at that point, and handed each of them a cup of strong black coffee, which she had brought on a tray, along with two croissants and two bread rolls. "That'll wake you up," she said. "Do you want me to go out again now, so that you can continue this discussion tête-à-tête?"

"If you wouldn't mind," said Paul, mildly, "I think that might be best. I'd like to resume work on the painting as soon

119

as possible, but I would like to hear what Talia has to say, and if she..."

"No," said Talia. "Don't go. I don't have any right to ask you to go."

"Oh, don't worry about me," said Juliette. "I'm like you, just an instrument. I put on a chemise and pretend to be Jeanne d'Arc, and he paints me. It makes a change from drawing spirits, I suppose."

That speech only served to increase Talia's already-deep embarrassment.

"If you wouldn't mind," Paul repeated, with ostentatious mildness, "would you leave us alone for half an hour, Juliette? I really am anxious to get on with the painting, but I think that I also need to hear what Talia has to say."

Juliette pursed her lips, but she nodded her head, and left without slamming the door. Talia sipped the coffee, but refused the croissant that Paul invited her to take. "I'm sorry," she said. "But..."

Paul waved the apology way. "We have half an hour," he reminded her. "I think I've grasped the explanation of why, although you're a genuine medium and Zosima is a genuine magnetizer, you have to put on an act in order to make a living and conduct your own research into your abilities. Let's focus on what happened last night. Why do you think that I was reading our mind?"

"Because of what you drew...things you couldn't have got from anywhere else, since Zosima assures me that I didn't say anything aloud. And I truly am sorry, about the young woman who drowned."

Paul felt as if his heart had just stopped.

"Martine?" he said, anxiously. "Why do you say that she drowned?" His mind, meanwhile, was racing. Obviously, Talia knew about the lifeboat. She had had plenty of time to jump to conclusions...or to formulate tests and challenges. He reminded himself that Talia, an admitted performer, might be performing now, that all of this might be an act.

"Because I felt it," Talia said. "She was drowning while we were entranced. It was horrible"

"And that's why you screamed?"

Talia didn't answer. She was staring at him. "You didn't know, did you?" she said, faintly. "You didn't know that she was dead? At least, you knew—I saw that you knew—but you didn't want to admit it. You didn't want to accept it."

Paul fought hard to control the turmoil of his emotions. Keeping a firm grip on the level of his voice, he said, as calmly as he could: "Why did you scream, Talia?"

"Because it frightened me," she said, "when I realized that you knew. Nobody knew but me, you see...nobody. Until you read it in my mind. I didn't know that was possible. I was amazed, frankly, when you drew Martine, Charles Cros and Madame Scrive, but I wasn't concerned at that moment with the how, and I was about to start on the script when...when you drew the baby. That's why I screamed."

"Baby? You mean the fetus? Why did that make you scream?"

"You mean you don't know that either? I assumed that you knew...I thought you had to know...but you didn't did you? You didn't know that the girl on the boat had drowned, and you didn't know about the baby?"

"It wasn't a baby," Paul said. "It was just a fetus. Nobody recognized it as a fetus, except for Cros and a few other doctors familiar with anatomy textbooks."

"You can call it a fetus if you like," she said "but it was a baby. And what you didn't know, I've just told you, haven't I. You know now."

"I didn't know anything," Paul told her. "I have no memory at all of making the sketches. When I came out of the trance and saw them, I recognized Martine immediately, and I suddenly panicked at the thought that if I really was drawing spirits, then she must be dead—but I didn't know...and Doctor Cros spent the next two hours trying to convince me that I wasn't drawing spirits at all, but just drawing images out of my unconscious memory...including my sister."

"Your sister?"

"Yes. I had a twin sister who died in the womb. According to Doctor Cros, I drew a fetus in the womb because I felt guilty—unreasonably guilty—about having caused her death in a competition for maternal resources within the womb, which I won: the survival of the fittest."

"Your sister?" Talia Cadelan repeated, incredulously. "It wasn't your sister, it was my daughter."

"How do you know?" said Paul, slightly bewildered.

"Because I recognized her!" There was a distinct hysterical edge in the young woman's voice

"You couldn't have," Paul objected, rationally. "One six-month fetus looks much like any other...it has nothing much in the way of differentiating features, no individual identity." Even as he said it, though, he saw the logic of the mistake...if, in fact, it was a mistake. Antoine Cros and the other people at the séance who had identified what he had drawn had done so on the basis of generalized depictions in medical textbooks, but Talia Cadelan had never looked at a medical textbook. She had only ever seen one fetus in his her life: the one that she had delivered. And when she had seen his drawing, she had not seen a generalized fetus but a very specific one, which she had had no hesitation in recognizing.

"You gave birth to a stillborn baby...a very premature stillborn baby," he deduced. "Not really a childbirth, more like a miscarriage." *If only my mother had been able to do likewise*, he thought.

"I killed her," Talia said, flatly. "I thought you knew. I thought you had read my mind."

Perhaps, Paul thought, the girl—surely she must have been a girl at the time although she was a young woman now—had actually contrived an abortion, but it was surely more likely that it had been an accident of nature, a mishap, for which she had assumed the guilt...needlessly...wrongly...just as he had assumed unnecessary guilt himself in a different situation.

"I didn't read your mind, Talia," he said, softly. "Doctor Cros is right. I drew a fetus because of my sister—my twin sister, who died alongside me in the womb. She was blurred because I was imagining her still in the womb, still floating in amniotic fluid. If it had been your daughter that I drew, the features would have been clearer, as distinct as the features of Charles Cros...and Martine...and Martine's features were distinct because I wasn't drawing her under water. I wasn't drawing her drowning. Some of this, at least, is in your imagination. I don't know why you think I got the image of Charles Cros out of your mind, but in view of what you said earlier about you and Zosima having to make preparations for your audiences, I think I can guess. It's just a coincidence, and...." He stopped, as the argumentative train derailed. He paused for several seconds before saying: "Did you just mention Madame Scrive?"

"Yes," she said. She was abstracted now, thinking about what Paul had said, and wondering...

Paul tried to focus his thoughts, knowing that he had to do everything he could to match the standards of hypothetical invention that Antoine Cros had displayed the night before.

"Talia," he said, carefully. "When, exactly, did you see the drawing I made?"

"When you made it. I was watching you. My eyes were supposed to be closed, but I was peeping."

"And then, when you realized what the fetus was, you screamed. Did you see the drawing again, after that?"

"No. Monsieur Flammarion took it away."

"He didn't show it to you again after Madame de La Vaudère and I had left?"

"No. Zosima and I went down the service stairs not long after you. She'd asked the coachman to get the rig ready, so we climbed straight into it and went to the hotel. I was still upset, and it was late, so I went straight to bed."

"Before you left, you were in the study while the doctor, Jane and I were talking to one another, and to Flammarion. Both Martine and Charles Cros were named as people in the picture, as well as the fact that Martine was aboard a missing lifeboat. But when did you hear Madame Scrive's name mentioned? Why do you think she was in the picture?"

"Zosima said so."

"Zosima told you that Madame Scrive was in the picture?"

"Not exactly. I heard her talking to Raoul."

"Who's Raoul?"

"Our coachman."

"A coachman who doubles as a professional eavesdropper—for the benefit of your performances?"

Talia Cadelan blushed. "Zosima asked Monsieur Flammarion for permission for him to be in the audience. There was nothing underhanded about him being there."

"That might be a matter of opinion."

"We're not charlatans, Monsieur Furneret. You know that. You're not a charlatan, and neither are we. Perhaps I've made mistakes, but what you did last night was real, and Zosima enabled you to do it. We're not fakers—none of us."

"But you feel obliged to package yourselves as if you were," Paul muttered, thoughtfully, "in order to carry out your own investigations as to exactly what it is you're doing."

"That's right," she said, "but your ability is real—and you really did read my mind, even if...even if you don't believe that you drew my daughter...and that I recognized her..."

She no longer sounded as certain of that recognition as she had a few minutes before. Paul had planted a seed of doubt that was already sprouting.

"Let's..." he began—but he was interrupted by a rap on the door, discreet but clearly audible.

"Damn!" said Paul. "I said half an hour. It can't have passed already." He realized, as he strode to the door, however, that he had not made a note of the precise moment when Juliette left, and he knew that she had no watch.

He opened the door, already preparing in his mind to ask her to give them another ten minutes, when yet another train of thought was derailed. The person standing outside the door was a woman wearing a long dark blue dress, a gray mantle, a broad-brimmed hat and a thick veil. Paul stared at her, uncomprehendingly.

"I'm sorry to disturb you, Monsieur Furneret, she said, in a soft voice, "but is Talia here, by any chance?"

Paul recognized the voice, and was not surprised when the woman lifted her veil to reveal her face.

"So even the suit is just part of the act, is it?" he said, rudely.

It was too late to slam the door, even if he had wanted to extrapolate his rudeness to that extreme. Although Madame Zosima had not crossed the threshold. She had only had to lean forward slightly and look to the left to see Talia sitting in the armchair by the window.

"May I come in, Monsieur Furneret?" she asked. "I have not come to make a scene, I assure you. Far from it."

Paul looked at Talia, who was sitting as if petrified. He made no move to give Zosima permission to enter, and she maintained her position.

"I gather that she has told you enough to deepen your prejudice, in her customary garbled fashion," said the magnetizer," a trifle wearily. "I hope that you will allow me to fill in a few details that she might have left out. I really would like to speak with you, Monsieur Furneret, and I honestly believe that it would be to your benefit as well as mine. And to answer your earlier question, the suit is not part of an act; it is my normal attire; but if I go out incognito, I can hardly combine it with a veil—I have to don the costume that completes the veil."

"I believe that we have both been invited to dine with Doctor Cros this evening," Paul said. "Perhaps we can talk then."

"I'm sure that we shall," said Zosima. "I have every intention of explaining myself fully and honestly to Dr. Cros and his other guests. I shall not be wearing a veil then, and I shall be wearing the suit. But I do believe, sincerely, that it would be to our advantage to have a brief discussion before then.

And for what it might be worth, I beg you not to doubt Talia's sincerity. I do not know why she wanted to see you, and why she would not talk to me about what it was that frightened her last night. I promise that I will not ask her, or you, to violate any confidences you might have exchanged. But she sometimes misinterprets things that she sees, feels and hears; sincere as she is, her conclusions are sometimes unreliable. I am concerned for her, and I feel responsible for her. I will not try to take her away if she does not want to go, but I would like the opportunity to speak to her as well before I go. May I come in?"

Again, Paul looked at Talia. This time, she nodded. Paul stepped back and opened the door fully, to allow Zosima to enter.

The magnetizer went to Talia and said, softly: "I'm truly sorry, Talia, that you felt obliged to keep a secret from me, in order to discuss it with someone else, but I'm not angry, and I shall respect your secret. You and I need one another, and, for the moment, at least, we both need Monsieur Furneret. May I speak with him?"

Talia nodded again, and Zosima turned to Paul.

"Wait a moment," said Paul. "Before anything else, there's one matter I need to clear up. "Do you know what has become of Martine Lambrunet?"

Zosima met his gaze squarely. "Talia believes that she has drowned," she said. "I don't doubt her sincerity, and she has had intuitions of a similar kind in the past, some of which, but not all, have turned out to be accurate—all I can say is that no, I don't know for sure what has happened to the missing lifeboat and its passengers, but every hour that goes by without news increases my anxiety, as it must increase yours."

Paul supposed that he ought to be glad that uncertainty still existed, but it seemed a meager relief.

"And what do you know about Madame Scrive?" he demanded.

"Raoul informed me that Doctor Roimantel told Antoine Cros outside the study door last night that he believed he had recognized Madame Scrive in your drawing. The name immediately seemed significant to me, because I knew that Scrive was Madame de la Vaudère's maiden name. I therefore thought it a hypothesis worthy of investigation as to whether anyone else who had known Madame Scrive in the days of the Second Empire might be able to recognize anyone in your drawing. I intended to ask your permission for you to make a copy for me tonight, assuming that Flammarion brings the drawing to the doctor's dinner."

"Raoul being your coachman, commissioned to mingle with the audiences at your séances...in order to gather intelligence for you that might be useful in your act?"

"That is one way of looking at it, but not mine."

"What's yours?"

"The reason that I carry out research into people who have been identified as probable participants my séances, and ask Raoul to gather intelligence, to borrow your phrase, is to assist me to interpret and evaluate the revelations and manifestations made in the course of the séance—which rarely speak explicitly and articulately for themselves, alas. Given that you know from personal experience how deeply puzzling magnetically induced experiences can be, are you really surprised that such measures are necessary? Have you not spent the greater part of the last twelve hours, in fact, gathering as much intelligence as you can, as quickly as you can? Is that not what you are doing at this very minute?"

"Touché," Paul conceded. "And you are tolerating it with such good grace because every question I ask adds to your store of intelligence?"

"Precisely. If we do not understand one another already, Monsieur Furneret, I believe that we can certainly reach such an understanding swiftly, with the aid of a little good will on our part."

"I remain to be convinced of that. Am I correct in assuming that you had notification in advance that Doctor Cros and Madame de La Vaudère were both likely to be in attendance at last night's séance."

"Yes—and our research certainly extended far enough to consider the possible relevance of Doctor Cros's late brother, and the fact that Madame de La Vaudère had been orphaned at an early age. That is merely standard research. Investigating your background was less easy, as your biography has not yet reached any standard reference books, or even newspaper archives. We had nothing to go on but second-hand reports of what happened at Henri Lemastur's last séance—and that, I must admit, seemed like very dubious evidence. You were an enigma, Monsieur Furneret, and you are even more enigmatic now than you were yesterday evening. That is one of the reasons why I am here. Without your own testimony, I have no basis for inference regarding your...performance. I assume that you would take it as an insult if I called it an act?"

"Paul felt tempted to laugh. "You haven't heard the anecdote that's been running around the salons of the city, then?" he said.

"About you? No. I've heard nothing of that sort—but I was in Nice until very recently, and have not had the opportunity to visit many Parisian soirées as yet. I don't suppose, by any chance, you would care to enlighten me as to the substance of the anecdote in question?"

"Why not?" said Paul, sardonically. "Everybody else has apparently heard it, even if not everyone could put a name to the student of Jacollet's featured therein. Unwisely, in jest, I remarked more than once that I was a double murderer before I was born, having stifled my twin sister in the womb and thus cased the death of my mother, who gave birth successfully to me but then failed dismally to repeat the trick with my late sister."

Zosima blinked. "You poor boy," she said. "You really should not make jokes like that. It is bad enough to be what you are without adding further burdens of unnecessary guilt. In fact, though, that would not have assisted me to draw any inferences with regard to what you drew last night, unless you are implying that the second woman you drew might have been phantom of your late sister, extrapolated to the prime of life?"

Paul glanced at Talia, but he was careful not to let the glance linger. After a pause he said: "You didn't recognize the fetus then?"

Light dawned in Zosima's eyes. "Is that what it was?" she said, wonderingly. "The idea never occurred to me. I thought it might be one of Flammarion's imaginary extraterrestrials. So did he, if I overheard correctly."

"I didn't recognize it either," Paul admitted. "It was Doctor Cros who did."

"And that's why he denied Flammarion's conjecture so definitely," inferred Zosima, instantly, and then started slightly. "Wait a minute...are you saying that he tried to persuade you that what you'd drawn was your dead sister, on the basis of some stupid joke that had gone the rounds of the salons? The swine!"

Paul laughed, dryly. "I don't think he thought of it as a hostile or insulting hypothesis. His interpretation might be incorrect, but it was certainly sincere, and had no motivation other than intellectual curiosity."

"He's a surgeon, not an alienist...and even if he were an alienist, he would have had no right to put such ideas into your head. It's nonsense, by the way. I don't even believe that it was a fetus—I still prefer Flammarion's hypothesis."

"That's very charitable of you. But Cros is something of a psychologist, as every good doctor has to be. Perhaps he's taken the latest fashionable theories coming out of Austria a little too seriously, but his argument makes sense. On what grounds should I prefer your expertise to his?"

"Because you know that I have abundant experience of the phenomena in which you were implicated last night—admittedly as a magnetizer rather than a medium, but no single viewpoint is adequate to the understanding of such a cryptic phenomenon. You can't consider me a friend yet, I know—and far be it from me to suggest that Doctor Cros might be the kind of friend with whom you wouldn't need enemies, given that I hardly know the man and he has such a fine reputation, but please, don't write off my opinions without giving them a fair examination."

A stray thought crossed Paul mind. "By the way," he said. "Did your background research of Doctor Cros happen to include mention of the Kingdom of Araucaria and Patagonia?"

"Was he involved in that? He was a friend of Tounens, then? But that was long ago—more than twenty years."

"I don't know," Paul confessed. "It was just a joke that Madame de La Vaudère made, that I didn't understand Who's Tounens?"

"Orélie de Tounens—A French adventurer who proclaimed himself king of Araucania and Patagonia in South America. The Chileans deported him to France, but he kept trying to go back and claim his realm, before he died. But that was a long time ago. Are there still French pretenders to the imaginary throne in Paris? I can believe it of Nice, the pretenders' capital, but I thought Paris more reasonable."

"Apparently, there are. What did your research tell you about Madame de La Vaudère, then?"

"She used to be a firm believer in spiritism, especially the version involving serial reincarnation—hence her long acquaintance with Flammarion—but she seems to have wavered slightly of late. An immensely successful novelist, but I feel bound to disapprove of her."

"Why?"

"Have you read *The Demi-Sexes?*"

"No—not yet."

"Well, when you do, you'll understand. Don't you think that it's my turn, now, to ask a few questions? Given that you might obtain as much insight from my questions as I've obtained from yours?"

"Go ahead," said Paul, after another glace at the silent Talia.

"When did you first figure out that you're a seer?"

"Late last night. Approximately ten o'clock I suppose, although I lost track of time somewhat. Until then, I was under the impression that I just had a vivid imagination. Baron de Rochemure hadn't really shaken that conviction, although he had given me pause for thought."

"Good. When would you like me to magnetize you again? Will tonight be too soon, do you think? It exhausts poor Talia, but you seem far more robust."

This time, Paul turned to look at Talia directly, in order to measure her reaction to that slightly brutal judgment. Zosima was swift to add: "Please don't be alarmed, Talia. Nothing that Monsieur Furneret and I might attempt together will affect our relationship. You know that I would never abandon you. I love you too much ever to think of that."

That had not been Talia's opinion, Paul remembered. *Just an instrument*, she had said. *She doesn't love me.*

But all that Talia said now, in a conspicuously colorless fashion, was: "I know."

Paul was still hesitating over what answer to give Zosima, wondering whether to risk a straightforward "Never" or to play safe with a judicious: "Tonight will be too soon; I need time to think," when there was another discreet knock on the door.

This time, Paul had no doubt that the thirty minutes he had requested had elapsed. He went to open the door, and let Juliette in. Paul escorted her over to the window.

"You've met Talia Cadelan, briefly," he said. "This is Madame Zosima, the celebrated Egyptian magnetizer. My model, Juliette Scarran."

Nobody offered a hand to be shaken. Zosima bowed politely; Juliette only managed a slight nod of the head, while looking the hypnotist up and down.

"This really has been most interesting," Paul said, "but I'm part-way through a very important painting—my submission for this year's Salon—and I'm working to a demanding schedule. Nor can I afford to waste my model's time, for which I'm paying a very moderate but not insignificant fee. I really must get on with my work now. I'll see you both this evening at the doctor's dinner, and we can talk then about the possibility of arranging further appointments. Please don't think me rude."

"Not at all, Monsieur Furneret," said Zosima, resignedly. "I apologize for taking up so much of your time. She looked at Talia, but did not have to utter any word or gesture of command. The young woman simply took her leave, politely, and left with her companion.

When the door had closed behind them, Paul said: "Sorry, Juliette. I thought half an hour would be enough. I didn't expect the other half of the double act to turn up. I should have done."

"Is that all of them now?" the model asked. "Everyone who's likely to call, that is?"

"Unless Victor comes back—but if he does, I won't let him hold me up. I'll get the palette and the colors ready, while you get into costume."

"It's about time," she opined. "I ought to make some effort to earn my modest but not insignificant fee, after all...not that it's really necessary for you to pay me, as you're providing board and lodging and not collecting rent in kind."

"I think you can stop going on about that now," Paul said. "We know what the situation is—although everyone in Montmartre will be acquainted with the wrongly-jumped conclusion before long, it seems. Madame Cambourg is a legend among concierges, Jane says. Apparently, she knew Jane's mother, at least by sight, back in the good old days, before her last house fell victim to Baron Haussmann and she was exiled from a decent upper class quarter to decadent Montmartre."

"Is this the way it's going to be from now on?" Juliette asked, as she came back down the spiral staircase having slipped into the chemise in a matter of seconds. "Jane says this and Jane says that? Do you call her that to her face?"

Slightly embarrassed, Paul said: "I haven't yet, but I could. She addresses me as Paul."

"Not the same thing—but I won't bring it up again. When you say 'a legend among concierges,' do you mean that

Mère Cambourg is one of those that always knows everything, even if she has to make it all up?"

"That was the inference I took."

"Damn. Still, we expected that. If reporters start calling, though—as your friend Victor and the doctor both said they might, she'll have a ball. Concierges love newspaper reporters, and vice versa."

"Probably—but at least she might intercept them and keep them out of my hair...our hair. And if fantasies are going to be concocted anyway, they might as well be hers as anyone else's. At least she has some interest in managing my image, given that she has to live with me, as it were. That's good— right arm slightly twisted, plus a saintly expression. There's my Jeanne d'Arc."

And at long last, Paul was able to resume his real work, and his true vocation.

CHAPTER IX

Juliette could not contain herself for long. "Will it break your concentration if I talk?" she asked.

"I don't think so," he said, uncertainly. "This is an entirely conscious painting; I'm not magnetized. I don't think Zosima even tried. She's trying to recruit me by stealth, for the moment. You can talk—but if I ask you to shut up while I concentrate..."

"I'll be as silent as the grave from then on. So the weird woman with the big hat and all the black gauze is the hypnotist, and that poor child is her instrument? She doesn't look much like a Svengali."

Paul had not read *Trilby*—the new one by the English author, not the Nodier classic—but he understood the reference. On that point, he was not out of tune with what "All Paris" knew.

"You haven't seen her in a man's suit." he said, rather absent-mindedly.

"That's true. Maybe I ought to cultivate her acquaintance. Perhaps she could hypnotize me into becoming a café-concert star? On the other hand, I suspect that poor child's career isn't exactly thriving. If I had to bet, I'd say that you'll be following her coffin long before you'll be applauding her at the Opéra. She's in a worse state than I am...but not so different. If I'm the lady's type, maybe she'd take me on as a replacement. Not that she's my type, but I'm versatile enough. And the kid might be slipping through her fingers anyway, although I don't suppose the reason she was so desperate to talk to you is that she's looking to convert and was drawn to your awesome masculinity"

"She thinks that I read her mind last night while we were magnetized, and discovered the darkest secret of her life," Paul remarked, absent-mindedly

"And did you?"

No, Paul thought, *but I know it now—poor child.* He added the further thought: *If that's what repeated magnetization makes of a seer, perhaps I'd be very well advised to steer clear of Zosima*; but he said nothing aloud.

When Juliette decided that he wasn't going to reply to her question, she went on: "Well, at least while you've got me you won't be tempted to ask her to model for your next picture. A mercy for her. If the Egyptian loves her, she ought to take her back to the Riviera, or all the way to Egypt. Parisian air won't do her any good. Maybe that's another reason why I should volunteer to let her hypnotize me, and train me up as a partner for the little girl. I'd be afraid that Talia might scratch my eyes out, though. *She doesn't love me*, she said, plaintively. The little waif act—I've seen it before. I'd say *don't let her fool you* if I thought you'd be capable of taking the advice."

"I wish I had read her mind last night," Paul said, aloud, but talking to himself rather than reacting to anything that Juliette had said, "and seen what she had seen, and felt what she had felt. As things were, I don't even know what I saw and felt. Perhaps I *should* take Zosima up on her offer and let her magnetize me again tonight at the doctor's dinner, to see what else I can draw. I'm sure that Cros and Flammarion would be all in favor, in the interests of experimentation..."

"Not that I have a vote, being a mere instrument," Juliette put in, when he paused, pensively, "but I'd rather you didn't—not before you finish your picture, have it accepted for the Salon, and make me immortal, at any rate. If you're going to take the other painting with you to the doctor's dinner—the one Madame de La Vaudère said she'd buy but made sure to leave behind—you'd better make sure you get the cash. Fake aristocrats always forget to pay their bills. She'll probably send a lackey over to pick it up, but you can be sure he won't have the louis in his pocket. Anyway, you've probably made the mistake of drooling over her dirty book to her face, so she'll expect you to make her a present of the picture and be glad...and to get down on your knees to beg her to pose for your next painting, as the Madonna...or Messalina. Feel free not to make any comment—I shouldn't really be trying to provoke one, or you'll be telling me to shut up."

Paul made no reply, concentrating on the face of Jeanne d'Arc.

"Would this be a good time to mention that my appointment is today? I'll have to leave some while before you set off for your dinner, but as you'll have to get dressed you won't lose too much time, and it'll be a full session if we don't take a break. I'll go out afterwards, so don't worry if I'm not here when you get back. Don't wait up—I'll try not to wake you when I come in. You'll have plenty on your mind anyway. If I were you, I wouldn't tell your friend Jane that while you were having your heart-to-heart this morning, little Talia was hiding upstairs hanging on her every word. I don't think you need worry about her giving anything away—she's not very chatty while Madame Svengali is around. Not that I suppose that you and the lady said or did anything untoward—but I know you. The question is, what might Madame Cambourg say, given that she doesn't know that you had a chaperone, and that she's a legend among concierges? But you're not even listening to me, are you? I'm talking to the wall. But that's just as well. Be grateful, Juliette, that he's not telling you to shut up, yet...or maybe not, given that the sensible thing to do would be...."

Fingers snapped.

Paul started, and for a second or two, he had no idea where he was, even though he was standing up, with a palette in his left hand and a brush in his left. He looked dazedly into the fact that was staring into his own from less than a foot away.

"Victor?" he said.

"Jesus," said Victor. "I've seen you entranced a dozen times and more, but never as deep as that. The girl said not to disturb you, because you were on fire, but that was obviously a joke. Put down the brush, will you, and all that messy paint. There's news, and it's not good."

"Martine? She's dead?"

"We don't know that. I've come straight from the tele-graph office, and there's no real news, although every hour that passes...no, when I say the news isn't good, I mean *this* news."

Victor held up a sheet of paper before Paul's bewildered eyes. It was only a single sheet of newsprint, smaller than a page of *Le Matin* or the *Petit Parisien* and the title was one he had never seen before, so far as he could recall: *Mercaba*. It only had four columns instead of the standard six, the left-hand column being headed: PROOF THAT THE DEAD LIVE ON EARTH AND OTHER WORLDS and the one to the right headed LIFEBOAT DISASTER—ALL FEARED DEAD. Much of the upper half of the page, however, was taken up by four sketches: three faces, one male ad two female, and a strange image that resembled a bloated and distorted human head, with bulging eyes and something vaguely resembling the tentacles of an octopus dangling from the neck.

"That's not my drawing!" Paul exclaimed. His eyes scanned the three portraits. "None of them are my drawings! I only saw them for a moment before Flammarion whisked them way, but those aren't my drawings!"

"It doesn't actually claim that they are," Victor said. "All the text says is that you made four drawings, of Charles Cros, Martine Lambrunet, Madame Scrive and an extraterrestrial. It doesn't say explicitly that these are the drawings in question, and the one that's supposed to be Martine doesn't even resemble her very strongly. I wouldn't know about the others."

Paul, completely at a loss, said: "What the hell is the *Mercaba*? "

"It's a weekly spiritist rag, which usually prints a few hundred copies, almost all of which go to subscribers through the mail. This is an extra, of which they probably ran off a couple of thousand to begin with, and hired a handful of camelots to hawk them on the boulevard. As soon as they sold out, they started printing more, and half the gamins in the city suddenly decided that they were camelots for the day and formed a queue outside the offices. It's snowballing. The *Mercaba* will probably keep the monopoly for a couple of hours yet, and probably won't be able to print more than six or seven thousand, but as soon as one of the evening editions of the major papers picks it up—and they will—the big presses will be printing tens of thousands. Tomorrow's *Parisien* will print a couple of hundred thousand, *Le Matin* a hundred thousand. They won't say that it's true—ostensibly, the fact that the *Mercaba* has gone overboard will be the story, rather than the allegations they're making—but that's the kind of fine distinction that much of the public doesn't notice. Ordinarily I'd say that all publicity is good publicity, but in this instance..."

Paul was trying to scan the text as rapidly as possible.

"Where did they get all this stuff from?" he complained. "Flammarion?"

"Not directly, that's for sure—but the *Mercaba* obviously had what the jargon calls 'a correspondent' at the Observatory last night, and he appears to have had sharp ears. He lists the people present, and although he doesn't quote anyone directly, he certainly implies that his judgment about the pictures is a consensus view, that Charles Cros, Martine and Madame Scrive, whoever she is, really appeared, not in the flesh, and a Martian straight out of *Uranie* along with them. It's been a while since it was a best-seller, but people haven't forgotten *Uranie*—and the Flournoy book and that English novel about a Martian invasion of Earth have stirred the mud up again, even though they give completely different accounts of Mars and its naïve life."

"But it's not an extraterrestrial! My drawing didn't have tentacles, damn it! Flammarion did ask the question, but Doctor Cros squashed the idea there and then. Nobody thought that it was a Martian—certainly not Oliver Lodge, or Charles Richet...they'll be furious! And this is all over Paris?"

"Not yet...not quite...but it's only four o'clock. By six...eight at the latest, it really will be the only topic of conversation from the Faubourg Saint-German to Belleville."

"What do you mean, four o'clock?" Paul objected. "It's only just past noon. He reached for where his watch-chain would have been had he been wearing a waistcoat, but only found the fabric of his smock. Victor took out his own watch, and showed the face to Paul. The hands stood at five past four.

"You mean that you've been in that trance for four hours?" Victor queried. "That must be a record, surely, I've seen you drift away for half a hour, maybe three-quarters, but all afternoon? And you've been painting the whole time? No wonder the girl said...."

"Juliette!" said Paul. "Where's Juliette?" His eyes searched the empty divan.

"I told you—she's gone to her appointment. She said she's told you...but she did mention that you weren't really listening."

"Of course I was!" Paul snapped. "Yes, I remember. She said that she had an appointment, but that we'd get in a full session before she had to go. But..."

His eyes had returned, mechanically, to the canvas—the canvas on which he had been working, it seemed, for longer than four hours—and which must have been entirely visible to his eyes ever since Victor had snapped his fingers, but which he had somehow not actually *seen*. He saw it now.

He had made a lot of progress—more than he would have expected, in a single sitting, even a protracted one. Jeanne d'Arc's upper body was almost complete, only requiring a few delicate finishing touches. The arms were properly positioned, and fully expressive, as were the features and their expression. But the real difference between the painting as it leapt to the eye now, and as it had been last time that he had registered its appearance consciously, was in the pyre. Barely sketched before, the flames were now leaping up, blazing aggressively. He understood, belatedly why Victor's comment about Juliette's observation that he was on fire qualified as a joke.

But where was Juliette?

"What appointment?" he asked, talking more to himself than Victor. "She said she had an appointment, but she didn't say what."

"*The* appointment," said Victor. "She wouldn't spell it out, would she?" Paul assumed that he must have looked utterly bewildered, because Victor only paused momentarily before elaborating: "At the Permanence. She's a registered prostitute. The law requires them to have a medical check-up once a month. If she shows signs of venereal disease, she'll be obliged to stop working until it clears. You've been in Paris for nearly two years—do you serious expect me to believe that you didn't know that?"

"Yes," Paul said, vaguely. "I knew...I just didn't think..." It occurred to him, as he spoke, that when Juliette had told him that she had an appointment, she had also told him that she would be going out afterwards, and not to wait up. He had been listening, he had been conscious, he remembered...but somehow, he had not taken it in. He had already been half-entranced.

"Zosima," he murmured, but weakly. It was not Zosima, he knew, who had done this to him; he had done it to himself.

Victor picked up on the name. "She'll do quite well out of it, I dare say," he said. Even a splash in the *Mercaba* qualifies as a result in her line of work. When the morning dailies pick it up, she'll have her pick of soirées at which to do her act. You know, if you could actually bring yourself to team up with her..."

"I'm not a café-concert conjurer!" Paul snapped.

"I know," said Victor. ""That's why I said *if*...and in truth you're right. Not the right image at all. Stooge to an ugly fake Egyptian lesbian...gross."

"Actually," said Paul, scrupulously, "she's not ugly, or gross, and she's only part charlatan. On reflection, I wouldn't be entirely surprised if she really were Egyptian. And it's not impossible that she could help me...not impossible, either, that she's the only one who can...except that that would be a direly dangerous route to follow. Four hours! I was painting in a trance for *four hours?* And painting the Salon piece, which is supposed to be completely conscious, perfectly planned? I'm going crazy, Victor."

"I've been telling you that for years," Victor said, uneasily. He was trying to be flippant, but evidently anxious that there might be truth in the jest.

Paul looked back at the newssheet, which Victor was still holding up for him, the painter not having freed his own hands yet. "Oh God," he groaned, "They've even put that in. Even though their extraterrestrial nonsense renders it irrelevant, they've put it in."

"What?" Victor asked.

"That stupid joke about murdering my twin sister in the womb. They even picked up on that—and it's practically the only things they say about me, except that I had a painting of Mourgue la Faye at the last Salon, and they only say that to make me out to be a crazy Bohemian."

"You did paint it," Victor pointed out, stopping short of suggesting that, by comparison with a respectable dandy like himself, Paul actually was a crazy Bohemian.

There as a knock on the door then, but Jane de La Vaudère did not wait for anyone to answer it; she opened it herself and came in. Her gaze took in Paul, Victor, the *Mercaba* and Jeanne d'Arc in a single sweep.

"Ah," she said, "you've seen it. That saves explanations. Sorry to interrupt you at work, but you need to get changed. Joseph's waiting downstairs with the doctor's carriage."

"But it's only ten past four," Paul observed, while Victor stepped forward, bowed, and said: "Victor Marvaud. It's a privilege to meet you, Madame de La Vaudère. I'm a great admirer of your work.

Jane de La Vaudère inclined her head very slightly, and replied, with what Juliette would probably have termed "look-what-the-cat-dragged-in politeness": "Thank you, Monsieur Marvaud." Then she practically cut him dead, turning to Paul. "Please hurry, Paul. Clean your equipment as rapidly as you can, and put on some decent clothes. The doctor thought it

141

best to bring our conference forward, in view of that"—she indicated the *Mercaba* in Victor's hand with a flick of a gloved forefinger. "Poor Camille is utterly distraught. You can be sure that the *Mercaba*'s so-called correspondent will never set foot in the Observatory again. Go, please!"

Galvanized into action, Paul ran toward the sink, leaving Victor and Jane de La Vaudère standing by the easel. The lady began to examine the painting with the utmost care.

Victor, utterly disconcerted, said: "Have I done something to offend you, Madame? I'm truly sorry, if so." Although he was on the other side of the room, Paul could hear everything they said.

The author condescended to look at her interlocutor. "I suppose that I ought not to hold it against you," she said, "as you had no idea what the consequences of your action would be." Paul assumed that she must have looked at the newssheet again.

"I can assure you, Madame," said Victor, sounding genuinely wounded, "that I had nothing to do with this."

"It was you, was it not, who asked Doctor Cros to take Paul to Juvisy?"

"Well, yes, but..."

"It was therefore you who were responsible for that fact that the doctor and I were sucked into this affair far more intimately than we would have been had we merely been two observers sitting at the back of the crowd. Had I not been in Camille's study with Paul, that imbecile Roimantel would have come to me with his ludicrous whisper, instead of telling Antoine, in a manner that must have attracted every curious eye and pricked ear in the room—which would have saved me an enormous quantity of unwelcome embarrassment."

"But...," Victor began.

Jane de La Vaudère cut him off with a gesture. "On the other hand," she said, "Had you not been so presumptuous as to ask Doctor Cros for that favor, on the basis of such a slight acquaintance, I would not have met Paul, which I am glad to have done, so I suppose that balances the account somewhat.

You may consider yourself forgiven. Now, please go away. I want to have a word with Paul before we go down to the carriage."

Paul could not imagine how Victor must feel, having been summarily dismissed from the studio twice in one day by two people of the status of the doctor and the author, but he was too intent on cleaning his brushes and his hands to turn round. When he eventually did, Victor was no longer in the room, and Jane de La Vaudère was standing behind him.

"I apologize for that," she said. "He is your friend, after all."

"He'll get over it," Paul said "He says that the headline in the *Mercaba* is false, and that there's no news as yet of the lifeboat."

"True," she said, "but this is one occasion when no news is not good news. If the lifeboat were merely adrift, it would have been spotted by now, given the density of shipping in the Manche nowadays. Let's not lose hope, though. You seem to have made good progress with your painting. I presume you've been working on the flames since dismissing your model for the day?"

"So it seems," Paul agreed, as he finished the cleaning.

"Seems?" the lady queried.

"I've been...absorbed. I literally didn't know what I was doing. I'm afraid I'll have to go upstairs in order to change. If you'll excuse me..."

"Go, go," she said. As he was climbing the spiral staircase, however, she added: "Has Zosima been to see you?"

"Yes," he called down. "But she didn't hypnotize me again...at least, I didn't think so. Talia was here too."

"Ah! So you know why she wanted to see you. Would it be indiscreet of me to ask what the reason was?"

Paul hesitated, half way through changing his trousers. "I'm sorry, Madame, but I can't tell you that. It's a secret that she gave away by mistake, and I feel obliged to keep it."

"I see. Well, there are things you know about me now that I'd rather you didn't repeat, so I'm glad to find you so scrupulous. I wish I had much confidence in Madame Cambourg's promise not to say anything to anyone about my mother if anyone should ask. She's already seen the picture in the *Mercaba*, and is in no doubt that it's fanciful, and not a real portrait, but that's not very helpful in determining whether the face you drew might be my mother. Camille has showed me the drawing again, of which I only caught a glimpse last night, and I can see what Antoine meant about a family resemblance, but it's very vague."

"I only caught a glimpse of what I'd drawn myself," Paul said, "and my attention was wholly absorbed by the drawing of Martine. If you want me to make copies of the other image, to show to Madame Cambourg, or anyone else...."

"In fact," the author said, "I'd rather you didn't. To be perfectly honest, I'd rather the *Mercaba*'s fake were copied and circulated and circulated as widely as possible, given that the cat is already out of the bag, so that anyone else who knew my mother can say, as Madame Cambourg has—to me, at least—that the caption is a lie. That way, her name might be dropped from the story."

"I'll do everything I can to assist that result," Paul promised.

"Thank you. Will Zosima be a problem in that regard, do you think? Or Talia? I'm sorry to be so egocentric...especially since Antoine's amateur psychoanalysis must have been more painful for you than for me."

"Actually," said Paul, attempting to tie his cravat neatly and failing, "it wasn't—or rather, it was, but only temporarily. I'm not sure that he was wrong about my carrying a burden of unconscious guilt, and I think that bringing it out into the open might help to dispel it."

"If only things were that easy," she said, in a voice so low that he could only just make out the words from above. He decided that the cravat would do as it was, brushed his jacket swiftly, and put it on. While he came down the spiral staircase, Jane de La Vaudère moved to meet him at the bottom.

"You friend Victor wouldn't approve," she observed, "but you'll pass. Let's go."

As they went down the gloomy stairway, Paul said: "Forgive me for mentioning it, but in view of Madame Cambourg's reputation, do you think it was entirely wise for you to come up to my studio unescorted twice in one day?"

"Twice is no worse than once," she replied, with a brief laugh. "If it's my reputation you're worried about, there's no need. It was tarnished long ago. If it's yours...to be honest, you're a Montmartrean painter from the Midi, so there's really no brightness to tarnish. I'm sorry if you thought otherwise. The heroines in my novels would never dream of going to pose for a painter without taking a chambermaid as a chaperone, of course, but that's just convention...absurd in the context of scandalous texts like *Les Demi-Sexes*. I'll come to pose on my own, if you don't mind. I'll even drive my own carriage, as I've been doing for years, although even that was considered scandalous at one point. We have Joseph to preserve appearances today, though. Bonjour, Madame Cambourg!" She pronounced the last phrase as she swept past the concierge's lodge on to the sidewalk, where Joseph was already holding the carriage door open. Paul hastened to offer her his arm as they climbed up. She took a seat facing the direction in which the carriage would travel and when Paul moved as if to it opposite she dismissed that possibility with a gesture and obliged him to sit beside her.

"What will you say," she asked, as the vehicle moved way, "if Zosima proposes holding another séance tonight?"

"She already has," Paul told her, wryly. "Fortunately, I was saved from having to answer immediately because Juliette came back just then—but I would have stalled, in order to have time to consider whether it's wise ever to allow myself to be hypnotized again."

"And?" she prompted.

"I seem to have lost any time I might have spent thinking about it by hypnotizing myself—which I shouldn't have done while I was working on the Salon submission. But Flammarion will presumably be all in favor of a further experiment in automatic drawing, to substitute for the one that's been compromised, and the doctor probably won't be averse to the idea."

"They won't pressure you. They know that you're anxious about the Lambrunets, and they know how much more anxious you're becoming as time goes by. The only question you have to ask yourself is what you want to do. "

"I wish I knew. The frightening thing about it isn't what I might see or draw but the fact that I won't be conscious of what I'm doing. Perhaps I shouldn't be alarmed, given that when I lost consciousness of what I was doing this afternoon, I didn't do anything that I wouldn't have done while conscious—I just carried on painting, and didn't spoil the Jeanne d'Arc in the slightest. But the mere fact that, even before my memory stopped recording, I heard Juliette talking to me without taking the slightest notice of what she was saying...it's a state of consciousness I'd rather avoid, if I can, at least until I can learn to control it. If I could do that...but I can't help suspecting that the more I try, the more I might fall victim to it. Before you came into the studio, Victor was just saying that he'd been telling me for years that I was going mad...and he has, but always in jest...until then. Then, for the first time, he sounded anxious that it might be true. And so am I."

"You're not going mad, Paul. Antoine, playing at psychology, would probably tell you that fading out of consciousness this afternoon was just a reaction to the stress of not knowing what has become of Martine—that it was a kind of retreat. Perhaps that's true. Perhaps it's the case that your painting, with all its varying degrees of concentration, has always been a retreat. My painting was, in the day, and my writing still is. A lot of people think that I just do it for the money, that I write the kinds of things I write in order to pander to an audience, and an audience with low tastes at that, but it isn't true. Perhaps it qualifies as a defensive obsession—but I'm not mad, and neither are you. In fact, you and I are saner than most, and even the sanest of us has hauntings with which to deal—as witness Antoine and Charles.

"As to what the best way to deal with it might be, I wish I could give you some sound advice, but I can't...and my observations suggest that anyone who pretends that he can is a liar—perhaps a liar fooling himself as well, but a liar nonetheless. All I can say is that you're not alone...and Camille and Antoine are on your side too. Zosima I'm not so sure about...and even if she thinks she is on your side, that doesn't mean that she isn't capable of harming you. Whatever power she has, I don't believe that she's in control of it, or that she understands it. I've met a lot of magnetizers and mediums in my time, some of whom have pretended to have the wisdom of the ages at their fingertips, but if all their knowledge were pooled, it probably wouldn't fill a thimble. A hundred years of science hasn't made more of a dent in the mystery, as yet, than a thousand years of intuition. The power is real—but in the circumstances, that might be regrettable, not just for its immediate victims but its possessors. Oh, we're here—sorry, I got carried away."

"Not at all," said Paul, not merely for the sake of politeness. "You've been very helpful."

As he offered her his hand to help her down from the carriage, he thought yet again how effortless idolatry might be.

CHAPTER X

Paul and Jane de La Vaudère were shown into a drawing room by a manservant, who withdrew immediately, leaving them alone with Camille Flammarion. The astronomer hastened to shake Paul's hand.

"Thank you for coming," he said. "Antoine is otherwise occupied for the moment, I fear, but I asked him to summon you early in order that we could make up for the time we lost last night. Jane was kind enough to volunteer to fetch you, as she had been to your studio before. Have you seen this?"

The astronomer held up a copy of the *Mercaba*.

"Yes; Victor brought a copy round as soon as it came to his attention."

"Completely unethical behavior. I know who's responsible, and I will inflict what penalty I can, but there really isn't any way to counter it. Denials are futile in such cases, as I know from long experience."

While he was speaking, Paul had already noticed a large sheet of paper set out on a side-table, which could only be the drawings he had made, and he had already begun to edge in that direction, as had Jane de La Vaudère.

"Yes, of course," said Flammarion. "You've hardly had a chance to look at it closely, have you, and none at all to compare it with this?"

Paul inspected the four drawings that he had made under Zosima's influence curiously, making swift comparisons with the images in the *Mercaba*. The two sketches of Charles Cros resembled one another closely enough, one, if not both, having presumably been copied from an existing image. The sketches of the two women, however, bore little resemblance to one another, the *Mercaba*'s artist evidently having no idea what Martine looked like, or the appearance of the sketch that Paul had made of the woman tentatively identified by Doctor

Roimantel as Madame Scrive. He had not even bothered to reproduce a "family resemblance" to Jane de La Vaudère, of whom he would have had little difficulty locating a picture had he made the effort. On the other hand, Paul saw readily enough what Cros had meant by the resemblance in question—which made it plausible, he surprised, that he his unconscious mind had employed Jane's features as a basis for extrapolation, but, by the same token, did not deny the hypothesis that the sketch might actually be an image of her mother, as she had been prior to her death more than forty years before.

The blurred image of the "Martian" reproduced by the *Mercaba* bore only the vaguest resemblance to the fourth sketch that Paul had made, in which the artist, prejudiced by the doctor's identification, now had little difficulty seeing as a human fetus afloat in amniotic fluid. But surely, he thought, that was strong evidence for the image having been dredged from his unconscious mind, given that he had never heard of spiritists reporting apparitions of fetal ghosts, or mediums summoning such spirits from the beyond.

On the other hand, he mused, if one looked at the matter logically, many more human beings died in infancy than in the prime of life, and if their souls really did survive that death, and really did preserve some semblance of what they had been when alive, why should there not be infantile spirits? Whether there could be fetal spirits, he supposed, depended on the moment the soul entered the body, but if it was earlier than birth, while the body was still developing in the womb, then why not? Talia Cadelan, it seemed, was still haunted by the memory of the child she had lost while still little more than a child herself. If any hauntings were real, why should that not be as likely as any other? And if any spirit could be vengeful, why should his sister not have as much right to posthumous resentment as any victim of foul murder...?

"Do you still think that the fourth image might be an extraterrestrial beneficiary of interplanetary reincarnation?" Paul asked Camille Flammarion.

"Antoine has certainly pointed out its resemblance to a fetus," the astronomer replied, "and his judgment might well be sound. Do you have any memory or intuition that suggests *why* you might have sketched...whatever that is?"

"None at all," Paul said, "save for the suggestion made by my stupid joke, that I might feel guilty about the death of my twin sister in the womb."

"Do you think," Flammarion suggested, "that you might be able to remember why you drew the four images if you could be returned to the same state of mind that you were in when you drew them?"

"It's possible," Paul admitted, a trifle reluctantly. "But when I returned from it again, would I not simply forget again?"

"What if you were interrogated under hypnosis?" the astronomer persisted. "That way, even if you forgot, a record could be made of your testimony."

"But would it be reliable?" Jane de La Vaudère put in. "You have tried it before, Camille, have you not?"

"I have," Flammarion acquiesced, with a slight sigh. Paul gathered that the results had been ambiguous, at best.

"Have you had a chance, as yet, to show this image to someone, other than Roimantel, who knew Madame Scrive?" he said, pointing to the relevant sketch.

"Not yet," the astronomer said. "And in all honesty, could we trust any memory of that antiquity? Forty years is a long time. Septuagenarians are scarce enough; those with accurate memories are rare birds indeed. And now that the *Mercaba* has publicized the identification, it is bound to function as a powerful suggestion. Even if half a dozen individuals came forward and said: 'Yes, that is Madame Scrive as I remember her,' how far could we trust their unanimity?"

"How much credence do you place in the theory of animal magnetism to which Lemastur adheres, Monsieur Flammarion?" Paul asked. "You have been researching the matter for a long time. Do you believe that magnetizers really radiate some kind of fluid, or that they can project some kind field of force with an effort of the will?"

"There is certainly some suggestive evidence for the magnetic analogy," Flammarion said. "Exactly how close the analogy might be is difficult to determine, but yes, I accept that the hypothesis of fields of psychic force might explain many puzzling phenomena."

"The reason I ask is that Talia Cadelan believes that a link was formed between her mind and mine when Zosima extended her supposed field of force, and that I might have plucked one or more of the images I drew out of her visual memory rather than my own. But if that were true, it might open up the possibility that I might have mined other minds as well—yours, for instance, or Doctor Roimantel's. It is not implausible, is it, that the sight of Madame de La Vaudère might have prompted Roimantel to nostalgic remembrance of her late mother?"

"It is a hypothesis worth considering," sad Flammarion, judiciously.

"Not as worthy as the hypothesis that it's not my mother at all, but someone else entirely," the lady said bluntly. "Perhaps Paul might remember the person concerned, if the memory could be triggered somehow. Or perhaps, if she is a spirit, she comes from a remote era of history, when no portraits existed: Cleopatra, Semiramis or Mary Magdalene."

"Or Ennoia, Delilah or Eve," suggested Flammarion, with mild sarcasm. "The possibilities are endless...alas."

"A moment ago," Paul said, "you suggested that if I could be interrogated under hypnosis, a record could be retained of what I said. Did you record what Talia said last night? Presumably you have a phonograph, and use it routinely in your séances?"

"Yes, I did," said the astronomer. "I have played it back several times without being able to make out any coherent speech; the recording is not very clear, and not very long. You worked on the drawings with such remarkable rapidity, and

Talia interrupted herself with the scream just as she seemed to be on the verge of settling into coherency."

"But it did record what Zosima was murmuring?" Paul queried.

"Yes, of course, but very faintly—and that too seems to be gibberish, almost a kind of vocal music rather than language. I can play it for you if you wish."

"I'd be curious to hear it," Paul said. "Including the scream; if anything could trigger a memory, that might do the trick."

"The apparatus is in another room," said Flammarion. "I'll fetch it."

"As soon as he had left the room, Jane de La Vaudère said: "Are you sure this is safe?"

"Of course not," Paul replied, "but I presume that it will be safer than waiting for Zosima to arrive and repeating the experiment more exactly, as she is bound to want to do."

"Shouldn't we wait for Antoine?" she suggested.

"In case one of us requires urgent medical attention?" he queried.

"We are in his house," the lady pointed out. "He might think it a little rude to proceed with an experiment without him."

Paul did not want to concede the point. "It isn't an experiment," he said. "I merely want to hear the recording. I won't attempt any hypnotic drawing before he's here to observe."

The author still seemed a trifle uncertain, but Camille Flammarion had no hesitation, when he returned, in winding the apparatus and setting the wax cylinder on the turntable. He barely looked around to check that his audience was ready before activating the machine.

The quality of the recording was indeed poor, but Zosima's voice soon became audible as a faint whisper, somewhat reminiscent of a distant prayer recited in a foreign language, or what Paul had heard reported of the phenomenon of glossolalia. Then another voice became audible, or perhaps more than one—but Paul assumed that it was, in fact, only

Talia who was making the sounds, although she too was producing a kind of glossolalia: what had once been called
"speaking in tongues," thought by neoplatonist philosophers to
be a gnomic species of prophecy. It was not difficult to imagine that three or four distant and different voices were compet-
ing to be heard, overlapping and becoming confused.
Zosima's murmur was still faintly audible in the background.

Paul did not feel anything out of the ordinary within
himself. He listened hard, and thought that he could also hear
a scratching sound, which he took to be the movement of his
charcoal over the sheet of paper, but he was not sure that it
was not a construction of his imagination, seeking to find
sense in a blur of sound that was literally incomprehensible.

As Flammarion had said, there seemed to be a development in the glossolalia, whereby syllables seemed to become
gradually more distinct, and to form sequences that were
word-like, without actually being graspable words—at least
not words in French or any other language that Paul could
recognize.

Then the scream cut through the soundscape, driving out
everything else. It did not seem to Paul to be a very loud
scream, to the extent that the apparatus had been able to capture and preserve it, but it did seem penetrating, as if it were
cutting into his sternum. It did not arrive with any hint of a
vision, or trigger any nostalgic memory.

After a momentary silence, other confused and overlapping voices became audible: the voices of members of the
audience reacting to the scream. Movements could also he
heard—and this time, a memory *was* recalled, as Paul remembered the struggle that had formed around him, and the jos-
tling, as people endeavored to looked over his shoulders—and
then the voice of Doctor Cros, clear and decisive, demanding
passage in order to reach his beleaguered patient.

Flammarion switched off the machine, and the cylinder
stopped rotating.

"Interesting," said Paul, wishing that it had been more so. "What do you make of the voices, Monsieur Flammarion—the voices that Talia was synthesizing, that is?"

"Glossolalia is by no means uncommon in mediums," Flammarion said. "It has a long history, linked in Christendom with divine ecstasy in such well-known instances as that of Hildegard of Bingen. Other writers, of course, associated it with demonic possession. Modern spiritists differ in their interpretation too, but one common suggestion is the spirits speak various languages of their own, and have difficulty in adapting to the usages of mediums in order to address living human beings."

"It's hard to understand, though, why the unconscious mind should be speaking in tongues, if the phenomena mistaken for apparitions originate there instead of in the spirit world?"

"I'm unsure as to whether the dichotomy between the rival theories is as clear as the adherents of one or the other sometimes assume," said Flammarion. "Philosophers make a sharp distinction between the subjective and the objective, and psychologists between the real and the illusory, which might not be entirely justified. The mental states of dreaming and wakefulness can overlap considerably—as you, being an artist are perhaps more aware than many people. At any rate, proof that an apparition of the dead takes place entirely within the mind of a seer, rather than in the external world, would not demonstrate, *ipso facto*, that it was not an apparition of the dead.

"Thus, the fact that no one but you saw the ghost of Charles Cros in the Observatory last night is not absolute proof that he was not actually there. Ghosts might be all around us, but find it difficult to bring themselves to our attention, let alone communicate with us effectively, without the help of seers of one kind or another; but even with such aid, they are far more likely to be manifest as voices or images in a medium's mind than as tangible physical presences. That is an elementary feature of spiritism, in theory and practice. The skeptics who take it for granted that everything manifest in the mind must be a product of the imagination are excessively simple-minded."

"So Jeanne d'Arc's voices might really have been those of the saints she named?"

"The evidence is not such as to permit any conclusion, but I do not rule out *a priori* the possibility that what she heard did not originate spontaneously in her own imagination."

"Perhaps Jeanne d'Arc is employing me to depict her," Paul mused, thinking of the four hours he had lost, and the face and the flames he had developed in that interim.

"And using Juliette," added Jane de La Vaudère. "Don't forget your model."

Paul felt a twinge of pain at that reminder, as he thought of Juliette queuing at the Permanence for her legally enforced medical examination, and then "going out," once certified disease-free. Had he not been going to dine at the doctor's house, he wondered, might she have dined with him at the restaurant, and then gone home with him? Except, of course, that it would not have been "going home" in any true or metaphorical sense of the term. And why should he care, since he was only borrowing her features to represent a saint and martyr, and had no right or reason to expect her to behave in the manner of a saint...or even a martyr.

Then he thought about Talia, similarly pale and afflicted, perhaps a fraction closer to sainthood...and martyrdom. What selection, he wondered, might that impose upon the hypothetical spirits desirous of using her as a mouthpiece...assuming that she had any power of selection at all, and was not merely a hapless instrument, an unloved victim of some kind of struggle for temporary re-existence in which the strongest of the dead prevailed over the weak? But if Talia were a mere instrument, a kind of fleshy phonograph, even less efficient than the crude machine that he had just seen in operation, was he not akin to her? Was he not brutally banished from his own consciousness, while something else took over his right hand, using his fingers and his learned skills to do its own work.

She doesn't love me, Talia had said, flatly contradicting what her principal living manipulator had said. Which of them was lying...or mistaken? And whether it was true or not of Zosima, how could it be true of the spirits of the dead, even if they were capable of love? In the unlikely event that Jeanne d'Arc really could use him as a medium, in order to reinsert something of herself into the material world, what feelings could she possibly have for him, a mere machine of transmission? The same argument surely applied to Charles Cros and Madame Scrive—or whoever the image identified by Roimantel really was.

And what of his sister? He had assumed readily enough that she might hate him, but what if the reason that she had sought to employ him to express her image was because she wanted to tell him that she forgave him? Or—surely far more likely?—she simply found his hand a convenient device for laying claim to a momentary, shadowy fraction of the existence of which fate had cheated her before she had had a chance to savor it.

It was easy enough, he had to suppose, that his poor long-dead sister might not love him, but what possible grounds could there be, he wondered, for suspecting that Charles Cros had not loved his elder brother dearly, or that Jane's mother had not doted on the daughter whom she certainly had not wanted to abandon by dying? What might their motives have been for grabbing momentary possession of his hand in the midst of the spiritual melee? What had they wanted to communicate—given that Antoine and Jane both seemed intent on refusing even to admit the possibility that they might have been trying, the believer denying it just as strongly as the skeptic?

And what of Martine, who might well have been unaware of the love he had for her, or imagined he had, and might hardly have spared him a thought since the course of events had separated them nearly two years before? What could have motivated her to jostle for possession of him, if only for an instant...?

No, he thought, decisively, *that way lies madness. Cros is right; it was all the work of my own perverse imagination, drawing on the deep, muddy, poisoned well of unconscious memory...which might, alas, be only a different route to madness...*

Mentally, he heard fingers snap. No one had actually done that, his present company being far too polite, but he imagined it, deliberately, in order to drag himself back from his reverie.

He became aware that both of his companions were watching him curiously, observing him, semi-expectantly. Even without the dissuasion of their politeness, neither of them would have snapped their fingers; even Jane, despite her quasi-maternal pose, would have been more interested in studying his self-hypnotic state, had he descended any further thereinto, perhaps interrogating him, even without much hope of his making sense, because he was such an imperfect phonograph of the beyond...

"Sorry," he said. "My mind drifted there, for a moment."

"So we observed," said Jane de La Vaudère. "You had us on tenterhooks, waiting for a memory to surface, or a intuition to form, At the risk of being indiscreet, what were you thinking about?"

"Love," he said, uneasily, "and the lack of it."

The lady seemed surprised. "And my mentioning your model triggered that?"

Paul blushed, barely remembering the remark that had launched his speculative excursion. "No," he said. "There were several intermediate stations at which the train of thought stopped, including Martine. It was Martine that I was thinking...wondering...about before I snapped my fingers mentally to bring myself down to earth. It will be dark again soon, and the weather tonight might not be as mild as it was last night. If that boat's still adrift, heading further into the Atlantic...but this is 1901, and it isn't the raft of the *Medusa*."

"Nor will it encounter any sirens or Lorelei in the Manche," said Jane de La Vaudère, speaking softly but perhaps unable to resist the literary quip. "Neither Scylla nor Charybdis."

"According to Talia," Paul replied, with an edge in his voice that he could not evaluate himself, "if I really had read her mind, I could have felt her drown."

"But you couldn't," said the author." Couldn't read her mind, that is."

"Probably not," Paul agreed. "I can't even read my own."

"It's a common problem," Camille Flammarion said, mildly. "Studying the heavens is a great deal simpler, but only if you restrict your attention to the positions of little dots of light. On the other hand, even they become a great deal stranger as soon as a telescope can resolve a few of them into disks, and stranger still when one has a spectroscope. How can we know whether or not there are ghosts on Mars, when we aren't even sure that there are canals? The evidence of mediums like Catherine Müller—or Hélène Smith as the Swiss psychologist calls her—is hardly persuasive."

"Flournoy is very hard on poor Catherine, in my opinion," Jane de La Vaudère put in. "Even if her visions are simply, 'romances of the subliminal imagination,' as he puts it, does that obliterate their interest and merit? Does he think that composing and writing romances of the subliminal imagination is easy? He should try it some time. And what does it matter if she made up her Martian language rather than discovering an interplanetary Rosetta stone? Does he think that kind of invention child's play?"

"In fact," Flammarion observed, with his customary mildness, "her imagined Martian language bears a striking resemblance to the one that Hildegard of Bingen invented. I wish I'd had the opportunity to get to know Miss Müller a little better, so that I could make my own thorough analysis of her so-called cryptomnesia."

"You have me at your disposal," the author told him, "and my works to analyze—my double star, my victims of Kama, and very soon you'll have my King of Siam's amazon.

You have Paul too, now. Similar phenomena, according to Antoine. Paul has hardly begun to follow his chimera yet, though, from what I've seen in his studio and what I remember of his painting at the last Salon—perhaps as well, as his heart is still intact."

Paul recalled the seductive chimera in Jane's story, and its manner of collecting human hearts. Aloud, though, he exclaimed: "Hardly started! I'm terrified that I've already gone too far. Twice in the last twenty-four hours I've got completely lost, and if Victor hadn't snapped his fingers this afternoon, or Zosima last night..."

He stopped, aware that they were both still looking at him again with the same observant concentration, as if with the aid of mental magnifying glasses.

"Don't stop," said Jane de La Vaudère. "The declaration was just getting interesting. Do you mean that if I'd arrived at your studio a few minutes earlier—before Monsieur Marvaud—I'd have found you still entranced?"

"Yes," said Paul. "But you'd seen what Zosima did— you'd have known how to bring me out of it."

"Oh, I've known that for a long time," she told him, "but I'd have been strongly tempted to leave you in the somnambulistic condition, at least for a while. If you'd turned out be able to talk...but you probably wouldn't. The research is essentially frustrating, isn't it Camille?"

"It certainly has been," Flammarion agreed, regretfully. "And I must say, Monsieur Furneret, that I'm glad that Zosima wasn't tempted to leave you and Mademoiselle Cadelan entranced for any longer last night, given that you both seemed to be in some distress. Such disturbances are usually brief and superficial, but they are alarming nevertheless for those who have provided a stage for them."

Not to mention the instruments—or victims—themselves, Paul thought, but did not say aloud,

The door opened at that point and Antoine Cros strode into the room. "I'm very sorry to keep you waiting," he said, "but the operation proved more challenging than I had anticipated. My hand is neither as steady not as swift as it used to be."

"Was the operation successful?" asked Flammarion.

"Yes—and the patient didn't die. That old joke never seems amusing to me, especially while I'm waiting to see what happens when the chloroform wears off. Sometimes, everything goes perfectly until that last moment. But let's not waste time discussing the stubbornness that certain patients put into dying, even though one has done everything necessary to save their lives. Zosima will be here soon, and we ought to decide in advance how we're going to receive her. Are we going to request that she undertake another experiment? If so, or if she asks to do so, do we let her dictate the terms, or can we negotiate with her to design a truer test. What's this?"

This was the copy of the *Mercaba*, which Jane de La Vaudère had brought from the other world and put down beside the phonograph. Apparently, Cros had been too busy all afternoon to have been apprised of that development. He gave the machine a disapproving glance before picking up the paper. He scanned the sheet, turned it over to check that it was printed on both sides, and then began to read the text more carefully, from the beginning. He soon stopped.

"Damn," he whispered. "Exactly what we were hoping to avoid. I'll have to post two burly men at the gate and the coaching entrance tomorrow, to repel the inquisitive. They can't have printed that many copies, I suppose, on their tinpot press, but at least a couple of the evening papers are bound to pick it up, even if they pretend to be protesting at the scandal. Martians, indeed! And the whisper about your mother blown up out of all proportion, Jane, Why couldn't that old goat Roimantel keep his voice down? If you're going to whisper, damn it, do it properly...otherwise you just attract attention. It's still treason on the part of your guest, though, Camille. Do you want me to send a couple of the Araucarian brotherhood round to break his kneecaps?"

Flammarion did not bother to reply to the ridiculous suggestion. "It's entirely my fault," he said, "I should never have invited the fellow to attend."

"You couldn't expect a trick like this." He put the *Mercaba* down again, in order to return to more urgent matters. "Well, Paul, what are we going to do about Zosima? Are you going to volunteer—or if not, what are you going to do if she puts you on the spot? Because she will put you on the spot, believe me."

"I know. She's already made her intention explicit. I'm very grateful to you for offering us this dinner; it saved me from having to give her an instant answer this morning, and it will ensure that when she does issue the challenge, I'll have seconds around me to make sure that the duel is fair. I've given it some thought, and it seems to me that the best thing to do is to accept the challenge, but to place conditions on my cooperation. As the challenged party, I presumably have choice of weapons. First of all, I'll demand that she give us a brief summary account of the results of her exploits thus far, and her expectations for the result of the experiment, in view of what she's already seen me do, and the fact that it went somewhat awry."

"It'll be a pack of lies," Cros opined. "You'll just be testing her ingenuity."

"Actually, I don't think it will. My impression is that she really wants to know what happened last night and why, precisely because she didn't expect it. She's as curious as we are—as curious as you, at least. When I've heard her out, I'll be better able to judge what I might be risking, but my thinking is that I need a diagnosis and a prognosis of my existential situation, and that I'll never have a better opportunity to obtain it than in the present company. The more I can help you inform yourselves, the better placed you'll be to be able to advise me subsequently. So, with those provisos, full steam ahead—and one for all and all for one, if you'll forgive the melodrama."

All three laughed, dutifully.

"Good for you, Captain d'Artagnan," said Cros.

"One more thing," said Paul.

"Name it," said Cros,

"Let's be careful of Talia. She's delicate, and it might be that the greatest danger in this is for her. I wouldn't want anything bad to happen to her by our fault."

"Goes without saying," said Cros. "We're all gentlemen here, aren't we, Jane."

"In your definition, perhaps," the lady replied, "but not in mine. That said, it does indeed go without saying—and that, unless I'm much mistaken, is the sound of the bell at your coaching entrance, so let's get the soirée started."

CHAPTER XI

Paul had attended numerous dinner parties in Toulouse, where, even though he had not belonged to the upper echelons of that city's society, his acquaintance with Victor and Gaston had gained him frequent access to respectable houses. Because provincial society was so carefully imitative of Parisian society, the rituals of the evening did not take him by surprise, and the legacy of his previous observations ensured that he felt more comfortable in the surroundings and the company than Zosima, and infinitely more so than Talia. It was understandable, however, that Zosima should feel somewhat outnumbered; she was only too well aware of the fact that the other four diners had met up in advance of her arrival, in order to conspire, and that three of them had a long history of acquaintance and common interest. She must also have been able to see, almost immediately, that the fact that Antoine Cros and Jane de La Vaudère had opposed philosophical convictions would not inhibit them in the least from forming a solid alliance.

To begin with, it was the conventions of dinner parties that governed the occasion entirely. Once the initial formulae were out of the way and they were sipping preliminary drinks from crystal glasses in the drawing room while waiting for dinner to be served, the conversation immediately focused on the mystery of the missing lifeboat. Zosima commiserated with Paul on the absence of news, and did not make the slightest reference to Talia's conviction that the *Mercaba*'s headline was accurate.

The *Mercaba*, not unnaturally, was the next topic of conversation. Zosima assured the assembly that she had had nothing to do with the appearance of the newssheet, and that she had not knowingly spoken to any reporters. Flammarion and Cros assured her that they believed her, that they had had no difficulty in identifying the person responsible, and that they were no strangers to the various kinds of distortions to which reportage of séances was subjected by committed believers of all stripes.

Somewhat to Paul's surprise, Zosima did not bring up the possibility of subjecting him to hypnosis again, and actually seemed to be avoiding the topic. She did, however, ask him how his painting of Jeanne d'Arc was going, and when he replied, cagily, that he had made good progress that afternoon in spite of the stressful circumstances, she asked him how he had made the thematic transition from Mourgue la Faye to Jeanne d'Arc. He did not imagine for a moment that she had seen the earlier painting, and he was certain that she had barely glanced at the canvas in the studio, but he answered honestly, as he had when Jane de La Vaudère has asked him a similar question.

After that Zosima began questioning Flammarion, about astronomy, meteorology and natural history—but Paul observed that she made no mention of the unfortunate zanglodon fiasco, in which Flammarion had innocently incorporated into his showcase account of the natural history of the earth an account of the recent discovery of a prehistoric saurian that had turned out to be the work of an American hoaxer. He would have been prepared to wager that the magnetizer was not unaware of the incident, and that her avoidance of it was purely diplomatic.

In the end—by which time the meal was well advanced—it was Cros who cracked first and introduced the question of whether Zosima might attempt another experiment after dessert.

Zosima immediately became pensive. "You want to test me again," she said. "Or rather, you want to resume the test that was unfortunately aborted last night. That's understandable. As I have already told Monsieur Furneret, I am anxious to work with him further, and I wish I had been able to discuss the matter more extensively with him this morning, but I also understand perfectly why he was hesitant then. If I were to say now that I would much prefer to investigate his ability further in private, with no one else present but Talia, in my own time, in conditions of my choosing, you would be suspicious of my motives, although it is the simple truth. So, yes, I am willing to conduct a further...experiment here, under Monsieur Flammarion's expert observation...but only on certain conditions."

Cros and Flammarion exchange glances. Paul turned to his left in order to meet the gaze of his neighbor, Jane de La Vaudère, who seemed amused by the unexpected turn of events, but she did not say anything, or even sketch a confidential smile.

"What conditions are those, Madame Zosima?" Cros asked.

"Firstly, that Talia is not involved. She can be present, because the drawing room where we took drinks a little while ago is large enough to permit an appropriate distance to be established between us without her having to be removed therefrom. I realize that the result of her exclusion from the full intensity of the force will be that the conditions of last night's event will not be duplicated, but an important aspect of experimentation is the variation of conditions, in order to study the consequent variation of outcomes, so I hope that you will not mind. In any case, as you also saw, Talia was upset and disturbed by what happened last night, and I cannot, in all conscience, expose her to the risk of a repetition so soon."

Not unnaturally, everyone looked at Talia, who had hardly said a word thus far. "In fact," the medium said, in a tone that Paul thought surprisingly firm, "I'd prefer not to be excluded. I'm not a child; I can make my own decisions. I want to try again." She looked directly at Paul, meting his gaze, but her expression was unfathomable. She was seated to Paul's right, at the opposite end of the table to Cros, but she was further away from him than Jane de La Vaudère, because of the angle of the table.

"The condition is not negotiable," Zosima stated, flatly.

Talia was still looking at Paul, and Paul wondered whether she might be appealing to him for support, or whether she was simply trying to measure his reaction to her suggestion, given that she knew that he was in possession of information in her regard that no one else had.

"The condition is acceptable," said Cros presumably having exchanged glances with Flammarion, who was seated opposite Paul, to Zosima's left. "Are there more."

"Yes. Secondly, I require Madame de La Vaudère to retire to an appropriate distance as well; perhaps she could sit with Talia. You, Doctor Cros, and Monsieur Flammarion, can observe as closely as you wish—or as closely as you dare. You probably both know better than I do whether and how you will respond to the effluvia to which I shall subject Monsieur Furneret."

"Might I ask why you want to distance me?" Madame de La Vaudère asked, in a tone that left no doubt as to her annoyance and resentment.

"The condition is not negotiable," said the magnetizer, flatly.

"Accepted," said Cros, peremptorily, certainly without consulting his guest. "Anything else?"

"Yes, thirdly, and most importantly, before we leave the table, I want you to hear me out. I want to explain to you why I do what I do, and why I do it in the way that I do it. You might well refuse to believe me, because you might well have already decided that I am a charlatan and a trickster, and will probably construe anything I say as part of my performance, but it is important for the sake of Monsieur Flammarion's research, and doubly important for Monsieur Furneret's ability to contribute to mine, that he does not go into the experiment with false expectations."

"Whether that condition is negotiable or not," Paul was quick to put in, "It's acceptable—but might I ask you a question?"

"Of course," said the magnetizer, although she had conspicuously failed to answer Jane de La Vaudère's question."

"You want to exclude Talia from the experiment," said Paul, "and are prepared to insist on that, even though she wants to take part. Is that because you are afraid that you might break a useful instrument, or because you are afraid that you might injure someone that you love?"

Zosima stared at him obliquely, across the laden table. "Are the two exclusive?" she parried, after a moment's hesitation.

"I believe so," said Paul, "But I find it interesting that you should challenge the assumption. You'll forgive my impertinence, I hope, given that I am being asked to fill the role of your instrument...again."

"There's nothing to forgive, Monsieur Furneret," she said, with a mildness that easily matched Flammarion's, with the aid of her softer voice. "I assure you that I find your challenge as interesting as you find my reaction. I confess that I had hoped...expected, even...that you would be enthusiastic to attempt another drawing, in the hope of obtaining some insight into what you drew last night...and I had certainly hoped, and even expected, to be able to make some contribution to that. We are not at odds, Monsieur Furneret; our interests coincide."

"What if I consider that it is in my interest to involve both Mademoiselle Cadelan and Madame de la Vaudère in the experiment? Would you consider that I am mistaking my own interests?"

"Quite frankly, yes, but I can understand that you do not know why. Will it be adequate if I say that it is desirable, given that intense reactions have already been provoked once, that we continue our investigation with relatively simple conditions, at least to begin with. I am attempting to distance circumstantial factors that might be confusing, if not...disturbing."

"You think that Talia might be capable of *disturbing* Monsieur Furneret?" Jane de La Vaudère put in. "And you think that I might too?"

Zosima simply retorted: "The condition of your distancing is not negotiable," although, Paul thought, she might just as well have said yes...and he also thought that she might not be wrong. He even felt that he ought perhaps to come to the magnetizer's aid in that matter.

"You want me to be able to focus my thoughts on Martine," he said. "You don't want me to be distracted by physical female presences that are too close...although your own is unavoidable."

"My own is irrelevant," Zosima told him.

Paul could not decently raise the question that sprang to mind in response to that comment, nor did he want to risk the flippant remark that occurred to him that he appeared to have had trouble with physical female presences that were too close even before he had been born. Instead, he said: "And if I were to draw Martine again, what would it prove, given that she is so urgently present in my mind, and we do not know, at present, whether she is alive or dead?"

"Perhaps it would be wiser," Zosima said, "if we were to see what you draw, if anything, before attempting to analyze it. And if you'll permit me to say so, this verbal fencing is wasting time that would be better employed meeting my third condition. What I have to say will probably answer at least some of the questions that are seething in all your minds, especially if you are prepared to believe what I tell you."

"Madame Zosima is right," Cros said, doubtless after exchanging another glance with Flammarion. "I, for one, am very interested to hear what she has to say—with your permission, Paul?"

Paul simply nodded his head, although he was well aware that his permission was unnecessary. Jane de La Vaudère reached out with her right hand to touch his left hand, in a gesture that their position allowed to be unobserved by anyone else. It was, he assumed, a simple gesture of reassurance, a reminder that she had taken his side, not an acknowledgement of the legitimacy of his finding her close physical presence disturbing. Talia kept her own hands in her lap.

"First of all," said the magnetizer, "My name really is Zosima, and I really was born in Cairo, in Egypt, although my father was a mariner from Marseille and the cast of my features owes more to him than my mother. He was away a great deal, but present often enough, for long enough, for me to lean to speak French as well as my mother's tongue—the principal incentive being to listen to his stories, which were abundant and fanciful, and doubtless mostly lies. I shall not trouble you with an account of the difficulties that my mother endured. One day, inevitably, my father went away and did not come back again. I missed him greatly.

"My abilities were beginning to develop then, but to begin with, being haphazard and incontrollable, they caused far more problems than any opportunities they might have provided in different circumstances. My mother, having accepted that my father would not return, suffered more than I did from the rumors that began to surround me, and she took me upriver to stay with her relatives, in what is now the city of Luxor but was once Waset, known to the Greeks as Thebes. It was not a wise decision. To be a reputed magician and someone manifestly attracted to my own sex had been awkward in Cairo; it was impossible in Luxor. The time came swiftly enough when it was necessary for me to leave, on my own, initially to return to Cairo, and then to leave Egypt altogether.

"My ultimate objective was to go to France—perhaps I had some vague notion of searching for my father—but the practicalities of travel initially took me to Naples, and there I encountered other seers and magnetizers, and I discovered that there was actually a place for such individuals, on the fringes of Italian society, as mediums and mesmerists, and I began lending my assistance to seers, serving my apprenticeship in spiritism, as it were. At the same time, I was able to carry forward a broader education, which my parents had only been able to commence feebly. There is a substantial French community in Naples, which is rich in intellectuals as well as outcasts of other kinds, and I was fortunate in the relationships I formed there, which provided the basis for the contacts I made subsequently on the French Riviera."

There was a general pause while the dishes of the main course were cleared away, the desserts served and the wine-glasses substituted. Then the magnetizer resumed her story.

"Those Neapolitan seers who were genuine—or self-deluded, as the likes of Professor Flournoy and Doctor Cros might prefer to express it—recognized my utility very rapidly, being inevitably avid to find means of improving the contacts they had with what they believed to be the spirit world, in order that they could make a successful profession out of what might otherwise be seen, and frequently is in many regions of Europe, as an unalloyed curse.

"I am sure that I have nothing to teach Monsieur Flammarion about the intermittence and unreliability of mediumistic communication—or experience, if Doctor Cros cannot accept the term communication—nor about the frequent desperation that mediums experience in being unable to control the communications they receive in a manner sufficient to answer the demands of their clients. He knows, I imagine, better than anyone, the incentives that mediums have to cheat, and to use every trick they can master in order to enhance the appearance of their powers—but I think, too, that he understands that relatively few of them are outright fakers. The vast majority are uneasy believers. Perhaps, as Doctor Cros probably believes, they are all self-deluded, victims of cryptomnesia, to employ Flournoy's coinage, and perhaps they are, desperation leading them in that direction as well as the direction of pure fakery. You will be unsurprised to learn that I do not believe that. I know for certain that some of them, some of the time, really do make contact with what, for want of a better term, I shall call spirits.

"Are the spirits with which mediums like Talia make contact really the souls of the dead? I believe that, for the most part, they are, but exactly what that assertion implies is a complex and dubious matter—far more complex and dubious that the simplest forms of spiritist beliefs assert. It is further complicated by the fact that some of them also seem to be what

English psychic researchers like Messieurs Gurney and Myers call phantasms of the living.

"Madame de La Vaudère, I know, is familiar with the ability that Indian fakirs are sometimes able to learn, to project what are sometimes called their astral bodies over long distances, while their bodies lie inert, or torpid, and she is also familiar with the notion that fakirs and other seers can sometimes form mental linkages that seem to be immune to distance—what modern jargon, again with encouragement from the English Society for Psychical Research, is beginning to call telepathic bonds. I believe, admittedly on slender evidence difficult of interpretation, that there are stranger phantoms too. Whether Monsieur Flammarion's proposal that souls can be and routinely are reincarnated on other worlds is true, I do not know, but I agree with the logic of his argument that if souls are reincarnated at all, then the range of possible reincarnations might be much vaster than our ancestors assumed, given what we now know about the vastness of the universe, which they assumed to be limited to the surface of the earth."

This time the pause was voluntary, while Madame Zosima appeared to collect her thoughts. She had been drinking very sparingly throughout the meal, but Paul noticed that she made more substantial inroads into the dessert wine than the Bordeaux served with the meat course. He deduced that she was more nervous than she wanted to appear. He took advantage of the pause to study the other diners. Cros and Flammarion, he observed, were drinking very sparingly indeed, as he was himself, considerably more so than either of his neighbors at the table.

Again, Zosima resumed her lecture. "To summarize briefly, spirits do exist, although there is room for debate as to exactly what they are, and contact with them is possible, albeit in puzzling and problematic fashions, just as other exotic mental contacts are possible. For the majority of people, however, all such contacts are very rare, and perhaps even impossible, because the defensive walls of consciousness are often too strong to permit them.

171

"That is understandable, in terms of the modern theory of evolution by selection, because there are definite benefits to be accrued, not merely in terms of physical survival, but in terms of fecundity and the successful raising of children, in being psychically limited, or even psychically blind. Mediums and other seers are often outcasts from their natal societies, and rarely become successful parents. Some, like Thalia and myself, are confused in their sexuality, but that cannot be reckoned typical; so far as I have been able to observe, sexual eccentricities are more common among the psychically limited and the psychically blind than is generally admitted, but they are better equipped to hide them from one another.

"That might be a more relevant point than you might think, because there are other things that the psychically limited find it easier to conceal, even, and especially, from themselves. Indeed, I suspect that psychic blindness is more often voluntary than innate, that it is often not so much an inability to make contact with spirits as a refusal to do so or to admit that it happens.

"You have doubtless observed, Monsieur Flammarion, that people are attracted to séances for very different reasons. Some, like Baron de Rochemure, appear to be very anxious to make contact, even at second hand, with spirits that were dear to them when alive, or with spirits whose forgiveness for real or imagined wrongs they are desperate to obtain. Others, who attend séances even though they pride themselves on being skeptics—debunkers, as the Americans put it—tell other people, and perhaps themselves, that they are trying to protect the innocent and gullible from cruel or insulting impostures, and perhaps they are sincere, but some of them, I suspect, are simply fearful. They go to séances not in order to make contact with spirits but to obtain reassurance that such contact does not and cannot happen, because they are afraid of the possible consequences of that fact. Some probably experience contacts that they want to deny or refute. At any rate, they have more in common with those in search of forgiveness than they can admit, the principal difference being that they consider themselves to be unforgivable, and fear the harshness of the unforgiving dead.

"I am making no accusations, nor even drawing implications. Some skeptics, I presume, are simply skeptical, and some interested investigators who appear to have no psychological ax to grind are probably nothing more nor less than interested investigators, but I want to put it to all of you—principally and primarily to Monsieur Furneret—that the matter we are dealing with is very complicated, both metaphysically and psychologically. It is a labyrinth of ideas in which we have, as yet, no reliable guiding thread, but which I have had the motive and the opportunity to explore with great attention and dogged determination, and if I am not more expert yet than anyone else in that navigation, it is certainly my ambition and determination to become so. I do not deny that part of the reason why I have come to Paris is because it might be easier for me to make a living here, but it is also because it is the intellectual capital of the world, and there is nowhere that has better facilities for philosophical research."

She paused again, and deliberately took the time to finish her dessert, which she had hardly been able to touch. Paul followed her example gladly; the others had all been making steadier progress while listening.

"To return to personal matters," Zosima went on, "having served my apprenticeship in Italy, while I served several notable mediums as an aide—an instrument, if Monsieur Furneret prefers that term, as Talia does—I felt that I was qualified to take the lead in further...performances. I immediately set out to complete my original intention to reach France, initially intending to search Marseille for a young seer who had raw ability but needed assistance in its development. At first, I assumed, arrogantly, that I merely had to locate one, and that I already had the native ability to guide her successfully. I underestimated the difficulty of the problem, and overestimated my ability to cope with it...indeed, I overestimated the control that I had over my own psychic magnetism. After several failed experiments, however, I leaned enough to be more successful with Talia. Our relationship has been far from unproblematic, but it has, I think been broadly successful, and it is a matter of great distress to me that she is in poor health, seemingly incurably.

"It is arguable that we should not have left Nice, remaining in the Midi, where the climate seems to be more conducive to holding phthisis at bay, but we have been, to some extent, victims of our own success. When rumor of our séances reached Paris, there was no shortage of invitations to come here. You may read what you wish into the fact that the first one that I accepted was far from the most lucrative, and was undoubtedly the most challenging. Monsieur Flammarion is doubtless aware of the intimidating reputation that his party of scientific investigators has in the community of seers, and the courage and conviction required to confront it—more aware, at any rate, than Monsieur Furneret, who, if he will forgive me or saying so, seems to be an curious and anxious innocent, who had no idea what he was letting himself in for when he accept the invitation that was made to him in haste when rumor of what had happened at Lemastur's séance ran around.

"If you will forgive me again, I also beg leave to doubt that Monsieur Furneret was fortunate in being escorted to Juvisy by Doctor Cros and Madame de La Vaudère, whose kindness, although perfectly sincere and well-meaning, might well have added a further dimension of confusion to the situation. On the other hand, I can readily understand why he was exceedingly grateful to fall in with them, and still is. I certainly would not want to dissuade him from soliciting their opinions and heeding their advice in future, in spite of the condition I have imposed on my imminent attempt to enable him to produce further automatic drawings, in whatever quantity he is able to produce them—the more the better, given that I have not previously encountered anyone who could produce so many with such rapidity and such dexterity.

"And that, I think, is all that I want or need to say, for the present. Am I correct in assuming that, at this stage in the proceedings, we would be moving to the drawing room in any case, in order for coffee to be served?"

"Indeed you would, Madame Zosima," said Doctor Cros, playing the role of host with familiar ease. "And thank you, for a most enlightening account of your previous endeavors. Might I offer you my arm, as is customary in the circumstances?"

"Of course," the magnetizer replied, although she must have known that, clad in a man's suit as she was, they would make an odd couple.

Following the seating plan, Flammarion offered his arm to Talia, while Paul offered his to Jane de La Vaudère, and they proceeded to the drawing room with an ostentatious formality that every one of them, so far as Paul could tell, was making an effort to exaggerate to the point of caricature.

"I suspect," Paul's companion whispered in his ear, "that the lady might be more concerned with the disturbing effect of my physical proximity on her than on you."

"That would be understandable," Paul murmured, "but not accurate."

"Gallantry," she countered, dismissively, "but thank you."

Was it? Paul thought. *And what does it signify that I do not know?*

When they had all taken coffee cups, Talia immediately parted from Flammarion, leaving him free to engage in a three-way conversation with Cros and Zosima, while she came to speak to Paul and Jane de La Vaudère, a short distance away.

"I'm sorry," she said. "There's no arguing with her."

"Sorry because she's sending me to the back of the room, or sorry because she's sending you?" asked Jane de La Vaudère.

Talia blushed. "I was apologizing to you," she said, "although I'm regretful on my own behalf too. She doesn't like you, I'm afraid."

"Really? I thought that I was small enough, slender enough and frail enough to appeal to her esthetic sensibilities, and although I'm no longer young, I doubt than I'm older than she is."

"Oh, I'm sure she thinks that you're very beautiful...but she didn't like your book."

"The *Demi-Sexes*? It gave her the idea that I'm prejudiced against female homosexuality? Suggest to her that she might read my next book, *L'Amazone du roi de Siam*. It will correct her misapprehension...although, I must confess that the lesbian heroine comes to a sticky end, just as every other character does, save for the heartless male whom the readers are supposed to despise. Sometimes, I worry about the impetus of my own imagination...but the world is the way it is, and my conscience will only allow me to misrepresent it to a limited extent, even in exercises in symbolist exotica. Not that anyone I have recently encountered in Parisian society, except perhaps Paul, seems to understand why *Le Mystère de Kama* is representing things as they are, or at least trying to figure out how they are, and why...although, now I come to think of it, I can't help wondering whether those flames you drew this afternoon, Paul, while deeply entranced, were partly inspired by the holocaust in *Kama*."

Paul knew that the author was being flippant—but he also knew that flippancy was sometimes employed to cover serious, if unadmitted, preoccupations. Talia presumably understood the flippancy too, but that was not what caught her attention.

"You were entranced this afternoon?" she queried.

"In a sense," said Paul. "Not magnetized...at least, I don't think so...but absorbed by my work a little more than usual. A psychologist would probably say that I was in retreat from the uncertainty of my situation, the agony of not knowing whether Martine and Amélie are alive or dead."

Talia stared at him. "I don't know who Amélie is, but I already told you that the girl you drew last night was drowning while you were drawing her. You didn't believe me?"

"No," Paul admitted, "I didn't. And you'll forgive me, I presume, for continuing to hope that you were mistaken, even though every hour that passes makes it more likely that you were right."

The young woman seemed deeply uncertain as to whether she could or ought to forgive him his lack of trust in her clairvoyance. In the end, she said: "Perhaps it's as well that Zosima wants to keep us apart. But I'm afraid for you anyway. She's right about you having no idea what you're risking. She doesn't care about you—to her, you're just experimental material, but I care."

"Of course you do," said Jane de La Vaudère, in a neutral tone. "We all do, if not quite in the same way. But what are you afraid of, exactly?"

"People like us can't choose what we see," Talia said. "That might not matter, if we only saw what other people wanted us to see, if we could only do what the people who come to consult us want us to do—but it doesn't work like that. More often than not, it works the other way around: we see the things we don't want to see, or what other people don't want us to see. We see the things that we, or others, are frightened of seeing. You don't believe me yet, Monsieur Furneret—but if Zosima can enable you to see something...you probably won't like it when you wake up and discover what it was. You're sensitive...I felt that last night. I might seem weak, because of the coughing, and because I'm so slight, but that's just my body. You're healthy and strong, but your mind, once it's stirred, might not be...and it obviously hasn't recovered from last night's agitation, if you had an episode this afternoon. If it's too soon for me, it's certainly too soon for you. I'm sorry if I seem rude...but I'm just anxious."

She fell silent, and moved away, after an intimidated glance at Jane de La Vaudère, heading for Zosima's side, and the apparent protection provided by her mentor.

"I didn't mean to scare her away," the author said. "I warned you, didn't I, to be wary of her? She *cares* about you?"

"So does everyone else, according to you."

"You know exactly what I mean. And she might be right about your being too sensitive for your own good, no matter what else she's wrong about. You fainted last night when you saw what you'd drawn, remember."

"I didn't faint—I was just slightly shaken. It took me by surprise. But I'm not agitated now; whatever I draw this time, it won't surprise me, and it certainly won't scare me."

"I hope you're right. I'll make sure that Antoine gets Joseph to take you home though, when he takes me. Will your...model be at the studio when you get there?"

"I don't know," Paul replied, defensively.

"You don't know? I thought she was staying with you. Pardon my indiscretion, but...I know she wasn't there when I picked you up this afternoon, but I rather assumed..."

"She had to go to the Permanence for her monthly medical check," said Paul, bluntly, "and this evening, she's working. She wasn't able to bring much away from her last place of residence, and the fees I can pay her for modeling won't stretch to a new wardrobe."

The gaze of the author's blue eyes bored into him, and he lowered his eyes.

"And you don't like it," she concluded. "Oh, don't worry, I'm not accusing you of anything. She's just your model, and you're just being kind. But you don't like her selling herself, do you? You don't like any of the poor things having to do it? Far too sensitive for your own good, as the little girl says."

"She's not a little girl," said Paul. "She's small and thin because she's ill, but she's right; she's an intelligent adult. So is Juliette."

"They're all little girls, Paul, however old and intelligent they are. And it's only a matter of time before one of them slips past your intentions and fastens on to you like a leech. Just try to make sure that it isn't one who'll bleed you dry...and don't let the coughing wring your heart too much. There's no end to the torment that kind of attachment entails.

178

Anyway, whatever happens tonight, I'll come to see you tomorrow, in my own carriage, to pick up that painting. I'll be sure to bring the cash...but leave the little model to furnish her own wardrobe, I beg you, and make her move on, as soon as you don't need her to pose any more...tomorrow, if you make as much progress then as you did today. You won't need her to fill in the background, any more than you needed her this afternoon to paint those flames"

He made no reply to that, but simply kept his eyes lowered. After a brief interval, she said: "Sorry. It's not much more than twenty-four hours since I first clapped eyes on you, and already I'm trying to dictate your life. I don't know why I think I'm qualified, as I've never been very successful with my own. But you're a reader, and even though I appear to have more than twenty thousand of them, I'm such a miser that I want to keep them all under lock and key, as if they were gold coins, so that I can take them out occasionally and fondle them...metaphorically speaking, of course."

Paul was not obliged to comment on that, because the doctor appeared alongside his companion, and said: "We're ready now, if you are."

"As ready as I'll ever be," Paul said, feeling that it was not exactly true, but he put down his empty coffee cup and tried to stride purposefully and proudly to the small desk where the doctor had ordered a large sheet of paper to be placed—even larger than the one that Flammarion had provided at Juvisy, with three pencils, a handful of sticks of charcoal, several sticks of white or colored chalk, and even a few sticks of colored wax. The doctor had evidently wanted to provide for all eventualities, and he had a competitive streak that made him want to set aside any possibility of being outdone in any future experiments.

"Flammarion will want the picture, of course," Cros said to Paul, quietly, "but this is my house, and it's my picture. I'll pay you a fair fee for it—I don't expect a work of art in exchange for dinner. Agreed?"

"You haven't seen what I produce yet," Paul replied, uneasily, "if I produce anything at all."

"After what you just heard at table? Believe me, the suggestion started more than half a hour ago, along with the performance. But don't bother with Charles this time. I've got that message, if it was a message. Concentrate on the girl in the boat."

"The same goes for family resemblances," Jane de La Vaudère put in, having approached them curiously, "if I'm not far enough out of range for you to put me out of your mind.

Paul did not tell her that he thought that putting her out of his mind would henceforth be a very difficult feat to achieve, even if he wanted to try. Nor did he tell Antoine Cros that if the spirit or the memory of his late brother appeared insistently, he probably would not be able to resist recording it, because he would no longer have control of his own right hand, which would be free to offend anyone, including himself. He still refused to believe that Talia had seen Martine drown, but he did believe her assertion that he and she could not choose the spirits that came to them, no matter how hard they tried to prepare the inspirational ground for them.

Even so, he accepted that the doctor's advice was sound. He needed to concentrate on the one female presence—or absence—that was really important to him. If his wayward talent could tell him anything beyond the temptations of cryptomnesia, he wanted to know whether Marine was alive or dead...and whether he had been deluding himself for years in believing that he loved her, profoundly and exclusively.

And that, he realized, was the real issue, for him. The paramount question haunting his confused mind was not what he might learn about events that had happened to other people, other spirits, but the possibility of penetrating the defenses of his own self-delusion. Like all the people who attended séances in search of the forgiveness of those they had wronged, or to shore up the confidence that those who were unable to forgive them were impotent to harm them, what he wanted, or needed, to know, was whether other people, other spirits, wanted to make contact with him...whether he actually *mattered*, to Martine...or, indeed, to anyone...

He took his seat at the desk.

"Don't look round," Zosima said to him, softly but insistently, with a suggestion that was plainly striving for command, for empery. "Just look at the blank sheet. Don't try to focus on what you can hear—it isn't anything comprehensible. Just relax. Try not to think about anything in particular. Look at the white sheet, and imagine that your mind is a blank sheet. Don't pay any attention to the pencils or the colors; concentrate on the emptiness, the beautiful void.

"You must be very tired, after your long night and your testing day, but that's all right. It's all right now to let it go, for the moment, to envy the condition of the blank sheet, that miraculous, blissful blank sheet. You have my permission to become the blank sheet, and that's all you need. You know that I'm in control here, and that I won't let anything happen to you.

"You're very tired, and very confused, but you can relax now. You can forget the blackness and the color of existence, and relax into the whiteness, the softness of the blank sheet. There's nothing to be afraid of, not now or going forward, and when the time comes, I'll snap my fingers, and you'll be able to come round. You're perfectly safe, so you're free to be the blank page, to savor its bliss, its emptiness."

Paul did as he was told, and did not look round; he simply took it for granted that Jane and Talia had retired to the far side of the room, and that Cros and Flammarion were sitting in armchairs to his left and a little behind him, while Zosima was stationed to his right, focusing her "effluvia" on him. And the condition of the blank sheet did, indeed seem enviable to him, and not just because he was a painter, for whom every blank sheet or canvas was a potential capable of containing the flood and fantasy of his inspiration, the depiction and detail of his chimera...

Come to my aid, O Chimera, O Cryptomnesia, he said to himself, sarcastically. *Let me put on a good show for these worthy people, in order that they might not feel that I've been wasting their time...*

Zosima was still murmuring, very softly, but there were no longer any words in what she was murmuring, although the meaningless sound expanded nevertheless to fill his consciousness, to fill the space where black and flame-colored meaning might have been, and to occupy his whole sensorium, as if he could actually see the nonsensical syllables, and feel their silken touch, and even smell them: a strange, faint smell of burning...

CHAPTER XII

Paul woke up and opened his eyes to find himself lying on his side, facing a wall hung with green fabric, and his sense of touch informed him that he was partly unclothed. He woke up entirely, instantaneously, surprised that he had been asleep. But where was he? The sense of touch told him, in more detail, that he was still wearing his trousers, and his socks, but no boots, no waistcoat, no jacket and no cravat—and he was covered up to the neck by a soft woolen blanket.

Where was he? It was not entirely dark; the reflection of candlelight was illuminating the green fabric softly. But what was that fabric? He was sure that he had never seen it before...but how much was such certainty worth, now that he had been introduced to the notion of cryptomnesia, which would probably haunt him indefinitely now...

He rolled over, and pushed the blanket back as he freed his arms.

He was in a small bedroom that he did not recognize. There was an armchair positioned beside the bed, for the occupation of a *garde-malade*. Jane de La Vaudère was sitting in it, fully dressed and draped in a shawl. She was asleep, but as soon as Paul sat up on the bed she woke up abruptly, as if startled to find that she had been asleep, apparently more confused as a result than he was.

"Where am I?" he asked, when he thought that she would be able to answer him.

"Still in the doctor's house," she told him. "How are you feeling."

"Fine," he said, honestly. "What time is it?"

"Two o'clock."

"In the morning?"

"Yes."

183

"I've been asleep for hours? Why didn't Zosima snap her fingers?"

"She did. So did Antoine. Snap, snap, snap...it was like a volley of firecrackers, You didn't wake up. Antoine examined you, but he said that your heart was beating steadily and you were breathing comfortably. You were just asleep...asleep, and presumably entranced. Zosima said that it was nothing to worry about, that she'd commanded that you go to sleep because you were very tired, and that people sometimes took the instruction to heart, and didn't want to hear the fingers snapping, because they really did need to sleep, to have permission to forget everything for a while...but it was always temporary, she said, an hour, or two at the most. I didn't believe her. Just because others had woken up, I thought, there was no guarantee that—how did you put it?—that she'd seen the full range of phenomena.

"Talia didn't believe her either. In fact, Talia was positively hysterical. The distance wasn't enough apparently. She was convinced that you wouldn't wake up. She had been connected to your mind while you were drawing she said, because you and she had made a bond, shared secrets, and she said that you had gone to Hell, and that you wouldn't be able to get back, and that nobody would be able to bring you back, because your beloved Martine was dead and because even though you had a bond with her, she couldn't love you and you couldn't love her. She told me that I didn't even have a bond with you, but I think that was just jealousy talking. Anyway, she was insistent that you were all alone, horribly alone, in despair and burning. It didn't do any good to show her that you were breathing peacefully and didn't seem to be in the slightest distress. Then she started coughing, horribly— coughing blood. In the end, Antoine had to give her a sedative, but he's very worried about her.

"I don't mind telling you that I was scared for you. Even though the nasty little bitch said that we didn't have a bond, I knew that we did, that you were far more like the kind of seer that I am than the kind of seer that she is, and I was frightened for you, even though you were breathing peacefully and definitely not in Hell. That's why I'm here. I was frightened for you."

"But I'm fine," Paul said. "I feel fine. Perhaps Zosima was right, and I just needed the sleep, just needed to let go for a while."

"You don't remember being in Hell, then? You don't remember any burning...or despair...or blood?"

"Absolutely none," Paul confirmed. "There was a slight odor, while I was looking at the blank sheet, but I think it was coming from the coffee pot, or the dining room, or the kitchen, and it didn't seem to matter at the time. I was focusing on the blank sheet, wondering what was going to fill it...where's Talia now?"

"We put her to bed in another room; she'll be asleep for hours. Zosima's with her. Flammarion's on a divan downstairs. He had a vision too, but he remained conscious, and was able to describe it briefly. It shook him up a little, I think, but he said that it's nothing he hasn't experienced before. Personally, I didn't see anything. Rather disappointing, in a way, given my long experience...but I didn't come here tonight in search of imagery for a work in progress; my chimeras and panthers are safely stabled. In any case, I was all too well aware that Zosima was deliberately trying to exclude me, to punish me for an imagined offence...but if it worked with me, I don't know why it didn't work with Talia, who was right beside me, and who really doesn't have any bond with you at all, in spite of the seductive potential of the little girl act..."

Paul interrupted her. "Did I draw?" he said. He looked around the room as he said it, half-expecting that the sheet of paper would be there."

"Yes, you did."

"For...how long has it been? Five hours? Six?"

"No, you drew for about two minutes, very rapidly. Then you went to sleep."

"What did I draw?"

"That's a matter of opinion. Probably Jeanne d'Arc—but after what you'd told me not long before Zosima put you under, we couldn't be sure. For safety's sake, Joseph took one of the valets to Montmartre with orders to wait in your studio, and Antoine went to the morgue."

"The morgue?"

"Yes. We couldn't be sure, you see, whether you'd drawn Jeanne d'Arc, or your model, or both. You drew the face twice, although the images overlapped, and were very confused. You drew her in the flames, much as you'd depicted her this afternoon...except that she was no longer reaching up with her arms imploringly toward Heaven, but writhing in agony...very graphic...almost as graphic as the image with which it was confused, which showed her supine, bleeding from what were presumably stab-wounds, her face similarly contorted in agony. It would have looked horrific enough in charcoal, but Antoine had kindly provided you with red and yellow chalks and red wax.

"Paris isn't London, obviously, but it's not unknown for streetwalkers to be brutally murdered here, by pimps who take the appellation of Apache far too seriously, and after what you'd told me about your model going to the Permanence and then to work...that's why Antoine went to the morgue after Madame Cambourg let him into your studio and there was no one there. Hopefully, it was all anxiety and imagination...especially given that Talia was obviously wrong about you being in Hell.

"But there is bad news, I'm afraid. Two female bodies have been found washed up on a beach in Guernsey. Neither is Martine or Madame Lambrunet, but both had been passengers on the *Palatine*. It certainly looks as if the lifeboat has come to grief...which still doesn't mean that Talia was right about seeing her drowning."

Paul tipped his legs off the bed and on to the floor, casting the blanket away completely. "I want to see the drawing," he said.

"Of course. It's still on the desk downstairs. Let's be quiet, though. If Zosima has gone to sleep, we don't want to wake her, and Flammarion is in the small drawing room, hopefully asleep as well."

"What did Flammarion see in his vision?"

"Stars and planets. He's an astronomer, and a popularizer, who's made one of his several careers out of imagining what life on other worlds might be like. He even wrote a history of such ideas—I've read it. How grateful he'll be to Zosima for inducing it, I'm not sure...but as he says, it's nothing that he hasn't experienced before, on his own imaginative impulsion."

They made their way downstairs. Still in his stockinged feet, although he had put his waistcoat and jacket on hastily, without buttoning them up, and carrying his boots in one hand, Paul had no difficulty in going quietly. Jane de La Vaudère had taken off her ankle-boots, which she was carrying in the same fashion, and her feet were clad in silk. She gave the impression of gliding, and might easily have passed for a specter as she moved along the corridor—only illuminated by a single candle that she had brought from the bedroom—had she been wearing a white dress instead of a blue one.

The large drawing room was silent and deserted. It was also dark. Paul squinted into the gloom, wondering where the commutator that controlled the electric bulbs in the chandelier might be located, but Jane de La Vaudère, who presumably knew where it was, ignored the modern refinement, and used the candle she was carrying, carefully, to light the candles in the candelabra that were still stationed proudly on the mantelpiece, not yet intended purely for decorative purposes. She brought one of the candelabra to the desk, perhaps striving—consciously or unconsciously—to maximize the effect of the picture by means of the candlelight.

Paul stared at the drawing, which was like nothing he had ever drawn before.

He did not think that he belonged by conscious commitment to any particular school of painting, even though the label of Symbolist had been stuck on him automatically, and he had been instructed to paint in different styles while he was a pupil in Jacollet's studio. While following his Symbolist penchant he had normally aimed for dream and delicacy, but he had occasionally cultivated a hint of the macabre when dabbling in neo-Naturalism. He had, however, never drawn anything as frankly horrific or as stylistically hybridized as the double image of the supine Juliette butchered by some Parisian Jack the Ripper and the upright Jeanne d'Arc burning to death, both stricken by terror and agony, neither looking to Heaven for aid, neither offering themselves stoically to martyrdom.

It was repulsive, all the more so as it seemed so personal. He hardly knew Juliette, and he was convinced that his kindness in allowing her to stay in the studio while he finished the painting could not possibly constitute a "bond" in the sense that Talia had used the term. But he knew her. He was painting her, in the guise of a saint and martyr, and even though he had been forced to confront what she really was, he couldn't see her in that way—not completely—which was, he supposed, exactly what the drawing depicted: behind the assault of torture and murder, the flamboyance of fire and blood.

Is my unconscious mind really so sadistic? he wondered. *Or is Jane right, and I took my flames from the holocaust depicted in* Le Mystère de Kama?

He felt physically sick, and sat down in the chair, looking wonderingly at the pencils and chalks lying pell-mell alongside the double-drawing.

"And that only took a matter of minutes?" he queried.

"Yes—done at lightning speed. Only black, red and yellow, maybe half a dozen sticks of various sorts, but even so—I wouldn't have believed it if I hadn't seen it."

"And what did Zosima say? That I'd evidently been visited by the spirits of Jeanne d'Arc and Juliette, twin sisters in appearance, one in order to correct my romanticized idea of her martyrdom and the other to notify me of her murder?"

"No. She said that it was probably just your anxieties seeking exaggerated expression, that you had been in no condition to operate as a medium and that it was her fault for not realizing the fact. But she did tell Antoine to go to the morgue, just in case."

"In case he had to identify the body?"

"No—he couldn't do that, if the necessity arose." The author did not bother to add that that would be Paul's task, if the doctor did find a body in the morgue that resembled the stabbing victim in the drawing."

"I don't know anything about her," Paul said, "except her name. Scarran, with two *a*s. The other girls call her Scarab, apparently."

"It's too soon to assume that anything has really happened to her. It was just a nightmare."

"That's exactly what I thought of Talia's vision last night...but hers was true."

"We don't know that either. Something has obviously happened to the lifeboat, but that doesn't necessarily mean that everyone aboard died. You hear stories all the time about people clinging to pieces of flotsam for days before drifting ashore or being picked up by a ship. The Manche isn't freezing at this time of year."

"You hear stories," Paul echoed. "That's all they are...nothing real."

"And what's that if it isn't stories?" said his interlocutor, flicking a pale, ungloved hand at the atrocious compound image. "Do you seriously believe that the spirit of Jeanne d'Arc has visited you in order to correct your misapprehension regarding the facts of her death? It's a fantasy, just like the other. It's entirely my fault. I put the idea in your head before you walked to the desk."

"Why, then, did I sleep for nearly five hours?"

"Probably because you'd hardly slept at all the night before, and you've been wound up to maximum pitch all day, pestered by visitors, except when you were painting—and even then you blanked out, in spite of being as taut as a violin

189

string. As soon as you'd dispelled the excess of nervous fluid doing that drawing—at superhuman speed, remember—you suffered a backlash and went to sleep, and your body, wiser than your poor overtaxed brain, wouldn't let you wake up, even when fingers started clicking like gunfire. For a while, you were beyond the reach of suggestion."

"But breathing normally, with my heart beating steadily. So I didn't actually *see* these things; my hand just drew them."

"Jeanne d'Arc didn't draw her own execution, not Juliette her own murder, if, indeed that really is Juliette, any more than the other is Jeanne d'Arc, or your sister who died in the womb drew her own image...or yours...and whoever the woman mistaken for my mother was, she wasn't really there either."

"But you're the believer. You're the one who believes that spirits really do manifest themselves at séances, throwing flowers, playing toy flutes, gushing ectoplasm and producing voices and more voices, and everything else. Why have you suddenly turned into a hardened skeptic?"

Jane de La Vaudère was still standing up beside the chair in which Paul had been forced to sit down; she was looking down at him. She turned away, but only for a moment, took a step and hesitated, as if uncertain which way to go, and finally sat down on the edge of the desk. "Weren't you listening to Zosima's lecture?" she said. "Some people go to séances hoping to get messages from their dead relatives and some go dreading that they might. Everyone wants to be forgiven, but some dread that they might be unforgivable. Why do you think I felt for you so much in the train back to Paris last night? Because I understand how it feels to be unable to get past the feeling that you ought to feel guilty, that you can't be forgiven, even though you know consciously that you haven't done anything so very terrible...or anything, at any rate, that justifies the depth of your feeling...and unlike me, you really haven't done anything wrong. You really are innocent."

"As innocent as they day I was born," said Paul, sarcastically. "And don't take the doctor's psychoanalysis too seriously—sometimes, at least, a joke is just a joke, and isn't covering up any deep layers of guilt. And you can't possibly have anything to feel guilty about—your mother didn't die giving birth to you; she just died when you were young."

"And she's been watching me ever since, from Heaven, according to the nuns at the convent, watching everything, seeing everything...and I never believed it, not for an instant...not consciously. But beyond the layer of rational thought, she's there, in my conscience, and she's seen everything...every sin, every failure. So no, I don't want her to visit me in my dreams, and I don't want her to speak to me through the voices of mediums, because I know exactly what she could, and would, and sometimes does say. And that's really a vey banal story, because I don't know anyone...anyone...who could stand up to that kind of inspection, if they believed in it. But they don't: their rationality is backed by their quiet, plaid, ignorant unconscious. Mine, on the other hand...well, you've read some of my work. If you read more, you'll see more of my unconscious at work in the interstices of my contrived plots, many fragments of semi-automatic writing. Even the little vignettes I dash off for newspapers, about flirts and frauds and animal trainers...it's there in the green eyes of the black panthers, in the blue or black eyes of pale or dark little whores, and in the insistently virtuous too, all yearning for love but never, ever, able to find it for more than a fleeting moment. But the sphinx deliberately shoved me out of tonight's little charade, just because she thinks that I don't like women in men's suits, so now, I can be utterly and completely rational, and I can tell you with heartfelt conviction, that *this did not happen*. You made it up.

"You were under pressure to perform, and you performed. But all of this came out of your own mind, your own anxieties. It didn't happen *out there*. Jeanne d'Arc is a saint now, enjoying eternal bliss, with no memory of what befell her on earth. And your pale little whore is in bed in some cheap hotel, servicing some drunkard after a late supper following an evening spent at a café-concert, laughing at the dirty jokes and bawdy songs. And she'll turn up at your studio tomorrow as bright as a button, ready to pose, at least wearing a new hat with ribbons, if not a new dress. And some English fishing-boat, which picked up survivors from the *Palatine*'s lifeboat, including your substitute mother and your imaginary lover, will have taken them back to some godforsaken Cornish coastal village where there's no telegraph, where they're fast asleep right now in dirty but comfortable beds.

"And all of that's a story that I just made up, but there isn't any reason at all why it shouldn't all be true."

Nor any reason at all why it shouldn't all be false, Paul thought, remembering what she had said earlier about her next book, in which everyone died except for the despicable male, because that was the way she saw the world when she let her visionary self off the leash.

Aloud, he said: "You're right. This isn't evidence. It's just my lurid imagination."

At that moment, they heard, in the distance, the main door of the house open and close, and whispered voices in the vestibule. Paul recognized the voice of Antoine Cros a few seconds before the drawing room door opened and the doctor came in.

"Oh, you're both awake, and here," he said. "Why didn't you switch the electric light on? It's not as if I make a point of banishing everything from the house that Edison had anything to do with. Anyway, I'm glad—it's a relief. We thought you might have turned sleeping beauty, Paul, doomed to wait forever for your princess to come. I've just come from the hospital. Your model is there, but she'll live, as long as the shock and the filthy water she drank doesn't precipitate a pulmonary crisis like Talia's. She's lucky, I suppose—but I think you need to go and see her when you can, and try to persuade her of that. At the very least, I think you ought to tell her that you need her to recover so you can finish your painting, whether it's true or not. That's a formal prescription."

Paul looked down at the image he had drawn, the macabre, confused image that confused his model with the figure that he had hired her to represent, full of blood and fire.

"She was stabbed?" He queried.

"No, of course she wasn't. I just told you that she took a filthy drink. She jumped off the Pont-Neuf into the Seine, but a boatman pulled her out. She was taken to the hospital, where they found a bill of health from the Permanence tucked inside her bodice, which had the address of your studio inscribed as her current domicile. They sent an errand boy round in search of a next of kin, and he found Robert—my valet—waiting there. He came to find me at the Morgue, and Joseph took us to the hospital. I examined her, and told the intern to make sure that she was kept warm and watched carefully, to make sure that she didn't try to run. Now, it's up to you, but they won't let you on to the ward until nine o'clock, and only then because I gave them firm instructions to bend the regulations. Just show my card at the guichet, and say you've come on my behalf."

"Did she tell you why she jumped in the river?" Paul asked, dazedly.

"No; she was semi-conscious, but incoherent. She mumbled something about putting out flames, but it didn't make an atom of sense. For what it might be worth, though, a streetwalker was murdered by an Apache in Montmartre last night, not far from your studio, further up the hill. I saw her body in the Morgue, with multiple stab wounds. I was afraid at first, obviously, that it must be your model, whom I'd never seen in the flesh, but they had her handbag, which had her number and certificate in it, in case she was stopped by the police, so the orderlies at the Morgue had already identified her, and the name didn't match—and that's when Robert arrived. It's not inconceivable, given the timing, that your girl saw the murder, or the body on the street, and that's what tipped her over the edge. You can ask her tomorrow.

"For now, I need to check up on the young woman who's in the worse danger, and then I need to get some sleep—and I dare say that Jane does too. Joseph is waiting in the courtyard with the rig—he'll take you both home. I'll look in on Camille and Zosima, but with luck, they'll both be fast asleep, and it's certainly best if the girl stays overnight. I'll come to your studio tomorrow, between eleven and noon—you should be back from the hospital by then, perhaps with the model if she's fit to be discharged. I'll bring Flammarion and Zosima, and Talia too if she's recovered from the crisis, but if I were you, I'd be a little wary of making any further appointments for magnetization in the near future. One mishap was unfortunate, but two is ominous, and the second was considerably worse than the first...perhaps it's better not to risk catastrophe. Speaking for myself, even though I was only looking on, tonight's episode was just a little too much."

He left, heading for the room where Camille Flammarion was probably asleep on the divan.

"Amen," Paul murmured, in response to the doctor's last remark. He looked at the horrible drawing, but he would not have been tempted to take it away even if it had not been agreed already that it would belong to Antoine Cros. Rather absent-mindedly, he put his boots on. Then he looked at Jane de La Vaudère, who had also taken advantage of the pause to put her footwear on.

"I said it was just a story I'd made up," she said, defensively. "And the real one could be worse—at least somebody fished her out."

"Let's hope that she managed to put out the flames," said Paul.

"You're hooked," opined the author, who understood the rules of melodrama. "You'll never get rid of her now. She'll be a millstone round your neck until Père Culose comes to claim her. You're not hard-hearted enough to throw her out. It might have been an act, though. She might have seen the boatman, known that he would pull her out. Little girls like that..."

"She isn't like that," said Paul. "And she isn't a little girl. She's an intelligent adult. She's even reading *Le Mystère de Kama*."

"They're all little girls, Paul. Juliette, Talia...all of them. Believe me, I know. I grew up in a convent. There's nothing I don't know about little girls...even ones who read books. I'll wager that she thinks *Kama* is just pornography."

It did not seem diplomatic to reply to that remark, or to challenge the blithe assumption that there was nothing that Jane de La Vaudère did not know about little girls, having been brought up in a convent under the imaginary watchful eye of a censorious mother. "We'd better go," he said. "The doctor is probably right—and poor Joseph needs to get some sleep as well. He'll have to do it all again tomorrow."

"Half the time that coachmen spend on the seat, they're asleep. Personally, I drive my own carriage, for fun, but to them it's just a job. And for every hour they spend on the road they spend another waiting. But the doctor is right: while you were fast sleep I was wide awake, and it's late. Let's go."

Paul did not challenge that assertion either. He offered his arm to the lady, in a ceremonious fashion, and escorted her into the courtyard, where Joseph was waiting dutifully, holding the door of the carriage open. Paul helped Jane to climb in, and sat down beside her.

As they headed for the river, of which Paul could not think without imagining dirty water, and the possible ill-effects of inhaling it, his companion said: "Don't be upset about that drawing, Paul. Please don't let it put you off. You need to be aware, and to remember, that in spite of the unfortunate effects, you're fortunate—blessed, even. You can't choose what you see, and you might not like what you see, but being able to see is a privilege, and you have a great advantage in being able to draw like that. Very few people can draw at all, and to be able to do it so rapidly, even if you can only do it when you're unconscious, is a very precious gift. You can not merely see spirits, but record what you see, instantly, or almost. I couldn't do that when I tried to be a painter. Writing is much, much slower, infinitely more bogged down by consciousness."

She paused, looked out of the window of the carriage at the street-lamps of the city of light, yellow-tinted by nocturnal mist. Then having drawn breath, she continued.

"So what you and I can do is hard...but it's a privilege. It's frustrating, and sometimes painful, but it's something that the people Zosima calls the psychically limited and the psychically blind don't have, and can't understand, and it's a treasure. Maybe it isn't a good idea to be miserly with it, and maybe there are risks in letting it run so freely, letting it use us as instruments, but it's still a gift. Don't ever be tempted to give it up, Paul. Don't ever be tempted to bind it in chains, to suppress it, or to confine it within technique, routine and reiteration. Don't ever go to work in a bank, or become a mechanical repeater of formulae...but don't hand yourself over, bound and gagged, to someone like Zosima, either. Be your own man."

As if by way of emphasis, she had put her hand on Paul's knee, and the contact caused a frisson to run up his leg and through his soul, like a dart. But this time, hardly pausing at all for breath, she went on with increasing urgency.

"You have that advantage as well as the advantage of being a painter, you see. It's much easier for men to own themselves, and you need to take advantage of that. Be despicable, if you have to be, but don't be a little girl. Nobody should be a little girl, least of all little girls. When you paint my portrait, don't try to be a photographic apparatus. Look inside. And when you think about that drawing—which you'll probably never see again, as I can't believe that Antoine will thinking of hanging it, although he'll probably keep it in a drawer, with his anatomical drawings—see it for what it was: a work of art; not a depiction of a mere event, but a work of art, reaching for the reality behind appearances, brutal but unafraid. You need to be unafraid, Paul. When the terror takes hold of you momentarily...and it will, believe me...steel yourself. Refuse to be afraid. Be a man, since you can. Only little girls jump off the

Pont Neuf, or shoot themselves in the heart, or overdose on chloroform. You understand what I'm saying, don't you?"

"Yes," Paul said, diplomatically. "I do."

"And you know that I know, don't you? Better than Zosima ever can, or Talia, or Antoine Cros, or Camille Flammarion. *I know*."

"Yes," said Paul, "I believe you do. But we're in Montmartre already. You should have allowed Joseph to take you home first. The doctor should have told Joseph to take me home before taking me home. That's what convention demands."

"Antoine knows how to write a prescription. Trust him on that. And trust me too. Joseph will see me safely home; he's done it many a time before. Bonsoir, Paul, and I'll see you tomorrow—with money in hand."

Paul climbed down from the carriage in front of his building, which seemed as silent as the tomb. He wondered whether the blood was still visible on the pavement where the streetwalker had been stabbed by the Apache, but he knew that the legendary street-cleaners of Paris would have washed it away before the city woke up Paris was a city rapid in forgetfulness, a city that reveled in selective psychic blindness.

"*Au revoir*, Madame de La Vaudère," he said, as he closed the portière.

"Call me Jane," she said. "The hell with what convention demands. Call me Jane. That's an order."

"*Au revoir*, Jane," he said.

And the carriage drew away, while Paul went to ring for Madame Cambourg to lift the cordon, hoping that he could find enough money in his purse the next morning to give her a suitable tip, and still get a fiacre home from the hospital, if Juliette was fit to be discharged.

CHAPTER XIII

Juliette was asleep when Paul arrived by her bedside—but only asleep, not in a coma. The intern reported to him that she had settled down after Doctor Cros had left, and that she would probably recover rapidly, but that she had to be monitored in case she showed any signs of developing pneumonia or began coughing blood. Mercifully, she hadn't shown any sign of either symptom.

Paul sat down beside the bed and studied her, wondering what on earth had happened when Zosima's hypothetical magnetic force had provoked psychic currents in his oversensitive brain. He had been supposed to be thinking about Martine, inviting her spirit to visit him, from wherever it might be, if it were anywhere at all. Talia, apparently, had not been out of range on the far side of the room, and had evidently still been under the impression that she was bonded with him, capable of reading his mind...albeit mistakenly. Logically, therefore, Jane could not have been out of range either, and her strange behavior after the event could surely be interpreted as an effect of a bond of some sort, perceptible by her as an excessive quasi-maternal concern. But Juliette had presumably been in Montmartre, until she had run to the Seine, and if he had somehow read her mind, even at that distance, or made contact with her spirit, why had he not seen her running through the streets, or jumping from the Pont Neuf, or being pulled out of the water by the boatman? Why had he seen her being stabbed, which had not happened, at least to her, and why had he superimposed that image on the image of an agonized Jeanne d'Arc?

He was still wondering, and no closer to an answer, when Juliette opened her eyes, and saw him.

Her first reaction was one of alarm and dismay, perhaps with hints of other emotions, but certainly not pleasure. He could not help feeling a trifle insulted.

After a pause, during which she studied him, and the expression on her face changed, she said: "I'm sorry. I was crazy. I was stupid. I should have known that it was a hallucination...I *did* know that it was a hallucination...but somehow, for the moment, the hallucination seemed...not more real, but more meaningful...than the real. Crazy. I'm sorry."

"So I should think," he said, gruffly. "I need you in order to finish my painting. It was very inconsiderate of you to try to kill yourself before I'd finished."

She frowned. "Was I trying to kill myself? I don't think so, but..." She stopped. Her voice was hoarse as well as weak. She coughed, and then looked at the hand into which she had coughed, in a manner that must have come to be reflexive. She seemed surprised that there was no blood in the palm, for the moment, but glad of the absence.

He was puzzled too, and also a trifle guilty at having made the accusation—which had been motivated, at least in part, by the suspicion that he might have been in some way responsible for what Juliette had done. "Can you tell me what happened?" he said, softly. "I need to know. I'll explain why later, but I need to know."

She considered that speech, still frowning, and then said: "I don't know where to start."

"At the beginning," he said, aware that it was a cliché.

"Yes," she said, "but I don't know where the beginning is."

"You had an appointment at the Permanence," he reminded her.

"Yes, it was the day for my number—but that wasn't the beginning. You'll think I'm crazy, and I must be...."

"It's all right," he said. "Take your time." There was a cup of clean water on the bedside table. He held it out to her. She raised her head up from the bolster, and he held it to her lips. "I think they'll bring soup in a little while," he said.

"They're not supposed to let visitors in this early, but Doctor Cros left special orders. He's an important man here, second only to God. The intern will take good care of you. If it didn't begin when you went to the Permanence, when did it begin?"

"When I stopped posing. I couldn't hold the pose any longer, so I stopped. But when I came to look at what you were doing, you weren't working on the arms or my face: you were painting the flames, and you weren't even conscious. You were asleep—somni—whatever the Greek or Latin for painting is. And I was annoyed with you, because I'd been posing for no reason, and you could have told me to take a rest, but you hadn't. I kept staring at the painting, at me and the flames. I could see that you'd almost finished the head and upper body, all except the final touches, and I could see that you didn't actually need me anymore."

"Maybe not," said Paul, "But I would still have wanted you there while I was applying the final touches, for reference."

"Well, yes...but for the moment, you were painting flames...and I was burning in those flames. I could see myself burning...and...it seemed symbolic...of the moment...of everything..."

She took the cup from his hand and put it to her own lips in order to take another sip.

"I'm stupid," she said. "I didn't want to leave. In spite of the fact that you didn't want me...maybe in part *because* you didn't want me...I didn't want to leave. And the crazy thing is that I knew I didn't have to. I knew that you wouldn't throw me out. The other bastard owed me, had made me promises, had used me, and I'd always let him do it—never a word of protest—because I knew how much I needed him. But he threw me out, just like that. You didn't owe me anything, hadn't made any promises, hadn't even used me...but I knew you wouldn't throw me out. I knew that. I knew you were a soft touch. And I felt guilty. I felt guilty about taking advantage of you, when you were in a churning panic about the girl in the lifeboat, because not only wasn't it fair to take advantage of you like that, but because I might spoil it, when she eventually arrives. You didn't even know how she felt about you, and she probably doesn't either, and the last thing you need is to have me clinging to you like a leech when she arrives..."

She had to pause again. Paul was surprised that she'd been able to go on for as long as she had, but she seemed to be growing stronger as she talked, as if the effort were somehow drawing energy into her, motivating her.

"She's dead," he said.

"What?"

"Martine. She's dead."

"Are you sure?"

"Her body hasn't been cast ashore yet, and probably never will be, but yes; I'm sure."

"Oh, God! I'm so sorry. I wanted her to be alive. I wanted you to have her. I wanted you to get what you wanted. I knew it couldn't be me, and that if you...I knew it couldn't be me, and that was all right. I started out like all the girls, wanting to be loved, but I'd got way past that, knowing that it was impossible, and pointless. I knew that I couldn't even be useful any more, that all I could do was inflict myself...and then I saw myself, in your painting, going up in flames, and I thought: *That's me, that's me*...but that was just the beginning. It was the beginning, but only the beginning."

She had to stop for a while then. She was still trying to gather enough strength to start again when the orderlies brought in the soup tureen that served as the morning meal for the patients in the ward. It was ladled into bowls, and the orderlies began doing the round, handing out bowls to those who were capable of feeding themselves, and spoon-feeding those who were not. They moved steadily, doing the work with practiced ease.

Paul took the bowl destined for Juliette and assured the orderly that he would take care of it. They knew that he was there with the authority of the great Doctor Cros, whose whim was law, so he was allowed to do it.

"It's all right," said Juliette, sitting up. "I can feed my-self. I'm not a little girl."

"I know," Paul said allowing her to take the bowl. The soup had a pleasant odor; it had meat in it, or at least Liebig's beef concentrate. The recipe had doubtless been carefully de-termined to supply calculated nutritional requirements. It was the twentieth century, after all.

Juliette continued her story in between sips.

"There was a queue at the Permanence, as always. I was on time; they were late, as always...I went through the rigma-role—awful, as always, but you get used to it. I got my certifi-cate, and tucked it away in my bodice..."

"Having given my address as your current domicile."

She blushed, very faintly. "Sorry," she said.

"Don't be," he said. "It was true, and it enabled Doctor Cros to find you, and tell me where you were. That's how I'm here. Go on."

"Well, I came back from the quai to Montmartre...I got back just in time for the restaurant, so I had dinner with the usual crowd, and then went on to the café with the girls. You know the café?"

"I know the one you mean," said Paul, in a neutral tone.

"You don't come in, but you obviously know how things work, at least vaguely. It's a pick-up spot. Customers come in; sometimes they sit down and wait for a girl to approach them; sometimes, especially if they're regulars, they approach a girl...It works smoothly, it's rare for there to be any trouble, even among the younger ones, who are more avid or more desperate for custom. But there's always a bunch of girls at the back, talking among themselves, who don't chase the cus-tomers until time presses, and who don't get approached if they don't seem particularly attractive or welcoming...I didn't want to go anywhere. I just wanted to sit. I need new clothes, but...well, I simply didn't want to go, for whatever reason, so I just sat.

"I had plenty to occupy me, anyway. The word had gone round that I'd hooked you, and someone had picked up a copy

202

of that stupid *Mercaba* rag, which was going the rounds of the tables, with juicy bits being read out to those who couldn't, and I was supposedly the one with the inside dope...I told them that I hadn't actually hooked you at all, that you were in love with the girl in the lifeboat, and they believed me, because the opinion had been for months that the only possible reason you didn't bite, given that you obviously weren't...you know...was because you were in love with some girl back home in the province, and still had romantic delusions that hadn't fallen apart yet...I didn't know much about the drawings either—much less than whoever had written the story—but still, I was the one for whom they came for an opinion. *Is this true? Is this real?* Mostly I said I didn't know, but sometimes I gave them my opinion, uninformed as it was...And they lapped it up.

"I didn't step out of line. I painted you as a saint, because you are, and I even went easy on the woman who wrote the filthy book, even though I was tempted to tear her apart. I said what you'd said about the book, and I said that you were a person who would know...I didn't have to build up Doctor Cros or Flammarion, obviously—they're heroes hereabouts. Even thirty years after the fall of the Commune, people haven't forgotten what Cros did back then, and Flammarion's a legend...So you don't need to worry about the tone of the chat, it didn't reflect anything on you but glory, and I got to bathe in it a little, because even if I hadn't hooked you, and wasn't going to, I was sleeping on your balcony and I was in your picture.

"I told them about the painting, because they asked...perhaps more than I should...I went on for a long time...And I told them that you were still in mourning for your sister, who had died beside you in the womb, but that it was a filthy lie to say that you'd murdered her, and that when you'd said it, it was just student humor. They all understand student humor. This isn't the Latin Quarter, but it's the home of the café-concert...Everybody knows.

"And to tell the truth, I had a good time...except that I couldn't really enjoy it to the full, because of what was hanging over me, knowing that I'd have to leave even though you wouldn't throw me out, because I had to look after your best interests because you were too much of a saint...that I had to sacrifice myself, and because you wouldn't, even though you knew that you had to...even though, when you slipped into that trance, you stopped painting me and just painted the flames that were burning me up...symbolically...While you were conscious, I knew, you wouldn't be able to throw me out and that if I wanted to, I could even hook you."

She took a slightly longer pause at that point, in order to dig the last of the soup out of the bowl. Paul took the opportunity to say: "And did you want to?"

She was annoyed by that. "What sort of a question is that? Have you any idea what layers of meaning there'd be in saying yes or no?"

"I believe I do," Paul said.

"Well, don't flatter yourself. I'm not in love with you. I can't do that, not any more. If I wanted to hook you...which I have no intention of doing...it would be purely for reasons of self-interest...not financial interest, obviously, because I know that you don't have a sou, but in order to have someone to cling to, someone who wouldn't...but I'll get to that...

"Anyway, some time between nine and ten...not late, at all...I thought about going back to the studio and waiting for you, reading the book I'd started and trying to see what you saw in it, but Annette, who isn't exactly a friend but has been around as long as me, and to whom I'd given the occasional cuddle when she needed it, asked me if I'd walk up to the crest of the Butte with her because her man was angry with her...again...because of some argument that they'd had, and he's a crazy drunk, who'd said that he was sick to death of her and that he'd show her what happened to little girls who didn't know their place. I think she was angling to come to the studio with me, because I'd made it sound a little too good, but that wasn't on, so I said that I'd see her safely home and make sure that her man wasn't going to kill her...I actually said that, in so many words.

"So, we started going up the hill, past all the bright lights, up toward the old windmill. It was ludicrous. What did I think I was going to do if her man turned nasty? She never even got to her building. He comes out of some dive on a street corner, with three or four of his friends, roaring drunk, sees her, and he comes after her, and she tries to hide behind me, and I...I just got out of the way.

"I'm not Jeanne d'Arc, you see. I'm not a fighter. I'm not brave. I'm not a saint. I just got out of the way. But there was no sense to it at all, you see, and no reason for it. I don't even know what she was supposed to have done, but I doubt that it was anything out of the ordinary, and that it was all just an excuse for something going on in his stupid head, something that had tipped him over the edge. Anyway he had his knife, as they all do, and he just went after her. He had four or five friends with him, and they just watched. They didn't egg him on, and they didn't cheer him. They just watched. And so did I. God help me, I was supposed to be seeing that nothing happened to her, because I wouldn't take her to the studio, and I didn't do *anything*. Nothing. And that was when I realized why you'd stopped painting my arms, and my face, and stopped seeing me looking up to Heaven, because you knew...in your trance, you knew...that I was only good for Hell, only fit for the flames. And I knew that you couldn't forgive me, that I didn't deserve to be forgiven, because I wasn't Jeanne d'Arc, and I was just useless, pointless,...and I felt the flames. I felt the flames burning me, and I got out of the way. I got out of the way...

"And that's all I remember.

"I didn't try to drown myself. Someone...I don't know who...told me that I'd jumped into the Seine, but I didn't believe him at first. Me, run all that way, and not even know it? Not possible. Only, he told me again, or someone else did, and I began to believe it...I even think I might remember it now, vaguely. But I wasn't trying to kill myself. I was trying to save myself. I was trying to put out the flames. As I said, I'm crazy. And you shouldn't have come. Doctor Cros shouldn't have told you where I am, because he must have known you'd come.

"I didn't do anything. Do you understand? I didn't do *anything*, and after he'd done it, after she was lying there, on the road, with blood all over her, still oozing from I don't know how many wounds, he turned to his friends and he said: 'There! That's how it's done.' And he looked at me. He looked at me with such utter contempt, because I wasn't even worth killing. Because I hadn't done *anything*."

"Actually," Paul said, as he pried the empty bowl from her fingers and handed it back to the orderly who had come to collect it, "You had."

She looked blank. "What?" she said.

"You drew a picture," Paul told her.

"I can't draw," she protested.

"I can," Paul said, "you borrowed my hand. You were under the influence of magnetic power, and you were bonded with me. It's what English psychic researchers call a phantasm of the living, apparently. In moments of crisis, so it's said, people can sometimes project...well, their spirits, if you bend the meaning of the word slightly...something, at any rate, that can make contact with another mind, provided that it has a special sensitivity. You drew what you saw, and what you felt. And for a moment or two...perhaps as long as three or four minutes—I felt what you were feeling. I felt the flames...but I wasn't conscious of it. Someone else who was bonded with me did...probably more than one, but they reacted in different ways, having interpreted the sensation in different ways. That's a problem, you see: interpreting the contacts from the world of spirits. They don't speak or act for themselves. We have to speak or act for them, under their influence. But you're right in one sense: you really didn't do anything for which you need to feel ashamed, or guilty; you didn't do anything that requires forgiveness, by God or by anyone, least of all me. The only person who has done anything wrong is the madman with the knife. Nobody else...except me, a little."

"Don't say that. It's not true."

"You're a model, Juliette. All you had to do was pose, lending me your features and your stance. You didn't have to pretend, to play the part. That was for my imagination to do. But I overstepped the mark. I wanted too much."

"You didn't do anything."

"Yes, I did. But I have to go now—I'm expected at the studio. I'm sorry—but Doctor Cros promised that he'll come and see you later today, and if you're fit to be discharged he'll bring you back to the studio. If not, I'll come to see you again, tomorrow at the latest—and again, if you're fit to be discharged, I'll take you back to the studio. I need you there."

She looked at him for a long time before saying: "To finish the painting."

It wasn't a question, but he answered it anyway. "Exactly," he said. "I need to finish the painting."

CHAPTER XIV

When Paul arrived back at the house he called in at the concierge's lodge to collect the mail, which he hadn't taken upstairs as he went out. The stack seemed to have grown somewhat in the meantime. The previous day's wad had been thick; today's was twice as abundant. He riffled through the pile rapidly, and took out a note from Victor, which he opened and scanned rapidly.

"Some people are upstairs," Madame Cambourg informed him, laconically. "They said they'd wait. I let them in."

"How many?" he asked, when he had finished reading the note.

"Three. Four came in the carriage, but the doctor went away with it, saying that he'd be back as soon as he could. One of them is a woman dressed as a man, another an old man with white hair and a beard." She did not take the trouble to add a description of poor Talia, although Paul was glad to infer that she was with the others, not dead or consigned to the hospital. He deduced easily enough from the relatively satisfied tone of the concierge's narration that someone—probably Cros—had given her a sizeable tip to trek upstairs and unlock his studio door.

"Did Monsieur Flammarion show you a set of drawings, by any chance, Madame Cambourg?" he asked.

"He did. He wanted to know if I recognized anyone."

"And did you?"

"Of course. They didn't look much like the pictures in the *Parisien*, though. I recognized Madame Scrive and Doctor Cros's brother from the old days. Never saw the other woman before, though...nor the Martian."

"It's not a Martian," Paul told her. "Are you sure about Madame Scrive? It was a long time ago that you saw her."

"Certain. The eyes are old, but not dim. I remember her as if it was yesterday. They don't call me a legend among concierges for nothing. The old man told me not to tell Mam'zelle Jeanne, and gave me forty sous, but I wouldn't feel right about not telling her something like that, so perhaps I shouldn't have taken the forty sous, but it's not as if it's a fortune is it?"

"No, Madame Cambourg," Paul agreed. "But you haven't seen...what did you call her?"

"Mam'zelle Jeanne. That's who she was when I knew her mother, when she was barely out of swaddling clothes. Got married, I hear, when they took her out of the convent, that being the way of these things, but her husband never comes to Paris and she only uses the bit of his name that has the *particule* in it, and she calls herself Jane. Not me. To me, she's Mam'zelle Jeanne."

"Have you seen her today?"

"No."

"You will."

"And do you think I ought not to tell her that I recognized her mother?"

"That's entirely up to you, Madame Cambourg," Paul assured her, not about to part with ten sous in order to support Flammarion's futile bribe, let alone forty.

Madame Cambourg did not seen unduly concerned. "In case you hadn't heard," she said, "that chit you're living with threw herself in the river last night. At death's door in the hospital, they say, won't be coming out. But you didn't have time to get fond of her, did you?"

"In fact, I've just left her. She's making a good recovery. She'll be back tomorrow, or perhaps this evening."

"Time was when this was a respectable house," the concierge observed, with an artificial sigh, "but I'm broad-minded, and one has to move with the times. It's 1901, after all."

"So I've heard," Paul said, dryly. "Bonjour, Madame Cambourg, and thank you."

She did not say that he was welcome—which was only fair, since, in her reckoning, he probably ought to have given her an extra forty sous not to tell Jane that she had "recognized" her mother.

Flammarion, Zosima and Talia were all in the studio, some way apart. Talia, looking pale but determined, was sitting in one of the armchairs by the window, Zosima was going through the paintings on the shelves, inspecting them in turn, while Flammarion was standing in front of the canvas on the easel, having removed the dust cover that Paul had put over it carefully in the early hours of the morning.

It was to Talia that Paul went, immediately. "I'm very sorry," he said. "If I had suspected..."

"It wasn't your fault," she said, interrupting him. "They all think it's mine—that I got it all wrong and made myself bleed, but I didn't."

"No," he said, "you didn't. I've just come from the hospital. It was Juliette that was in Hell, not me, but I put her there and it was through the lens of my mind that you saw her reflected. You weren't at fault in any way. Thank you for being concerned about me, and I hope with all my heart that the coughing fit you had hasn't made your condition worse."

It was, he knew, a very frail hope, but the young woman seemed grateful for his effort.

"It's nothing that hasn't happened before," she said. "The doctor said I was fit enough to come within him, when I begged."

Paul nodded, and turned to Zosima and Camille Flammarion, who were now standing patiently behind him. "I'm sorry to keep you waiting," he said. "As I was explaining to Talia, I had to go to the hospital."

"How is your model?" Flammarion asked. "Your concierge appears to fear the worst."

"Recovering well," said Paul. "We were able to talk, and I think that helped. I hope I was able to diminish her anxieties slightly."

"Did she tell you why she tried to drown herself?" Zosima asked, curiously.

"She didn't. She doesn't seem to have swallowed as much Seine water as Doctor Cros feared, and none seems to have got into her lungs."

"Why did she jump off the Pont Neuf, then?" the magnetizer persisted.

"She had a hallucination. She was hypnotized, and then she had a bad shock."

"She wasn't hypnotized by me," Zosima was quick to say.

"I know. She was hypnotized by me—or, to be strictly accurate, my painting."

"That painting?" said Flammarion, indicating the canvas at which he had just been staring.

"Yes. She cooperated, of course; I doubt if the painting could have done it without the aid of her collaborative self-suggestion, but she searched actively for the symbolism within it, and saw herself reflected there, in the image of Jeanne d'Arc. The phenomenon might be unfamiliar to you, Madame Zosima—but it's not uncommon in Paris, and Monsieur Flammarion must have heard of it, even if he hasn't had a chance of observe it. There are works of art in the Louvre that are already becoming legendary for their hypnotic effect, and their capacity to haunt amateurs fascinated by them—the statue of Antinous Mondragone, for instance, Moreau's *L'Apparition* and Grasset's *La Vitrioleuse*. There's a rich literary mythology of such obsessions, with which Madame de La Vaudère must certainly be familiar. I fear, Monsieur Flammarion, that the two francs you gave Madame Cambourg as an incentive not to tell Jane that she had identified the image in last night's drawing as her mother was probably wasted—but the identification is surely worthless, given that she had already seen this morning's *Petit Parisien*, which had produced its own version of the *Mercaba*'s story, and she's known who the images were supposed to be since yesterday afternoon."

"I was aware of that," said Flammarion, with a sigh, "and I didn't suppose for a moment that I could buy her silence for two francs. I thought I ought to give her that much for acceding to my request, albeit with testimony that no longer has any value.

"Did the girl tell you that she'd been magnetized by the painting?" asked Zosima, incredulously, reverting to the matter of interest to her.

"No, of course not. I deduced it—and I might be wrong. She did tell me what she saw, though, and enabled me to piece together an account of why my hand drew the remarkable double image that Doctor Cros has. It's just a story, perhaps pure fancy, but it does explain why she might have communicated to me the idea of being burned alive, which I communicated in my turn to Talia—who, unfortunately for her, retained a memory of it, although I did not."

Flammarion was sufficiently rapid in deduction to say: "And that's why she jumped into the Seine? She had a hallucination that convinced her that she was on fire?"

"Yes. Again, she collaborated with it. She had already seen herself in the painting, and abstracted the metaphor. Then, when she saw her friend stabbed to death, the shock exaggerated the metaphor to the point that she actually felt the sensation. There's no doubting the intensity of the illusion; she ran all the way from the top of the Butte to the Pont Neuf. That's a long distance."

"You're convinced, though," Zosima persisted, "that there was a communication: a supernatural communication. One way or another, you were aware of a murder that was being committed on the Butte at the time when you made the drawing?"

"It seems so to me: but the corpse I drew was Juliette's, not that of the woman who was actually murdered. And there's a rich legendry of such murders, which invariably grip the imagination of the public...and even the imagination of drunks with grudges, who sometimes act them out. A skeptic like Doctor Cros would say that it's an intriguing coincidence, but that there are no rational grounds for thinking that it's anything more than a coincidence. He'd doubtless point out that everything contained in the picture I drew in his house was already in my mind, without even having to invoke the unconscious, or any trick of cryptomnesia, and that if I were afraid that something might happen to Juliette while she was walking the streets, I would be bound to imagine, first and foremost, her falling victim to a Jack-the-Ripper. There isn't an atom of objective proof of any supernatural event—it was all in my head, and Juliette, and Talia's. I'm convinced, and you're more than willing to believe me, but is there anything in what I've said, or could say that could persuade you, Monsieur Flammarion, let alone Doctor Cros?"

"I can sympathize with your difficulty, Monsieur Furneret," Flammarion said, judiciously. "It's by no means unfamiliar to me."

"But you didn't even know the girl very well, it seems," said Zosima, with a frown of puzzlement, "even if she was...a little more than a model."

"It depends what you mean by *a little more*," Paul said, "but the crucial point, if the story I've pieced together is true, isn't what she was to me, but what I was to her. As you say, she didn't know me very well, but the circumstances were such that, without actually doing very much, I was...a little more than a painter. Because of a fortuitous combination of circumstances, I acquired a sudden particular significance in her life. I don't know Talia at all, but again, by virtue of a singular coincidence. I suddenly acquired a seeming importance in her consciousness that created a bond—a link that the distance you placed between us last night was impotent to break. It will surely fade, though, as she realizes how irrelevant I am to her life and fate."

"That," observed Talia, "remains to be seen. If you're going to continue working with Madame Zosima..."

"I'm not," said Paul, flatly.

Zosima scowled. "That would be a mistake, Monsieur Furneret, from your viewpoint as well as mine...not to mention

Monsieur Flammarion's. If there's even a possibility that your interpretation of what happened last night is correct, it makes it all the more important that we continue the investigation. If you are, in fact, psychically bonded with Talia, even in a temporary fashion, that opens up a further spectrum of possibilities..."

"No," said Talia, "It doesn't. Monsieur Furneret is right. It's the correct decision, for him and for me. He's too sensitive. If you were to continue magnetizing him, especially in my presence, he would come to harm. If he values his art and his sanity, he might be well advised to keep a much tighter rein on the input of the other world...and keep away from magnetizers."

Zosima looked at her as if she had just committed an unforgivable treason, and the younger woman shifted in her chair, reflexively, in the direction of Camille Flammarion, as if requesting protection.

"Don't blame Talia," Paul said to the magnetizer. "She's the one who has been hurt in this disastrous affair, twice—but she's an intelligent adult, and she can make her own calculation as to the future of her relationship with you. As for me, the condition is not negotiable."

Zosima looked to Flammarion for support, but the old man immediately shook his head. "I only work with volunteers, Madame," he said. "I have no right to put pressure on anyone, for the sake of my personal curiosity, or for the supposed sake of science. Numerous artists have refused to work with me in the past, for various reasons, and I'm not unsympathetic to their anxieties. It's a truism that the act of observation affects that which is being observed, and when one is dealing with intelligent subjects, the knowledge that one is being observed, and the act of lending oneself to such observation, can have profound effects on the phenomena that are being subjected to scrutiny. Even in astronomy, where nothing we do can possibly affect the planets and the stars, the act of observation has profound effects on our notion of the universe, and hence of ourselves."

"What do you mean?" Paul asked, slightly puzzled by the digression.

The astronomer held up the scroll that he was holding. "Doctor Cros and I have been debating the results of my experiments for years, since he and his brother were present at some of my earliest experiments with automatic writing and drawing, in which they both took part. At that time, Charles gave a lecture to my group on a method of interplanetary communication that he had imagined, and which has since been featured in a number of speculative fictions, including one of his own. In my memory, at least, the idea of Charles Cros is not associated with the phonograph that he designed but never built, but with the planet Mars and Martians. And like many other people, I've read the recent English account of an imaginary war of the worlds, the Martians of which undoubtedly inspired the drawing that appeared in the *Mercaba*, and was copied in this morning's *Petit Parisien*. I'm certain that Madame Cambourg has not read that novel, but she had no more difficulty in identifying the blurred image on this sheet of paper as a Martian than Doctor Cros had in identifying it as a fetus. Perceptions are in the eye of the beholder as much as, or more than, the entity that provokes them. If we look for the supernatural, we can find it...and we can always improvise a story to justify our finding.

"I have every sympathy with your curiosity, Madame Zosima, and for the strength of your motive. You know, beyond the shadow of any possible doubt, that you have a supernatural power—but you told us last night, very succinctly, why you feel compelled nevertheless to support that ability with showmanship and with fakery in order to fit it to expectations that have been built up by previous showmen and charlatans. You are already well aware of the difficulties that lie before you in seeking to persuade others of the truth of your assertions. Monsieur Furneret is a artist; his only interest in the phenomena that interest us, is the contribution they might make to his art—and he fears, quite rightly, that the way that other people see his art, and him, had been drastically prejudiced by the grotesquely exaggerated publicity that has suddenly attached to him, through no fault of his own. I am not surprised that he wants to have nothing further to do with it and I certainly do not blame him for it. Nor should you."

"But I want to help him!" Zosima protested. "I want to put my power at his disposal, while he puts his ability at mine. I am not proposing anything that will not be beneficial to both of us—and Talia too."

"I'm sure your intentions are good," said Flammarion, mildly. "But I'm sure, too, that Doctor Flournoy intended no harm in his observations of Catherine Müller, and actually imagined that he might be helping her by ruthlessly lacerating her illusions. I'm sure that she has a very different opinion."

"According to the newspapers, his *lacerations* have helped to made her a fortune," said Zosima.

"So it's said," said Flammarion. "And cynics will doubtless consider that a marvelous result, being unable to imagine that she had any other in mind, but Monsieur Furneret, who is an artist, might not take the same view. In your impassioned speech yesterday evening, Madame, you reminded us that few mediums are outright charlatans, and in my experience, even the few who begin as outright charlatans eventually end up convincing themselves. This is not an arena in which success and personal fulfillment can be measured simply, and nor can the risks. There was an interval of several hours last night when the situation was completely out of your control, when you snapped your fingers over and over again without having the desired effect. Monsieur Furneret woke up of his own accord, not even able to remember the hallucination that had caused Mademoiselle Cadelan to believe that he was suffering the torments to Hell, but the fact that he does not remember it consciously does not mean that it has had no effect on him, not merely on his health but, equally importantly for him, on his art. I dare say that he can imagine risks that you cannot, Madame Zosima, and reasons why the help that you want to give him might seem direly dangerous. If he wishes to draw a line under this series of experiments, then I am not unsympathetic to his reasons, and I certainly have no protest to raise. If that makes me less of scientist, then so be it. I am certain that it does not make me less of a man."

Zosima turned back to Paul. "I'm offering you an opportunity," she said, "that you might not find again. You said yourself that I am probably not familiar with the full range of the phenomena that I want to investigate, and you have proved yourself to be correct. In collaboration, we can surely extend that range further. Who knows what we might accomplish? Are you really going to refuse even to try?"

"I am," Paul said, "for precisely the reasons that Monsieur Flammarion has just explained. Being a subject of observation in two experiments in a space of twenty-four hours has already changed me; I am already not the man, or the artist, that I was two days ago."

"Of course you are," the magnetizer objected. "It's the nature of human beings, and artists to change, to evolve, while remaining essentially the same."

"Perhaps so," Paul retorted, "but if I look at the matter simply, and selfishly, rather than in terms of high-flown philosophical generalizations, two days ago I was following a particular career trajectory, almost without thinking about it, which I had been following for two years. I had come to Paris, because that is what French artists do, in order to shape my painting, as far as I could, toward the criteria of success that determine artistic careers in Paris: the pursuit of medals at the Salon, the attentions of amateurs, dealers and collectors. I felt that I had to accept Monsieur Flammarion's invitation to come to the Observatory primarily because of the contacts I might make there, and my only worry as I traveled on the train was that I might not be able to produce a drawing that would pass muster among his friends an interesting example of automatic drawing. Had I been able to fake it, I certainly would have done, for exactly the reasons that you have cited, Madame. But Doctor Cros and Madame de La Vaudère had already begun to change my attitude simply by trying to reassure me, and the interest they took in me, then and thereafter, has given me an entirely different perspective.

"Between the two of them, they have literally changed my mind, and I shall be eternally grateful to them for enabling me to leave Paris with the consciousness that my sojourn here has been immensely profitable. But they, and you, have shown me entirely new and different ways of thinking, about mentality, about creativity, and about art—and it is in that context that I not only produced the two enigmatic works of art that I produced under the effect of your magnetization, but the continuation of my Jeanne d'Arc. Things are different now, for me; this morning's newspapers and this stack of correspondence"—he held up the pile that he had collected from Madame Cambourg's lodge—"are more than adequate evidence that if I stay in Paris the way that people look at my paintings, and at me, can no longer be the attitude that I wanted them to take. Even if I am and will remain, as you say, essentially the same person, it is not the person I believed myself to be or had ambitions to be."

"So you're going to run away," said Zosima, "like a coward."

"Precisely," said Paul. "I'm going to run away—like a coward. From you, and from Paris."

The magnetizer shook her head, but Talia nodded hers, approvingly. Camille Flammarion only said: "Not immediately, I hope."

"No, not immediately," said Paul, "but soon. I have a note here from Victor, informing me that my friend Gaston Lambrunet will not be coming to Paris, in the circumstances. He will sail from Le Havre to Bordeaux, and then travel overland to Toulouse. Victor will take the train from Paris to meet him there. The legal situation regarding the family property in Toulouse and in Spain will be complicated, if Amélie's body is not found, and arrangements will have to be made for some kind of memorial for Gaston's mother and his sister—who were, in a sense, substitutes within my life for the mother and sister I lost at an early age. It will not be possible to have an interment, I fear, but there will nevertheless be a period of mourning, not as intense for me as for Gaston, but intense nevertheless. I shall return to Paris for a while, but while I am in Toulouse I shall attempt to find a place to reside in the vicinity, with a view to moving there permanently. One can be a painter in the Midi as well as in Paris, and if the career opportunities are not as good, and the possibilities of being an *arriviste* are much poorer, then so be it. It is my homeland. I have just seen Hell in Montmartre, through the eyes and words of one of the least of its inhabitants, and it has chilled my blood. I cannot stay here."

Zosima shook her head again. This time, Flammarion nodded his. Talia Cadelan stood up, stepped closer to Paul, picked his right hand in both of hers, and squeezed it gently. "That is not cowardice, Monsieur Furneret," she said. "You know, I think, that I shall be with you in spirit in the Midi, even though we do not know one another, and our brief acquaintance has been formed almost entirely by errors."

"Thank you, Mademoiselle," he said. "My best wishes will go with you, wherever fortune takes you."

"Fortune," she replied, "has little to do with it, but thank you." She released his hand.

"These paintings," said Zosima, waving her hand vaguely at the array of shelves, "are not very good. You could do so much better. I've seen your hand at work. With the right guidance, it would be capable of great things."

"I agree with the criticism," Paul said. "These are mostly student work, a record of a learning process. I'm delighted that you think me capable of better, and I shall do my utmost to justify your faith. I shall follow the record of your future exploits in the press with the greatest interest, and I wish you every success."

She sighed, but then smiled wryly. "I'm sorely tempted to deploy other armaments in order to continue the competition, but it would not be fitting. I shall retire gracefully. Go in peace, Monsieur Furneret, and thank you for raising a tiny corner of the curtain obscuring the mysteries of the spirit. I shall attempt to take what profit from it I can." She put the palms of her hand together in from of her chin, and bowed.

"I would still like to see you at Juvisy again, Monsieur Furneret, before you leave for Toulouse, or when you return," said Camille Flammarion. "Not for an experiment, but simply a theoretical discussion, if you feel that it would be safe, and you can spare the time."

"I'd like that," Paul said. "I'll telephone you, if I may, when I have discussed our travel arrangements with Victor."

There was a peremptory rap on the door, then, and Antoine Cros came in without waiting for a response. "Sorry to have been so long," he said to the assembly. Everything always runs late, and now I'm in a frightful rush before my next appointment. I haven't had time to go to the hospital yet, Monsieur Furneret, but I promise that I will do so without fail before the end of the day, and will attempt to secure the safe release of your friend. Have you seen her?"

"I have," said Paul. "And I took your advice. There is no possibility of her leaping into the Seine again. It was a mistake, occasioned by a unique combination of circumstances. She seems to me to be recovering well, and I believe that I left her in better spirits than I found her."

"Monsieur Furneret is quitting Paris," Zosima was quick to put in. "There will be no further experiments."

Cros did not seem unduly disappointed by the announcement. "I can't blame him," he said. "Sometimes, it's not a good idea to go rooting around in the unconscious mind. The discoveries one makes there are not always welcome ones. Will you be following Monsieur Gauguin to Tahiti, Monsieur Furneret?"

"No," said Paul. "Not initially at any rate. I need to go to Toulouse with Victor in order to offer our support to Gaston. While there, I shall endeavor to make arrangements to relocate to the region permanently"

"It's a fine city for artists," said Cros, "surrounded by beautiful landscapes. Forgive me please, for running away so rapidly, but I promised to take Monsieur Flammarion to the

Gare du Nord and to convey Madame Zosima and Talia to their hotel—provided, of course, that you have concluded your discussions of the remarkable events at my house last night."

"We had hardly started," Zosima said, "but Monsieur Furneret has been kind enough to supply us with an explanation of sorts of what he believes happened, which he finds acceptable, although I strongly suspect that you, as a skeptic, would not."

"Indeed? Well, there might be time to discuss it later, if I can return here after my visit to the hospital, If not, I shall do my best to find another opportunity to hear his account. Have you anything further to do here, Camille?"

"Not for the moment," said Flammarion. "I really ought to get back to Juvisy. But I shall see you there soon, shall I not, Monsieur Furneret?"

"Indeed. It has been a great honor to meet you, Monsieur Flammarion."

"Likewise. I'll bid you *au revoir*."

Cros turned to Madame Zosima. "Do you wish to take advantage of Joseph and the carriage, while they're here?" he asked, "Or would you prefer to confer with Monsieur Furneret for a little longer, and take a fiacre."

"Alas," said Zosima, "I fear that we might already have overstayed our welcome, for the time being. If you change your mind Monsieur Furneret, it will be easy enough to find us. I'm sure that Talia will always be glad to see you, as will I. We too shall bid you *au revoir*, Monsieur Furneret, with the sincere hope that it is not *adieu*." She offered her hand to be shaken, and Paul shook it.

Talia did the same, but he felt more affection in the pressure, and then he listened to the four sets of footfalls descending the stairs, waiting until they had faded away before returning to his brushes.

CHAPTER XV

Paul had only just begun work again when he was interrupted for a fourth time. He decided to ignore the knock on the door, but he had not turned the key in the lock, and only half a minute passed before it opened. Jane de La Vaudère came in, her expression suggesting that she was more than a little angry as well as hurt.

"Am I *persona non grata* now?" she demanded. "Even though I'm bringing you money, as I promised."

"I'm sorry," he said. "I thought it was another reporter in quest of an interview. I've asked Madame Cambourg to tell them that I'm not at home, but I couldn't afford a big enough bribe. It was foolish of me not to answer, or at least to call out and ask who was knocking."

"Madame Cambourg told me that you had suddenly become very popular. She was in haste to tell me other news, which did not endear her to me. I wanted to come earlier, but I knew that Antoine had made arrangements to bring Flammarion and Zosima, and I didn't want to be part of a circus troupe. Perhaps I left it too long, but I thought you might have a lot to discuss and arrangements to make. Do you have news of your model?"

Paul had set down the palette and the brush, and made as if to usher his guest to the armchairs by the window, but she planted herself in front of the canvas and inspected the panting carefully. When he did not answer her question she looked at him sharply. "Not bad news, I hope?"

"No," said Paul. "Good news, so far as Juliette is concerned. I saw her this morning; she had a rude shock, but she wasn't coughing blood. Doctor Cros is confident that it will be possible to discharge her later today."

Jane inclined her head toward the painting. "You're working on the background, I see...but if necessary, you could finish the painting without her. You only need to put the finishing touches to the central figure."

"It's not strictly necessary," Paul admitted, "but it would be more convenient if she were present, for reference."

She leaned over in order to look at the picture more closely. "I'm sorry I made that comment yesterday about the relative dearth of fire in your paintings," she said. "I didn't realize that you'd take it to heart. I'm sorry, too, that I was a little...disorientated last night. Whether it was Madame Zosima's effluvia that affected me, or just the strangeness of the situation, I don't know, but I wasn't quite myself...no, that's not true. I was a little too much myself. I must have embarrassed you."

"Far from it," said Paul. "I was by no means myself...or perhaps I was a new self, to whom I was not accustomed. I've very grateful to you for staying with me while I was unconscious, and even more so for staying with me afterwards, and talking to me as you did. I needed it, and I hope that I can benefit from it. Please come and sit down—there's something I need to tell you."

She looked at him in surprise, and slight alarm. "You're going to tell me that you don't want to paint my portrait?" she guessed.

"Of course I want to do it," he said, as he led her to the window and gestured an invitation to sit down. "I'm sorry that I don't have anything to offer you, but things have been...disorganized." He sat down in the other chair. "I do have to go away for a few days, though, and I won't be able to start the portrait until I come back."

"That's all right," she said. "You're going to Toulouse...for your friends' obsequies?"

"Amélie was a substitute mother to me."

"I understand. I wish I'd had one. And Martine was, if not quite your lover, at least as dear as a sister."

"I'm no longer entirely sure what Martine was...or rather, what I was, in regard to Martine. But she was certainly very dear to me. I shall grieve for them both, and the impact will doubtless strike me more fully when I'm back in the places where I knew them, surrounded by reminders. Thus far, I haven't wept, but I know that I will, abundantly, when the last barrier of hope finally collapses. Notionally, Victor and I are going in order to give Gaston support, but he has an abundant extended family, and I suspect that I shall need him far more than he needs me."

"You don't have anyone else there?"

"Oh, yes—old friends and acquaintances, even a distant cousin or two. No one close, but a community of sorts. I won't be alone when I go back, after finishing your portrait."

"Go back?" she queried.

"Yes. I've decided that Paris isn't for me."

"The publicity will blow over," she assured him, in a neutral tone. "This is Paris. Sensations rarely last more than a week, and what happened a fortnight ago is ancient history. On the other hand, a reputation once acquired does tend to stick, and the temptation is always strong to exaggerate it rather than seeking to finish it. You could choose to exploit it, and you're probably clever enough to do it."

"No," said Paul, "I couldn't. And it's not the newspapers—it's more fundamental than that. Zosima thinks I'm a coward for running away, but when she made the charge, Flammarion supported me, and so did Talia, somewhat to Zosima's annoyance, Talia went so far as to suggest that I'm actually being courageous. Perhaps that's an exaggeration, but however it's evaluated, I need to do it...but not before I've painted your portrait. That, I need to do."

"Because the fee will finance your relocation?"

"I'll do it for nothing, if you wish," he said, "and you can have the siren for nothing too. You've already done more than enough to compensate me."

Her blue eyes, catching the light from the window, gleamed more intensely than the sky. "Because I've been another substitute mother, if only for a few hours?" she suggested.

"That might be what you've tried to be," Paul said, "but you've accomplished more than that."

"I was only pretending," she said. "Actually, if I were honest with myself, I'd probably suspect that I was unconsciously toying with the idea of seducing you...but the balance between the pros and cons keeps shifting. My self-esteem would probably never recover, though, if you didn't even make an attempt to seduce me while you're painting me, in spite of my age."

"I wouldn't even know how to go about it," Paul said. "Apparently, I'm a joke in the local cafés. All the local prostitutes laugh at me behind my back."

"Did Juliette tell you that?"

Paul felt himself blush, and knew that there was no point denying it.

"Don't forget that she has an ax to grind," said Jane. "How much time did you spend with her in the hospital?"

"Doctor Cros told me that I had to go. You were there."

"Don't use that as an excuse. I might not have told you not to go in so many words, but I think my advice was clear. You're too romantic by half, Paul—more than half. You've seen her lying helpless is a hospital bed, looking as pathetic as it's possible to look, and she's spun you her sob story, and hooked you good and hard. You do realize that she's just a cheap whore, don't you?—but even that that seems romantic to young men like you, thanks to Murger's mythologization of extinct Bohemia. You do know, don't you, that as soon as the money started coming in, Murger moved to a nice bourgeois villa in the country with a nice bourgeois wife and never went near another Mimi as long as he lived?"

"Authors aren't like their books," he countered.

"No," she said, "they're not—although not all of them are as spoiled for choice as to which one to imitate as I am. I've written novels about nuns as well as dancing-girls, and I came a lot closer in my youth to becoming the former than the latter. There, but for the grace of God...You do realize, don't you, that I couldn't even think about seducing you now?"

"I never believed that you would."

"No, you probably didn't—but that little whore did. She only had to look at me yesterday morning and her eyes stated flashing. You do know, I suppose, that you were in her sights from the moment you asked her to pose for you? You might as well have *soft touch* branded on your forehead."

"She did mention that. But the story she told me made sense to me. Doctor Cros would have no difficulty dismissing its evidential value, but one way or another, I made that drawing, and if the account she gave me of what happened before she jumped into the Seine is true..."

"If," the author interjected, in the tone of a professional manufacturer of bizarre stories.

""All right—if the story she told me isn't true, then not only does she have one hell of imagination, but she somehow managed to intuit what my hand was drawing at least three kilometers away from Montmartre. In any case, it's not really her story at all—she doesn't even know the half of it. She just provided some of the jigsaw pieces for my story. And even if that isn't true, which is probably not unlikely, at the very least it reveals something about me, the quality of my imagination, which is significant to me even if other people might misinterpret it. You, of all people can understand that."

"Doubtless you're expecting me to say *touché*, like a good sport. Doubtless I should. You'll forgive me if I don't, for the moment, even though I know well enough what young men are like, especially young artists. There's no way in the world I'd ever stoop so low as to throw myself off the Pont Neuf as a way of attracting attention, even if I were besotted...and I'm not. You know what Oscar Wilde said, don't you, about the would-be suicide he met on the Pont Neuf one night?"

"No," Paul had to admit.

"You really ought to go to salons. The way he told it, before he passed away, he was crossing the bridge one night and saw a man about to jump. 'Are you in despair, Monsieur?' he said, 'No,' the fellow replied, 'I'm a hairdresser.' It sounded better in an English accent, but you get the drift. Now there would be a spirit worth contacting. If only you'd thought of sketching Oscar at Juvisy, or at the doctor's house."

"I didn't get to choose," Paul reminded her. "Not consciously. And I'm not a charlatan. That's why I'm not going in search of more trances—the effects of the ones that come unbidden aren't entirely harmless, it seems, but those that are induced, whether by psychic currents or mere suggestion, I think are best avoided. Either the world of the spirits is chaotic, or I am...or both. And it isn't just me that's at risk, is it? Even if I'm not partly responsible for what happened to Juliette, I haven't done you any favors, have I? Even if Cros is right, and all I did was extrapolate a family resemblance, because your asking me to escort you from the railway station to Juvisy made such an impact on me..."

"Oh, shut up," she said. "Roimantel was right. Madame Cambourg is right. I knew that it was my mother as soon as I saw the picture, and I haven't even been lying to myself about it—just lying to everyone else. I have a portrait of my mother, just as you do, but I don't put in on display. I keep it hidden, secret, and private. So now you know. And I *know*, beyond the reach even of the indomitable skepticism of Antoine Cros, that there is no possible way you could ever have seen that portrait, or extrapolated its features from mine just because I gave you a little thrill by inviting you to pretend to be my cavalier, and practically fawning over you. It was my mother, damn it, just as it was Charles, Martine and your sister. You really did make contact with four spirits of the dead—but you'll never be able to prove it to anyone except the loyal readers of the *Mercaba*, and even they've put a spoke in your wheel by believing that your sister is a Martian. I know, and you know, but no one else can."

"Oh," said Paul, surprised, and just a trifle hurt. After a pause, he added: "I believed you when you said that it wasn't your mother."

"Of course you did. So did Antoine, and Camille. I've discredited you with them, for purely selfish reasons, and not

227

even good ones. And last night, when I saw that hideous drawing you'd made, not only did I take it for granted that your little whore was dead, but I *wanted* her to be dead, because of the way she looked at me when I called on you yesterday morning—nothing more than that. I didn't hold it against her, or you, when I assumed that she was your mistress, but I didn't like the way she looked at me. And even though my head is a lot clearer now than it was last night, I still wish that she really had been dead, because I think that, alive, she's a catastrophe waiting to happen to you, not Jeanne d'Arc or any other saint, but Nemesis."

"I think you're exaggerating," Paul said.

"Of course you do. Do you still want to paint my portrait?"

"Of course. You're the most fascinating woman I've ever met. If I can capture even a fraction of your soul..."

"Well, that's a risk I'm willing and ready to take. I suppose we'll have to wait until you return from Toulouse to arrange sittings—but if you don't come back, I shall never, ever forgive you. Now, I think I'm still suffering a little from whatever got into me last night...or perhaps it was renewed when I looked at your painting just now...and I ought to be on my way in any case. I don't have Antoine's excuses, but I do have a busy life. Anyway, I know we didn't agree a fee for the siren, but I hope this is more than adequate."

She took a black velvet purse from her handbag, and handed it to Paul. He weighed it in his hand, but did not think, even for a second, of opening it to see whether the coins it continued were silver or gold. That would have been poor etiquette.

"More than adequate" he confirmed. "I've wrapped the canvas for you. It should be safe even if it begins to rain—but you came in a carriage, I presume?"

"It's in the courtyard. I drove it myself, as usual. People have got used to seeing me now, and it's 1901, not 1887; I no longer attract undue attention in the street. I'll let you get on with your painting, and hope that you don't have any more importunate visitors."

"Only the others were importunate," he assured her. "You will always be welcome, I assure you."

"Likewise. Here's an invitation to my next soirée. The upper crust are shunning me, at present, but if you haven't set off for Toulouse already, you'll meet a few interesting people there, and they'll all be fascinated to meet you. I shall take it for granted that I can call on you here whenever I wish even if you're...in company."

"Absolutely."

"Good. I haven't given up yet on the possibility of your salvation. I shall send you some books, especially *Les Sataniques*, my little book of *femmes fatales*, full of perverse passions and uncanny revenants. You might find it amusing, if not edifying. I won't ask you to try not to think of me too harshly, because it would probably be best if you were to think of me very harshly, but were unable to resist me because of my strange magnetism." She stood up, offered him her gloved hand, and said: "*Au revoir*, Paul."

He lifted the hand to his lips and kissed it. "*Au revoir*, Madame," he said, and went to fetch the siren.

She did not instruct him to call her Jane.

CHAPTER XVI

It was already dark when Antoine Cros finally returned to Montmartre. Juliette was not with him. Paul was still at work, by lamplight.

"That really isn't wise, Monsieur Furneret," he said, as Paul set his equipment down. "You really must install electric lighting if you intend to work after nightfall."

"I've only been working on the background detail," Paul said. "It's meticulous work, but the lighting isn't crucial. I've been trying to make up for lost time; it has been a day of interruptions, most of them direly unwanted. Tomorrow, if I can make full use of the daylight hours, I might be able to finish it—but I need my model, in order to put the finishing touches to the principal motif—the soul of the picture."

"She wanted to remain in the hospital for one more night, but she promised that she would come tomorrow, at the usual time, for the final sitting. I've left some money for cab fare; although her clothes suffered badly from the dip in the river, they've been washed, and they're still serviceable, so she asked me to tell you that there's no need to worry."

"You talked to her at some length, then?" Paul queried

"Yes. She told me what had happened, and made other confidences. I'm only an amateur psychologist, except to the extent that every good physician needs to take his patient's mental condition into account as well as her physical condition, but she seems to me to be in a healthy state of mind now."

"Do you believe her story?"

"I do. She was undoubtedly among the witnesses to the murder, and although her account of the details differs somewhat from the accounts given in the newspapers, I suspect that hers is more likely be accurate than theirs. As to the nature of the hallucination, I cannot see any reason why she would lie."

"You don't think that it was all an act, then, and that she might have jumped into the Seine simply as a bid for attention?"

"Certainly not. I believe that she was in extreme distress, and understandably so, having just witnessed the murder of her friend. I examined her last night, and I am fully convinced that her symptoms were not feigned. Do you have some reason to think otherwise?"

"No, I agree with you."

"You've seen Jane?" Cros guessed. "Yes, she does tend to be a little hard on what she calls 'little girls.' She will tell you herself, in her charmingly doubly deceptive fashion, that it's pure jealousy on her part. Quite unreasonable, given that she's still one of the most desirable women in Paris, whereas most 'little girls' are...not...but we all have our irrational anxieties, do we not?"

"We do. Do you think that there could have been any connection between what happened in Montmartre yesterday evening and what happened in your drawing room, three kilometers away?"

"Certainly. Without knowing what you were thinking about when Zosima was subjecting you to suggestion, I could have guessed that you were still anxious about your painting, and anxious about your model. The mere fact that she had gone to an appointment at the Permanence must have brought her...other profession to the forefront of your mind, and laid the psychological groundwork for your superimposed images. It's a modern cliché, when we think about city prostitutes, to think of them as murder victims. The sensational reportage of the Whitechapel murders in England thirteen years ago has set the tone for Parisian reportage ever since. Prostitutes are only a tiny fraction of the murder victims in the city, fewer than wives, but that's not the popular public perception. The coincidence that enabled such a murder to happen at the time when you were imagining one is striking, but you are entitled to be thankful that your model was only a witness rather than the victim, even though the other poor woman is no less dead.

"It's perfectly natural, too that your mind should be unable to avoid forging a closer and more exotic connection between the two events than there was in objective terms. The human mind is organized to search coincidences for possible cause-and-effect relationships, because that is the bedrock of rational thought. It is not in the least astonishing that the alert mind sometimes perceives relationships where none exist, generating a vast legacy of superstitions. That you should perceive what happened as uncanny is entirely understandable—but you are an intelligent and rational man, in spite of being an artist, and I believe you to be capable of setting aside superstitious temptations and seeing the truth of the matter, even if it runs counter to your intuitions."

""You don't believe, then, that there was any kind of bond between Juliette and me, or between Talia and me?"

"Of course there was. They are young women, possessed of all the seductive qualities that Jane attributes to 'little girls.' They are not unusually pretty specimens, but you're a young man, organized to react to the stimuli they provide. In the same way, there is a bond between you and Jane. That is perfectly natural. There is even a bond between you and Zosima, in spite of the presumable lack of reciprocity. She is an attractive woman. That might well have contributed to the suggestion that she was able to plant in your mind."

"Which you also consider to be perfectly natural, and not evidence for some kind of psychic magnetism?"

"Perfectly natural. Perhaps it is analogous to magnetism in some ways—we routinely speak about magnetic personalities, as a common metaphor. There's no doubt that suggestion is real, that some people are better able to impose suggestion on others, and that some people are unusually suggestible, but people who think they're immune to suggestion are mostly deluded. There's a skill involved, and Zosima undoubtedly has it; it is fascinating to watch her at work, and I believe that were she to direct her efforts in that direction, she might make a useful and substantial contribution to medical hypnosis, but I fear that we might have lost her irredeemably to the entertainment industry. I am not in the least surprised that her own attempts to interpret and understand what she does have led her into the realms of the quasi-miraculous, but I do not see any need to follow her there. Given your obvious suggestibility, I think it might well be a wise decision not to place yourself under her influence any further."

"Even though, as an artist, I'm lost to the 'entertainment industry' myself?"

"A different branch. I'm not a philistine, Monsieur Furneret. I appreciate the arts, and even consider myself something of a connoisseur. Painting, music and literature are among the glories of the human mind, capable of making a enormous contribution to human wellbeing. Nor am I unreasonably prejudiced against Madame Zosima's art, or Juliette's."

"You mean, as a model?"

"No, I mean as a prostitute. I believe prostitution to be a good and useful thing, which does not deserve its reputation as a despicable vice, or even as a necessary evil, and it pains me that it is, in the main, such a scorned and dangerous profession. It has its villains, I suppose, like any other walk of life, but they are, in my opinion, far outnumbered by its heroines. There are prostitutes among my clients, both the high-paying kind and the beneficiaries of charity. I endeavor to treat them all with equal respect. Do you think that I ought to pander to popular bigotry instead?"

"Of course not," said Paul. "I agree with you."

"I assumed that you must, else you would not have been so kind to that girl in the hospital. I hope you will continue to be kind to her, to the extent that you can."

"Jane thinks that if I do, she will be my Nemesis."

"Jane often exaggerates, and sometimes melodramatizes. It's her profession. Juliette mentioned her while we were chatting; a mutual animosity seems to have sprung up between them literally at first sight. Not unusual—and again, quite natural. Don't read too much into it. But please be kind to Jane as well, to the extent that you can. You've already observed that she likes to give the impression that she doesn't need it, and perhaps she doesn't, but in my opinion, it's always better to err on the side of kindness, just in case. As your physician, perhaps I ought to advise you to be wary of both of them, but I know only too well how incapable young men like you are of being wary. Even kindness can lead to trouble, of course, but at least, if it proves be a road to hell, it is paved with the best intentions. Whatever proverbial wisdom might allege, most such roads are not—and there are, alas, precious few roads that lead in any other direction."

"You're a pessimist?"

"Certainly not. I'm a surgeon. All surgeons are optimists, and although the surgical knife sometimes fails, I believe I mentioned to you yesterday that when it is wielded skillfully, it saves far more lives than prayer or any other kind of magic. Unfortunately, one cannot take a scalpel to human relationships, and any such attempt, as the Montmartrean Apache demonstrated yesterday, only leads to ludicrous tragedy."

"Fortunately, I only wield a paint-brush. It can be unkind, but rarely draws blood."

"Fortunately, as you say. Will you use Juliette again, once your Jeanne d'Arc is finished?"

"Possibly. Jane has already reserved my next portrait for herself, but after that, who knows?"

"Ah. There's more than one meaning that can be attached to the phrase 'drawing blood,' as you demonstrated last night. Please be careful, Paul, even in kindness. Both women are my patients, as are you, and if there is one thing I hate particularly, it is seeing my patients inflict harm on one another."

"What do you advise me to do, then, Doctor?"

"I can only talk in generalities, I fear, but let me say that in my experience, there are two types of amorous relationships that very rarely end well: relationships between artists and models, and relationships between poor young men and relatively prosperous young women. Both kind of relationships tend to lead observers to jump to conclusions that, whether they are true or untrue, are insulting and injurious. Young men

234

in love, obviously, never care what other people think, in the beginning, and never think in the longer term, always preferring the possibility of present ecstasy over to the likelihood of future pain. But advice is futile in such circumstances; young men are organized in such a way as to fall in love in response to the appropriate stimuli, and even though, in my opinion, they have far more choice in the matter than the mythology of literary amour suggests, they are nevertheless subject to the effects of gravity."

"So you believe in psychic gravity, but not psychic magnetism?"

"I think it a better analogy, not so much because of the metaphor of amorous falling with a crash, which is brutally simplistic, as because of the Newtonian explanation of planetary orbits, whereby gravity maintains objects that would other follow a straight course in a closed loop around some attractive mass"

"And you think I'm in danger...?"

"We're all in danger, my boy, if you want to put it that way. That's the whole point of the theory: it applies universally."

"But some of us, metaphorically speaking, are suns, some planets, and some humble moons."

"If you wish—but the human world is no orrery; roles are much more changeable and variable. It would be ridiculous arrogance for a human being to think of himself, or herself, as a sun, and other people as mere planets or moons...although the phenomenon is not uncommon."

"It's not an error I'm likely to commit, I can assure you" murmured Paul.

"So I've noticed, and I didn't intend the comment as an admonition. You seem to me to be more likely to err in the other direction, in spite of the fact that all kinds of people are circling you at present, exerting uncomfortably contrary gravitational stresses upon your tidal fluids. There are worse problems—the worst of all being complete isolation. You might want to bear that in mind while you continue to weigh up the possibility of decamping to the environs of Toulouse.

"You said this morning that it was a good idea."

"So I did. I must confess that I was thinking primarily about supporting your decision to steer clear of Zosima. Talia agreed with me, although I'd be prepared to wager that she will be sorry to see you go. She probably cannot be attracted to you amorously, but that does not mean that she would be glad to be rid of you. Juliette will be heart-broken of course. As for Jane...but I ought not to talk about Jane in that context, for reasons of patient confidentiality."

"You just shared your prognosis of Juliette's future condition."

"The cases are dissimilar."

"Very. And, in my admittedly limited experience, each is quite unique."

"Do you think so? In detail, obviously, but Jane is not entirely wrong to say, as she frequently does, that all little girls are alike. It is not their fault, of course, and it's a tragedy, but it's the way our society works, unfortunately. No matter how heroically they struggle—and far more of them are heroic that common prejudice alleges—the circumstances are stacked against them horribly. No matter how intelligent or enterprising she might be, a girl born in Paris in the nineteenth century had no alternative means of survival than selling her body, one way or another, and that trade, at the highest level as at the lowest, is essentially frustrating, essentially degrading, and essentially heart-breaking. Will the twentieth century be any better? I believe in progress, but in that matter I fear that it might be slow."

"Some break free," Paul objected.

"You mean Zosima?"

"Actually, I was thinking about Jane."

"A pity. I can talk about Zosima...but she already described to you, last night, some of the ways in which she remains imprisoned by soil conventions, prejudices and expectations, and others are obvious in her person. But imagine a hypothetical individual who found herself, in the 1850s, in the situation of an orphan, with an inheritance in trust that would ensure her financial wellbeing, but devoid of other guidance.

"Her relatives, inevitably, place her in a convent, so that she might be decently educated, and as soon as she is of an age to leave, they shop around for a husband for her—a much older man, equally prosperous, in quest of a beddable beauty and heir. Perhaps he is a worthy fellow, undoubtedly he loves her—everybody does—and perhaps she tries, dutifully, to love him...but she has lived her entire life under the pressures of necessity and conformity; she has never been able to exercise a choice. Eventually, she wants to do that, especially if she is intelligent, creative and has romantic ideals born of childhood reading.

"There are any number of directions she might go, but the golden road, which the bravest of the brave can take, leads to Paris. There, as she moves through salon society, two-thirds of the male population are attracted to her because she is beautiful, and because a young woman on her own in Paris, with a distant husband in some provincial château, gives rise to all sorts of expectations. She is, of course, marvelously aloof, enjoying the abundant homage but jealous of her virtue. She paints, she writes poetry, she inhabits the fringes of Bohemian society as well as salon culture; she has the best of both worlds. She is a star. But is she free?

"Is she free from the pressures and expectations of society? Is she free from the pressures and expectations of her own heart? What if she falls in love? With whom? It hardly matters—it is not a relationship that can endure or end well. Having happened once, and gone awry once, is it not more likely to happen again, and to go awry again, at least until disenchantment sets is—and even then, does hope not persist stubbornly? Perhaps she is successful in one of her fields of endeavor, but in our society, how much esteem can a woman obtain as a painter, a musician or a writer? Even if she has genius, will it ever be recognized? If she has not, will she even attain respect?

"And inevitably, she will grow older. The homages that surround her continue to surround her, but their character changes. It is legitimate for everyone to adore a beauty of twenty, but a beauty of forty-five, no matter how beautiful? All adoration then becomes suspect, especially to her, and whatever relationships she forms, the eyes of onlookers become more censorious, more contemptuous. She becomes suspicious of all the hypocrisies that surround her, and all the sincerities too, and she becomes suspicious too of her own motives, her own ambitions, her own prospects. Is she free?

"I ask you Paul, has such a woman really broken free? Or has she simply broken, like all the poor little girls that she might affect to despise, because there is nothing about them that she does not know and understand?

"So, if you should every happen to run into such a hypothetical individual, my boy—and they are not so very rare—perhaps you can and ought to be understanding, wary and, if possible, kind. With luck, you will not fall in love with her, nor her with you, but luck cannot be trusted in such matters, and gravity affects every particle in the universe, none of which ever has a free choice as to which way it will fall, always being at the behest of the masses that surround it. And that is not pessimism, but realism. For myself, as I say, I'm a determined optimist, because I know that, however many insoluble problems life presents there are at last a few that can be solved by the skillful administration of a scalpel...and I do not rule out *a priori* the possibility that there are some that might be soluble by the skilful administration of a paintbrush."

"That," Paul relied, "really is optimism—but it's an optimism that I wish I could share."

"Can you not? You might think that I'm painting a bleak picture, metaphorically speaking, but insofar as you're my patient, I have high hopes for you. You're robust, intelligent, talented, and in a more salubrious environment that Montmartre, you will almost certainly attract the attention of women with whom you could for a perfectly healthy, rewarding and enduring relationship. I wish I could offer a prognosis as bright for all my patients. We can all fail, Paul, and few of us can resist temptation, when it is set before us, but the calculus of probability seems to me to be in your favor."

"Thank you, doctor. I wish I could afford to pay you everything that I owe you."

"You did me a fine drawing last night. I certainly wouldn't put it on my wall, but as a medical specimen, it's absolutely fascinating. If you're willing to call it quits, I suspect that I, not you, am the one who is getting the best of the bargain. But now, I really must be going. Don't do any more work tonight—that's a formal prescription. And if I don't see you again before you leave, be sure to come and see me when you get back, won't you? Socially, of course."

They shook hands. Then the doctor left, and Paul, deciding to follow the prescription, went to clean his brushes.

CHAPTER XVII

This time, Juliette was wide awake when Paul arrived in the ward, but she was still in bed. She looked at him with an expression he found difficult to read, but which did not seem to contain overmuch pleasure. She looked suspiciously at the parcel that he was carrying under his arm.

"I told Doctor Cros to tell you that I'd be at the studio at the usual time," she said. "You shouldn't have come here. It's not necessary."

"I didn't suppose that it was *necessary*," he said, "but I thought it might be helpful."

"I'm quite well. I can even take a fiacre to Montmartre. Doctor Cros left some money with the intern."

"I know; he told me. He also told me that the dress and underclothes you were wearing when you jumped in the Seine had been laundered, and I assume that your shoes have dried out too—but I thought that everything might be somewhat the worse for wear, so I bought replacements. I was paid for a painting yesterday, quite generously, and I thought it only appropriate to share my good fortune."

"Would that be the painting that you sold to Madame de La Vaudère?" she asked, dryly.

"It would," he said.

"I don't want anything from her."

"Why not?"

"I don't like her. Women like her..." She left it at that.

"As a matter of fact, she doesn't like you either, or 'little girls' in general. I told her that you were an intelligent adult, but she didn't seem to think the objection relevant. So, she would probably disapprove of my spending a tiny fraction of the money she paid me for my painting on this trivial gift...in which case, surely, you should be willing to accept it, just to spite her."

She laughed, briefly. "Typical," she said. "An answer for everything."

"Typical of men, you mean?"

"Good God no. Most men don't have an answer for anything, except a knife, which doesn't count. Typical of you."

"I'm not like other men, then, in your estimation? Because I'm an artist."

"Now you're just fishing for compliments. But you're right—palette knives generally do a lot less damage than the other kind. But I don't want your present. I don't want to be beholden. If I'd earned it, that would be different, but I haven't."

Paul sat down beside the bed and set the parcel down on the coverlet. "I don't want to be beholden either," he said. "My painting drove you crazy, temporarily. I don't want that on my conscience. It's because of me that your old dress got soaked in filthy water. I need to make amends."

"Don't flatter yourself," she said. "I went crazy all on my own."

"Is that what Doctor Cros told you?"

"No. In fact, he came pretty close to telling me what you've just told me—that it was looking at the painting while I was in a suggestive frame of mind, and trying too hard to involve myself in it. He talked a lot of nonsense about how natural it is for models to identify with the characters they portray, and how it can sometimes be dangerous to pose as Jeanne d'Arc unless you can wear a suit of armor and wave a sword. He said a lot of other things too. He talks a lot, for a surgeon."

"Yes he does," Paul agreed. "I like him, and he certainly talks a lot of sense. He might be wrong about some things, and probably is, but even when he's wrong, he still talks a lot good sense."

"What is he wrong about?"

"He doesn't think there's anything supernatural about the bond we formed. He doesn't believe that you used my hand to draw your friend's murder."

"Well, that *is* good sense. He's right about that—both those things, in fact."

"So you agree with him that the bond you formed with me—the bond that caused you to identify with Jeanne d'Arc and jump in the river to put out the flames of her pyre, was perfectly natural?"

"Now you're putting words in my mouth."

"Sorry. Actually, I don't think it matters much whether the bond we formed is natural or supernatural. What matters is that before and after I made that drawing—a drawing of you, twice over—I *felt* a bond. When Madame Zosima subjected me to her animal magnetism, I was thinking about you."

"Why?"

"Because I thought you were walking the streets, touting for custom, and I thought it was dangerous. As, in fact it was. The lunatic with the knife could have killed you too."

She was silent for a moment, and then she sighed. "What I ought to say," she said, "is that I don't want your pity. And it ought to be true. But it isn't. God help me, I do want your pity. And I don't like myself for that, but I ought not to take it out on you. Doctor Cros told you to be kind to me, didn't he?"

"Why do you think that?"

"Because he told me to be kind to you. He said it was a prescription, for me, that it would help me feel better. It wouldn't cure me, he said, but it might help me feel better. Did he say the same thing to you?"

"Not in exactly those words, but he certainly talked about kindness, and recommended it to me strongly. I suspect that he gives the same recommendation to all his patients. It's probably good advice."

"I'm glad you think so. You won't mind if I try to follow it, then."

"What do you mean?"

"Well, he didn't say so in so many words, but I got the strong impression that he thought that the best way that I could be kind to you would be to get out of your life forever—and I suspect that he's right."

Paul was startled by that, and had to pause to think about it for a moment or two. Then, more to himself than to Juliette, he said: "I'll wager that he gave exactly the same advice to Jane, that she interpreted it in exactly the same way, and that she intends to take it. That explains...well, not a lot, but a little. At least she's going to let me paint her portrait first—which is kind, because I really need the commission. But to be honest, I'd rather he didn't go around hinting to everyone I know that they ought to start treating me like a leper, for my own good—especially as it clashes with the advice he gave me...because if I'm going to be kind..."

"You've already been more than kind enough to me," said Juliette, in a low voice. "You can finish your painting—the part that needs me, at any rate—today. After that, I'd just be an encumbrance. I don't want to be. I can find somewhere else to stay tonight, and thereafter. You don't need to worry about me. And I don't need this." She pushed the parcel away with her right hand. "I'm not sure that I can take any more kindness...not from you."

"This isn't kindness," said Paul, pushing the parcel back in her direction. "As I said, this is guilt. Letting you stay at the studio when you asked was kindness, and that's a kindness I'd like to continue—but I don't want to be hypocritical about it. If you'd consent to stay in the studio for another couple of weeks, you'd be doing me a kindness...and unlike you, I can take all the kindness I can get right now."

For once her expression was readable, as astonishment mingled with puzzlement. "What do you mean?" she asked.

"I have to go away for a few days. I don't suppose for a moment that anyone will try to steal the Jeanne d'Arc or my other paintings, and I don't suppose you could stop anyone doing it if they did want to, but I'd feel a great deal happier if I knew that there was someone in the studio, looking after things."

"Where are you going?"

"Toulouse. Gaston Lambrunet is going by sea from Le Havre to Bordeaux, and catching the train to Toulouse from there. Victor and I are traveling by train from Paris. We'll give him what help we can with the legal formalities, and share his grief. It will be upsetting for me, I think, but I need it. Amélie was very good to me, and Martine...well, it will be difficult."

"And you want me to look after your studio?"

"If you would. You still need a place to stay, and you have a certain interest in the Jeanne d'Arc. If the building were to catch fire, I could trust you to try to save it. Perhaps, if you're willing, you could also serve as my secretary, and help to take care of my correspondence. It's piled up horribly over the last two days, and I suspect that more is going to pour in, at least for a few days. It would be very helpful if someone could at least handle the polite apologies for my absence. I could pay you for that—not much, but a little."

"To keep me from walking the streets?"

"If it had that effect, I'd be pleased, but you're a free agent.

"And you don't care one way or the other."

"I just said that I'd be pleased—but you might not care whether I'm pleased or not, and you're a free agent, as I say."

"And what happens when you come back?"

"Naturally, I hope that you'll continue to stay in the studio, and continue to help with my correspondence, if it's still burdensome. I'll be busy, because I have a commission."

"To paint Madame de La Vaudère's portrait?"

"Yes. And after I've done that, I'd like you to model for me again. I have an idea for another painting. It would be kind of you—very kind—if you'd consent to do that."

Juliette was evidently in something of a quandary. "Not another Jeanne d'Arc, I presume?" she said, presumably stalling to gain time.

"Actually, yes," he told her, "but not as a martyr, as a heroine. You'd have to wear a suit of armor and brandish a sword—so Doctor Cros's suggestion that you avoid the subject doesn't apply, given his own stated exclusion. Do you think you could do that?"

"I dare say," she said, uncertainly, but obviously wavering in regard to her earlier decision.

"There is one condition, though, and I'm afraid it's not negotiable."

"What's that?"

"I want to do the painting in the Midi, somewhere in the region of Toulouse."

"You want me to come to the Midi?"

"Yes, for as long as it takes to finish the painting. After that...I haven't made any further plans yet. I can't pay you much, I'm afraid, but I'll pay your return train fare, obviously, and provide what accommodation I can. You'll probably hate the Midi, being Parisian born and bred, but once the painting is done you'll be free of all obligations, and if you still think it would qualify as being kind...well, we can cross that bridge when we come to it. In the meantime, I need you. You're my Jeanne d'Arc. The picture will now be part of a diptych, an exercise in comparison and contrast. You'd be doing me a great kindness."

"You mean that you'd be doing me one. Out of pity."

"Partly—but also for art's sake, and that's more important."

"But nothing else."

"If you mean other obligations, no. But if you mean what you said about thinking that it would easy to hook me if you wanted to, I don't suppose that situation will have changed. Rumor has it that I might as well be walking around with *soft touch* branded on my forehead."

"Rumor? You don't listen to rumor. You mean Madame de La Vaudère, don't you?"

"She's not the only one who thinks so. I suspect that Doctor Cros thinks the same, but he tends to beat around the bush rather than say such things straight out, as you've noticed. I'm not sure that I agree with them—in fact, I'm sure that I don't, but sometimes other people see us more clearly than we see ourselves. I'll try to see Camille Flammarion at Juvisy before I leave for Toulouse, or when I get back if I can't manage it beforehand. I think he might be able to see more clearly than anyone, and although he's not nearly as loquacious as Doctor Cros, I still think he might be far better able than anyone else to help me understand what I am, and the way the world is, and he seems to be willing to try."

"You do realize, don't you," Juliette said, slowly, "that you're completely crazy?"

"Absolutely. I draw the spirits of dead people when I'm unconscious, and then forget all about it. How crazy can you be? If you really don't want to have anything further to do with me, I'll understand—but please don't call it kindness. It wouldn't be that at all, no matter what Doctor Cros might think."

"Do I want to have nothing further to do with you? Don't be ridiculous. At this moment in time, you're the only thing in my life that...but that's not the point. If it isn't a matter of obligation...and don't worry about being crazy...crazy is good...necessary. And where else would I find anyone crazy enough to hire me as his secretary? Not that I'm a stranger to earning money with my hand, but holding a pen requires a lot more dexterity, believe me—although it's not as messy if you suck the end. But all things considered, why not? I need a place to stay, so what the hell. I suppose I could give it a try, armor and all..." she stopped then, and became suddenly pensive.

"What's the matter?" Paul asked.

"I'd decided, firmly, that I wasn't going to do this—not this exactly, because I had no idea what you were going to say, but...well, *this*. I decided that I wasn't going to play the leech. As I said, when the Doctor said that I'd probably feel a lot better if I were kind to you, he didn't actually spell out what being kind might involve, and it's possible that I might have misunderstood him...but after thinking about it hard all through last night, I thought I'd come to the conclusion that the best way to be kind to you really would be to get the hell out of your life. Maybe I'm flattering myself, but after what you've just said...well, it's still the case that I might be dangerous to you, and I don't want to be."

"I know," he told her, gently. "But it's also the case that you might be able to help me, at least for a while. It won't be easy, for either of us, but it's a chance, isn't it? You don't have to decide now, and you can take everything one step at a time, all along the line. But I really would like you to take the clothes and shoes now. That would make me feel better. Please?"

After a moment's hesitation, she reached out, picked up the parcel, and began unwrapping it, but stopped almost immediately. "Thank you," she said, a trifle dully. After a brief pause, she added: "I'm really not used to kindness; it might take me a while to learn to accept it with a good grace...but I'll try."

"Good," he said. "I'll go outside and find a fiacre, while you get dressed...in whichever clothes you prefer. I'll meet you in the courtyard, and we'll see where it goes it from there."

www.ingramcontent.com/pod-product-compliance
Lightning Source LLC
Chambersburg PA
CBHW060352030726
47497CB00003B/682